OVERNIGHT DELIVERY

Raymond Parish

A HANK ANDERSON THRILLER

"*Overnight Delivery* is a clever, engrossing psychological thriller punctuated by wry humor and unexpected developments in a skillfully portrayed Iowa locale."
Ron

Copyright 2020 by Raymond Parish

This is a work of fiction. Names, characters, places, and incidents are either the product of the author's imagination, or are used fictitiously. Any resemblance to actual persons, living or dead, events, or locales is coincidental.

The psychotherapy sessions as written in this book are not intended to be exact depictions of the therapy process, nor to resemble any actual sessions; they are fictitious approximations of psychotherapy utilized to create this work of fiction.

Printed in the United States of America

In memory of, and with love to, Dad, who introduced me to Chandler, Conan Doyle, Hammett, Parker, and jazz. I hope you're dancing with mom.

In honor of the courageous people who practice recovery and the Twelve Steps in your daily lives.

AUTHOR'S NOTE:

Overnight Delivery began as a meditation; an exercise in relaxation. It evolved into a desire to challenge myself and finish a piece of work in a genre that captured my interest as a youth, a pastime that remains undiminished to this day. Finally, *OD* morphed into a project that I want to share with you during this time of uncertainty and, hopefully, positive change in our world.

PROLOGUE

In the generations before meth, this had been a working family farm.

Today, it was a John Deere graveyard.

The bleached-out carcasses of broken-down farm implements had been rendered ageless by the decay brought on by Iowa's four rigorous seasons. A rusted-out Chevy 4x4, once metallic blue, made for sorrowful lawn art. The once-upon-a-time sparkling white two-story farmhouse was now spackled with weathered gray primer where the paint had frayed, peeled, and dropped away. Sagging wooden steps led to a sagging, grossly mildewed front porch holding a mass of broken toys and the skeletal wrecks of worn-out home appliances.

On the heels of the visual assault, anyone foolish enough to happen down the pot-holed gravel road to this out-of-the-way place would also notice the oppressive quiet. No tractors, no combines, no cows, no kids. No sound but the never-ending whip of wind that recycles through every acre of Iowa countryside.

And then there was the smell. A violent stench emanated from the house, hanging over the property, as if contained by the rolling hills, evergreens and rock-strewn fields that separated this land from a better place. Harsh chemicals and harsher death.

It was not particularly unusual that tragedy had visited such a place. Cooking meth, with a heavy focus on personal consumption, is not a life choice associated with eventual retirement to Scottsdale or Orlando.

It was, however, the form of death here that would have given anyone deep pause. In most home meth labs, overdose or accidental explosion resulting from a combination of brain damage and bad chemistry are the likely stories. This scene was different. Two men and one woman, all dirty, disheveled, and severely emaciated, stared wide-eyed at the water-stained ceiling from where they lie on the filthy, chipped linoleum of the kitchen floor, each with one small, dark hole in their foreheads.

These were not ODs. These were assassinations.

Given their line of work, the three dead tweakers shouldn't have looked so surprised.

TUESDAY

Psychology sometimes says, "I am a human being, *not* a human doing. We are *not* our jobs."

People with plenty of money and privilege might believe that.

I'm from Iowa, where working folks often become what they do. Farmer, long-distance trucker, clergy, cook. These are not jobs. These are not careers. They are ways of life.

My way of life is a bit off the beaten path. Psychotherapy.

Why psychotherapy?

Reason one, I grew up as a townie, so farming is not in my DNA.

Reason two, I'm a natural-born snoop. I gained early infamy in the Anderson clan by hiding behind doors, sofas and in the occasional dark corner, waiting to overhear conversations, arguments, and intimacies between various family members. I kept my discoveries to myself. Since that time, I've come out from behind the couch, as it were.

Reason three involves a serious aversion to manual labor, which I developed in my youth and confirmed through a brief stint in early adulthood as an electrician's assistant, during a dangerous episode of poverty-induced insanity. After several near-incidents of knocking out the national power grid while punching my own ticket, I determined that this line of work didn't satisfy my requirements, which included the desire to live a long and ambulatory life.

My next obvious choice, after deceased Master Electrician, was Hank Anderson, Private Investigator. Along with my propensity for snooping, I had spent the better part of my adolescence devouring the classic mysteries of Raymond Chandler, Dashell Hammett, Ross McDonald, and Sir Arthur Conan Doyle. At a time when things weren't going so well at home, I spent hours and hours in the cool, sterile quiet of the county library. Phillip Marlowe, the Continental Op, Lew Archer, and Sherlock Holmes became good companions for a troubled bookworm.

Detective par excellence seemed a logical alternative.

Sadly, by the age of twenty it was clear that nature had betrayed me. I had topped out at five feet, seven inches in height. I weighed 130 pounds "soaking wet with a rock in my pocket," as Dad used to say. And then there was my aversion to guns and my desire to hug, not shoot, vulnerable critters. This is a somewhat unique stance here in the heart of pheasant and deer hunting country.

Whatever free time I spent away from reading was consumed by daredevil antics on my rattletrap ten-speed bicycle and carbon spewing ATV, not stalking dinner.

"Most Likely to Become Hard-Boiled and Suave" was not the caption under my high school graduation picture.

So, after finishing up eighteen years of a life uncertain in southwest Iowa, I turned my sights to a not-far-off university where I somehow managed to declare a major in psychology amidst my dedication to cheap pot, cheaper beer, and rock music. Giving up pot and serious drinking - but never music - I found psychotherapy, first as a client, then as a profession. With the absence of substance abuse, my eventual graduate program in counseling went far better than my undergrad.

Today, the benefits are many. First, I get to be a professional snoop without having anyone poke a gun in my ribs and say, "Put up your hands and turn around slowly, gumshoe." Secondly, I sometimes get to make a positive difference in peoples' lives.

I listen, empathize, question, encourage, interpret, and challenge. Often, like the detective I didn't become, I read between the lines. Most of the folks who find me already have many of the answers; they just aren't listening to their higher selves. I tell them what I hear and help them fill in the blanks.

It's pretty good work, if you can get it.

These were my thoughts on a crisp, cloudless Tuesday morning in October, as I set aside my paper copy of the *Des Moines Register*, after noticing the headline on the latest in a series of rural meth deaths staring up at me. Sadly, death and meth are not an unusual combination. This one was different. People had been murdered. The police were following all possible leads.

No online news for me. I'm no dyed-in-the-wool Luddite, but I find no joy in staring at screens, and still use terms meant for guys older than me, like, died-in-the-wool. Words about meth deaths are striking enough. Pictures are not required.

I was sitting in my office with a full view of lovely downtown Des Moines, sipping coffee, extra cream, and chomping on my first cruller of the morning. Word has it that I look like whatever they call YUPPIES nowadays, but you wouldn't catch me in one of those upscale bistros. Coffee, hot, with extra cream, not some flavored iced latte monstrosity, is the Bentley of caffeinated beverages.

Ah, Des Moines, Iowa. One of those cool places on the map passed through by the uninitiated on their way to overpopulated dives like Aspen and La Jolla. It's OK with me if most folks only come up with cornfields and hogs when they think about Iowa. We have plenty of both. Des Moines also has the river, the Iowa Cubs AAA farm team, the Drake Relays, the best bike trails in the U.S. of A., a renovated and updated downtown that borders on beautiful Gray's Lake, and Waterworks, a park that boasts more acres than Central Park. And, of course, there's the historic cow sculpted from butter that annually adorns the State Fair.

Sure, there's crime. Sure, young people are flooding in from small towns in search of jobs and adventure, white privilege colliding with rural white poverty. The gold dome of the capitol building can easily bring-to-mind tariff terror, nut-bar neo-conservatives, and institutional racism.

It's not all *Field of Dreams*. In my Iowa, Kevin Costner and James Earl Jones still have a lot of work to do on justice for all.

Still.

Dad would say, one could "lead the life of Riley" in this large small town.

A shrill and unanswered ring interrupted my caffeine meditation, reminding me that Belinda Clark, our office manager, and self-appointed mother figure, was taking the day off. Later it would occur to me that the Riley my Dad was referring to, whoever he or she was, may have had better judgment than me.

Probably didn't answer office phones.

"Anderson & Greenberg Counseling, Hank Anderson," I announced.

"You have a soothing tone," a familiar voice, rumbling from the same place Barry White used to sing, prodded me.

"Mental Health 'r' Us, Phil," I said.

"Well, then I called the right place. I have somebody for you, Hank."

"Uh oh." I paused. "Tell me more."

The basis for my "uh oh" is that Phil Evans is the source of some of my more unusual client referrals. Phil is a good friend. He's also a gold-shield detective, and a serious Methodist, which strangely doesn't seem incongruent with his being a big cop with a big gun. Phil takes both callings very seriously. Life's full of paradox.

We met some years ago at a crisis intervention training for mental health professionals and law enforcement. In a break-out session on the potential for embedding counselors in police departments, he showed a deep interest in better understanding the interaction of mental illness, addiction, crime, and incarceration. I learned that day that he was already a professional and personal expert on how race and racism featured as a central factor in this complex web.

Over lunch that day, we also discovered a common interest in coffee as our drug of choice.

To date, I only had one serious issue with Phil: He looked great in his ever-present brown fedora. A real noir detective hat. I'd given the fedora a go in my 20s, a vain attempt at Robert Mitchum cool. I just looked like a kid who was trying to hide the fact that he should be carded by every bartender committed to preventing underage drinking.

Phil has sent a colorful cast of clients my way. These folks are often both memorable and less than enthusiastic about the prospects of therapy. One such referral led us both down a very dangerous path several years past. In that time, I learned that underneath Phil's usual Zen-like demeanor lurks a cauldron of fierceness and vulnerability. No doubt; it's better to have him as a friend than an enemy.

The "Tell me more" portion of my response was in reference to the previously mentioned unflagging snoopiness. I'd hoped that by running around with Phil I would sharpen the point on my childhood dream of Investigator Hank. Instead, I'd become a referral source. Phil had detected that, although I've often complained about his unique collection of legally challenged referrals, curiosity tends to get the best of me. My desire to hear a good story, and help a person in pain create a healthier story, has been known to overwhelm my caution.

"I've got a guy who was arrested last week. His troubles are in your area of expertise."

"What would that be?"

"He drives a delivery van for Intercontinental Plus. IP is one of those house-to-house delivery companies. An unusual number of packages were coming up missing. The internal investigation went on for a while. They were all small shipments. A lot of the thefts were the same kind of products."

He had me. I switched phone ears. "What kind of products?"

"I'm getting to that."

Oh, he's good. Give me the details slowly. Draw me in.

"We were called in after the audit. I investigated, and found an unusual number of the thefts were on one young man's route. We got a warrant and checked out his place."

I reached for my coffee.

Here it comes.

"Turns out he stole more than five thousand dollars' worth of goods over several years' time. A felony. He had a whole room in his apartment stacked with open IP boxes."

I'm interested, not easy. "Why me? I don't do a lot of thief therapy."

"Most of what he stole was mail-order sex stuff. Anyway, he says he knows he has a problem and needs help."

There's the hook.

And Phil thought immediately of me.

Sure.

I eased back in my precious leather rocker as my thoughts drifted out the window.

Somewhere along the line, one of my specialties became working with folks who struggle with sexually compulsive behaviors. Contrary to popular opinion, there is sexual trouble in the breadbasket of America. It's probably the creeping influence of the East and West coasts.

As our understanding of gender identity, sexual orientation and healthy sexuality evolve, the complexity faced by young and old alike accelerates. Helping professionals are scurrying to keep up. Years of listening to stories about the intersection of escape, excitement, shame, and danger has given me a deep reverence for folks who cope with and recover from the challenges of any health-threatening compulsion. My compassion is grounded in the belief that there is no such thing as, "Now, I've heard everything."

"Hank, you there?" Phil called me back from my mental soapbox.

"Sorry, got lost in my reflections on sexuality in our culture and the courage of people in recovery. I'm back."

"Try to think out loud when I'm on the phone with you."

"Sure. Here's a thought. The prospect of jail time is usually not an authentic motivation to engage in therapy."

"Hey, it's a place to start," Phil said, without the strength of religious conviction in his voice.

"One of the reasons it's good you're a cop instead of a crook is that you're an innately lousy liar," I said. "You guys arrest thieves every day. You charge them, send them to the judge, and they get slapped on the wrist or sent up the lazy river. How come this man rates a big-time detective as his personal social worker?"

"I really don't know. The word came down from above that this guy was going to get probation on his charges, and that I needed to find him some help."

The tone of Phil's voice suggested he was less than happy about being left out of the full loop. "How high above, my God-fearing friend?"

His grunt echoed through the line.

"Not that high. I got it from the Captain. That's all I know."

He clearly didn't like admitting that fact either. He was displeased that he had also been appointed the client's ersatz probation officer, but Phil was a man who fervently followed the chain of command.

A way Phil and I were different.

"By the way, one of the reasons it's good you're a therapist instead of a comedian is that you're not that funny."

"I've been told that before, but remain undaunted."

I took a breath and pretended to struggle with his request.

"Because you are one of my favorite coppers and I know you will owe me a favor, send the fellow my way."

"Favor?"

"Coffee. Lots of coffee. And donuts."

I sensed the closest Phil got to a grin through the phone.

"It's a deal."

I grabbed a pen and pad as Phil gave me a name and told me he would have the man in question call me for an appointment ASAP. He'd already had the fellow sign a release of information, so he could be updated on whether my new client was showing up for appointments and cooperating. Of course, this meant Phil had assumed, before he even dialed the phone, that I would say yes to the referral.

Am I that predictable?

I didn't ask.

We agreed to get together soon for high-test caffeine. His treat.

After hanging up the phone I stood and did a little victory dance.

This could be a multiple cruller favor.

WEDNESDAY

Promptly at eleven the next morning, Kenny Jensen strolled into my office, taking his best shot at nonchalance. He'd called first thing, before I hit the door, and informed Belinda that Phil told him to get in right away. Belinda gave him a slot usually kept open for paperwork. She often did that when I neglected to leave her messages about new client referrals. It's kind of like being given an extra chore by Mom when you've screwed up. The difference is that Anderson & Greenberg gives this mom a paycheck every two weeks to treat me this way.

The data sheet Belinda had given Kenny to fill out in the waiting room said he was twenty-six years old and lived in a blue-collar neighborhood of southeast Des Moines. I walked him into my office. He had a smooth, shaved head and a small gold hoop in his left ear. He was wearing blue jeans, a jean jacket, and a gray T-shirt with a midnight-blue-and-gold IP, the Intercontinental Plus emblem, on his shirt pocket. He was, as my dad would say, a "wiry" young man, six foot or more and sinewy. He seemed to be going for the Michael Jordan look, if MJ had been a white guy who worked in delivery.

"What's this, Doc," he opened, pointing to my sofa. "A couch in a shrink's office?"

"It's OK to call me Hank." I smiled a welcome. "Almost nobody lies down on it anymore."

Kenny's nervous laughter blew the nonchalance cover.

"Yeah, I know."

"Oh, you've been in therapy before." He hadn't written that on his data sheet.

"Yeah."

Kenny's grimace indicated displeasure that the first personal disclosure of the session had occurred on impulse.

"Well, sit wherever you want."

"How about your chair?"

"Sure, but then you have to be brilliant."

"The cop said you thought you were funny," he responded, taking a seat in the wingback chair that sits alone in the far corner of my office. He was what Dad would call, "twitchy." Eyes darting. Shifting in his chair. Opening and closing his fists.

I sat in my desk chair. Relaxed and interested.

"What else did he tell you?"

"That you know a lot about guys with my kind of problem. I hope so. I need help."

So much for banter.

"Tell me about the help you're looking for."

He looked straight at me and crossed his arms.

Defensive?

I crossed my legs to give him space.

He's scared. No threat here.

"I steal stuff. Stupid stuff. Stuff I don't even need. And porn."

"Porn," I prompted.

"Used to shoplift from the corner mart, back in the day." He shrugged the information away. "Finally went big time at IP. They caught me stealing from my route. I don't know why," he added, shaking his head a bit. "I've been doing it for a long time. Never got caught before."

I doubt that.

"Never?"

"Well, one time. When I was a kid, my mom caught me on the computer. She was really pissed. Called me names. Smacked me around. Made me go to church. No big deal."

The blank stare into a not-so-distant past contradicted Kenny's claim. He had been shamed, hit, and humiliated for being a hormonally charged adolescent boy.

I softened my tone.

"Feelings still coming up about that time in your life?" Testing the waters.

"Not really." Crossed arms. Crossed legs. Like a cocoon.

"The past is the past," he monotoned.
I let the inconsistency go for another time and circled back.

"Was that when you got sent to therapy for the first time?"

"Mom took me to some guy she found. I don't remember his name. Dr. Somebody. A real dull pencil," he shook his head more vigorously. "We played checkers and he asked me questions about my parents' divorce. I didn't tell him about the computer stuff and he didn't ask. We had a few meetings. Mom decided it was a waste of time."

He gazed back into his mental time machine. "It got bad after that."

"Bad?"

"I started getting heavy into the porn."

At that, Kenny settled back into the chair and replayed the uncountable hours he had lost to fantasy during his youth. His face and arms relaxed, but his fingers drummed a constant rhythm on the cushioned armrests.

The explosion of the Information Highway had changed everything. Easy access. He got better at not getting caught. Porn on steroids.

The narrative was not unusual, in my work. Nor was the invisible emotional wall made visible by the disconnect between the flatness of his tone and the continuous motion of his body.

Who and why and when? He didn't just use porn for a while and then become a thief.

I steered the interview back toward Kenny's family.

Running his hand over his head, as if smoothing hair he didn't have, Kenny spoke chronologically. His parents divorced when he was eleven. He had infrequent contact with his alcoholic father. Kenny's overworked mother directed her pain and wrath his way for "being just like that bum."

No close friends as a kid. Spent a lot of time alone. Didn't date. Couldn't imagine how to talk to a girl he found attractive.

Kenny went on to share that his mom had died of a heart attack when he was 20, due, in part, to years of heavy smoking.

"I'd already moved out. We got along pretty well after I left home." He sounded matter-of-fact. "Can't say I miss her much."

Could be a lot underneath.

"Kenny."

His body stilled and he looked as if he was seeing me for the first time.

"Doc." He stayed with that.

"It sounds like some tough times that you had to handle on your own."

"True enough," he nodded to himself.

"You've been open and given me a lot of information about your childhood."

He made eye contact, smiling as if he had just been complimented for good behavior.

"I'm also noticing that you don't show much emotion as you tell your story."

"As I said, Doc, the past is the past," he repeated, parroting a statement I've heard from many clients over the years. "Just figured you needed the details. Should I stop?"

Now his look back to me was reminiscent of a chastised boy. The most distress I'd seen. I didn't know what was behind Kenny's recitation. My best early guess? I was seeing a young man who, at the very least, had spent years numbing his emotional pain with the behaviors that eventually led to his arrest.

He didn't wait for my response.

"I like talking. I'm not messing up right now, but sure as hell will again if I don't get some help. You're listening and I don't get much of that."

He was looking for a willing listener. A reasonable place to start.

"That's certainly a place we can start," I encouraged.

I finished the session asking for other history that would help me see Kenny as a whole person, not a thief with a sexual problem. He immediately shared his aversion for all alcohol and drugs.

"No way was I going to be like my dad. Don't drink. No drugs. Hell, I barely take aspirin."

OK. There's some juice.

It had yet to occur to him that he may have substituted stealing and secret sex for alcohol. I stopped the surge of energy from reaching my mouth. That interpretation could wait for another day.

Kenny reported he was in excellent physical health and had worked for IP for five years, after knocking around at a variety of odd jobs. He had an exemplary employee record.

"Until the stealing thing, Doc."

"I noticed you have an IP T-shirt on."

"Can't get used to the idea I've been fired," he lamented.

"Your job was important to you?"

He leaded forward and studied his hands.

"Work is the most important thing in my life."

"I get that."

Winding down, I shifted the discussion toward closure.

"Kenny, is there anything else you want me to know today, as we're beginning our work together?"

The sincere expression that Kenny had maintained through most of the hour shifted in a flash, replaced by an unmistakable look that Dad used to call, "a deer caught in your headlights." Fear, and lots of it.

"I can't think of anything, Hank. I've tried to be really honest about my problems."

I could have just taken note of the incongruity between Kenny's face and his words, and come back to this another time, much like my earlier decision about the substitute addiction theory. Or I could have admitted to myself that some days I'm more bumbling Dr. Watson than wily Sherlock Holmes, cleverly pushing to the truth.

Instead, I said "Maybe it's not about the troubles you were sent here for."

The fear moved from his face to a whole array of arm itching, voice trembling, and eyes moving to the escape hatch that was my door.

"Take my word for it, Hank. You don't want to know. It's better for your health if you don't."

He'd quit calling me "Doc."

I managed to reel in my curiosity.

"Maybe it's too soon to talk about. When you're ready, I'll be here to listen," I reassured.

"I don't think so," he said, looking me dead in the eyes and shaking his head with absolute certainty.

Kenny moved on with a sober countenance and an appointment to return in two days. We hadn't begun to talk about how to interrupt his possible compulsion, or other types of acting out that might accompany his troubles at IP.

Don't assume this was the whole story.

He knew he was in trouble and was clear that he wanted to get started on solutions. Fear was his current motivator, and experience told me that would fade in time.

With my thoughts still in the last hour, I wandered into our office suite's small kitchenette to get a reheated cup of the recycled motor oil Belinda claims is coffee.

Bad coffee is preferable to no coffee at all. Maybe.

I returned to my desk, stood with my back to the door, and commenced to seriously stare out the window onto Ingersoll Avenue. Late morning traffic trickled by like Iowa beef cattle wandering across the field to the creek. Perhaps it was the early crowd heading to lunch at the pub down the street. That free-association jumped to the idea of throwing a bit of table shuffleboard down at one of my favorite watering holes sometime soon. I mimicked the motion of sliding the hefty steel puck across my desk, minus the sawdust, then pulled my attention back to Kenny.

It wasn't a caffeine buzz that coursed throughout my body. It was the aftershock of the deep fear he had expressed, not because of what he said, but what he wouldn't say.

Two obvious possibilities. First, Kenny was well practiced at distancing himself from years of internal and external conflict. Other aspects of his history might carry deeper pain than he felt safe enough to disclose this early. Not unusual. Second, whatever Kenny didn't tell me was more frightening than being arrested and losing his job.

Lost in my silent meandering, I didn't hear Dennis Greenberg arrive.

"What's up, Marlowe?"

Dennis, knowing my penchant for mysteries, had long ago christened me Phillip Marlowe, Jr., a lesser version of the detective of Raymond Chandler and Humphrey Bogart fame. It saves him from having to treat me with the respect of using my real name.

I kind of like it.

"Post-session staring," turning toward him as I pointed to the window. "It's an essential part of the experienced clinician's repertoire. Stick with me and I'll teach it to you."

"And lose my standing in the AA community? No thanks," he snorted. "I put up with enough shit already for hanging around with you, a normie psychotherapist." He drew out the syllables of "psychotherapist" like he was a little slow on the intellectual draw. "If it gets out that I learned something from you, my credibility is toast." His smile softened the sarcasm.

Dennis is the Greenberg of Anderson & Greenberg. As usual, he looked exceedingly dapper, more like an old-school liberal arts college professor than the most revered and feared chemical dependency counselor in our great Farmland. He's all tweed-and-elbow-patches on the outside. Many are the fools who've been drawn in by this appearance of civility. Dennis is sometimes abrasive and confrontational, but seldom uncertain.

"Marlowe," he repeated, calling me back from memory lane.

A quick shake of my head and I was in the present, again. "New client."

"Another person digressing from cultural norms?"

Dennis was messing with me. "Possible sexual compulsion with other complications," I said with precise, professional diction.

"Dress up a 'compulsive drinker' in fancy duds, he's still a drunk."

"I see what you mean." I let my gaze move up and down his stylish garb.

He grinned, letting me know he could take it as well as dish it out. "Anyway, what's the deal? You only stare out the window when they get under your skin."

"This was one of those too easy initial sessions, until it wasn't. Lots of stories about his acting out. Almost no emotion through most of the hour. A little anger, but mostly like he was reading a book report on granular herbicides."

"Not unusual. Lots of people put their pain in a box and lock it down. Takes time for them to reconnect. You know that."

"Sure, but that's not what grabbed me about this fellow," I groused, impatient with the lesson. "At the end of the session I asked him the million-dollar closing question. He got quiet. Scared as hell. Completely serious. Staring off into the great beyond. He suggested there's stuff – big stuff – going on in his life that I'm better off not knowing."

"Once again, no huge news. Client comes in carrying a boatload of baggage, assumes his or her story is the most horrible you've ever heard. Says you can't handle hearing it, instead of admitting the shame of carrying it around."

"That's not it," I reminded him. "It wasn't shame that roared to the surface at the end. His fear filled the room."

"Got it," he said. "So, what's your plan?"

"See him again soon. Get to know him better. Build a working relationship. Continue to help him decide if he really is struggling with compulsive behavior. Develop an early treatment plan to interrupt his pattern of acting out. Talk to your brilliant self if I get stuck." I smiled back. "He signed a consent for me to consult with you and with Detective Phil, who referred him."

"And," I thumped the doodles that passed for session notes on my desk. "Hope to build enough safety and trust that he can talk about what is scaring him into silence."

Dennis nodded.

"That could take some time. Remember, Marlowe, moving at the pace he can cope with is how we work."

Dennis' need to play mentor.

"The last part of your plan, consulting with me, is insightful, though," he validated. "That's what we do here. Rely on each other. I've got your back. You've got mine."

He grabbed my pen off the desk as he moved to the door.

"In service of that teamwork, I need a pen," he said. "And now, I have my own clients to see. I'll check in with you if I need *your* expertise."

Nice parting shot.

I was roused from further mental ramblings by Belinda poking her head into my office.

"Jeff is here."

Jeff was a portly, married grocer from a nearby rural community, who had been fighting a private war with his own extramarital affairs for twenty-plus years. At the age of forty-four, he decided it was time to get help. He'd been winning the war, but his marriage was a casualty of the battles -- his wife was leaving him. He spent an hour sliding between gratitude for his progress and sadness for the impending loss of the woman he still loved.

My next client arrived as I replaced the coagulated axle grease in my cup with ice water.

I am deeply interested in more than sexual issues. Karen had been grieving the sudden loss of her mom to cancer shortly after Karen married. She had been pulled into her grief, shutting others out, and putting serious stress on the brand-new marriage. Her husband had been supportive, and increasingly frustrated.

By all reports, Mom had been a loving, warm, firm, and fallible human being who Karen loved with every fiber of her being. In the past months, she had taken inventory of her mother's strengths and shortcomings. She had gone deep into her anger about the "unfairness" of this death. She and I also had laughed over Mom's incongruous fondness for old Monty Python episodes.

After many months of courageous work, today would be our final meeting.

"I won't stop missing her, Hank." There was an edge in her voice as her eyes narrowed.

"No, you won't. And don't let anyone say you should, Karen."

"But I don't have to hide from my life to remember how much I love her, do I? She would want me to be happy with Anthony, wouldn't she?"

All that was required of me was a nod to validate the review of her insights.

Then, as she had many times over the past months, Karen cried. I wondered one last time why she always arrived with perfect makeup, knowing her tears would overpower her morning's efforts. I added a few tears of my own. So much for solving all the mysteries of therapy and unwavering professional detachment.

Karen had replayed and found healing in the conundrum of how love collides with loss. She thanked me, committing to return if she hit another stuck point. I thanked her for the privilege of being a part of her work.

Returning to the quiet energy left behind by a departing client, I rocked back in my chair and sighed, peaceful and a bit tired.

Time to put some fuel in the tank.

Having hit the floor running, therapeutically speaking, I decided to treat myself to a high-octane mid-day meal. A quality Iowa cheeseburger was on my wish list. Belinda declined my offer to bring her a takeout order.

I still long for the best chocolate malt in the Midwest. Quite a few years back, that was Stella's Diner. The downtown location, of course. At Stella's, the wait staff would gladly pour your malt for you, or occasionally on you. Any trusting customer could steady the glass on their head. The waiter would stand on a chair and pour that baby into the glass from several feet above. The truly bold would lie on the floor and hold the malt glass to their foreheads. The waitress would stand on a chair and pour from eight or nine feet above these adventuresome individuals. The staff rarely missed.

For reasons beyond my comprehension, Stella's had closed. After what others might say was more than enough time to move on, I still mourned. Today, in a best-case compensatory gesture, I headed for another diner of local repute. While waiting for a "table for one," my thoughts drifted back to Dennis, and I punched my internal repeat button on how the improbable partnership of Anderson & Greenberg had come to pass.

I met Dennis as a fledgling therapist, at my first job out of graduate school. I was young, carried a leather brief case, and was primed for action. On my third day, a psychiatric resident told me I ought to get to know Dennis. He sent me down the hall with a case to review. I can still imagine the snickering in the nurse's station as I, the lamb, hurried off to the slaughter that was Dennis Greenberg.

I did not know that the stories of Dennis' years working at county rehab were the stuff legends are made of in this field. Publicly dressing down a young internist in the nurse's station for prescribing a high dose Benzo to a "nervous" alcoholic two weeks off a binge of vodka and Codeine. Falling on the office floor to feign being devastated by a manipulative patient's coarse words. Dancing in group therapy to illustrate the importance of learning sober fun for the men and women who had been blessed – or burdened – with an alcohol-free field trip to see the Iowa Cubs play.

Dennis played along that day. He invited me into his office to hear my case summary and treatment recommendations. Then he told me I didn't have a clue about addictions and was incredibly naïve, in general. He strongly suggested I avoid him and his clients as much as possible.

It's difficult to remember whether my anger, fear or embarrassment was greater that day. But Dennis was right about one thing. I was naïve.

Proof? Deciding that I wanted to learn what he knew; my eagerness outdistanced my fear. I found every opportunity available to connect with him.

After several weeks of scowling at me, Dennis strolled into my office and appointed himself as my mentor. He said he was a sucker for strays. He offered me literature to read, introduced me to other addiction professionals, and took me to seminars. He sent me to open Alcoholics Anonymous, Narcotics Anonymous and Sexual Compulsives Anonymous meetings. He let me observe him at work. What I saw lurking beneath his gruff old-timer's exterior was a level of patience, empathy, directness, and knowledge that inspired me. For people new to sobriety, he is often barely tolerable. Those same people, days, months, and years into recovery, believe he's the most compassionate and smartest man on the planet.

When he and I left County to open our practice, Dennis suggested my name go first on the door, appeasing my, at times, fragile ego. He is often the most supportive person I know. Sometimes he's an obnoxious jerk. He's my best friend.

The growl in my stomach called me back as my table came open.

No malts. I had Andy bring a reasonable second choice, a soda fountain style Vanilla Coke. He always smiles when I wax poetic about the days of Stella's, but steadfastly refuses my advances regarding long distance pouring.

Taking the first sip of this more than adequate elixir, I felt soothed. Maybe there was a book in this, something for therapists on the merits of a diner diet for replenishing therapeutic stamina. I immersed myself in a fabulous cheeseburger, cooked medium, fully loaded. Side salad. Low fat dressing. No fries. A balanced meal, of sorts.

Reluctantly declining a soda refill, I returned to the office reinvigorated. An early clinical day was completed in the company of Mel, a man who had survived years of prescription drug addiction. We'd worked together on and off for a decade, as he moved in and out of sobriety and inpatient treatment. He had quit therapy more times than we could count. In the last three years he had begun to realize he was an intelligent, creative person. He was sober, had a good job in commercial real estate, and was a fixture in the local AA community, sponsoring younger men who reminded him of his former self. Of late, he was beginning to retrieve several key losses in his youth; grief that had only surfaced in the absence of substances to deaden old pain.

As Mel walked out of my office, I reflected on the day's clients and an early clinical supervisor of mine. Dr. Fleming assured me that as therapists mature, we become "neutral agents of change."

"Remember, Hank," he would caution. "You are only a mirror, there to reflect back the client's thoughts and feelings."

Yada, yada, yada.

The truth was, these people touched my heart. Mel and I had invested years in his recovery. This man, with his tough exterior and soft heart, was a miracle. I knew it, and now he knew it. Jeff was struggling and committed to change. Karen was re-engaged in her marriage, full of old love and new.

The respect I felt for each of them was a tangible force that gave meaning to many of my days.

What about Kenny? Mel. Jeff. Karen. And Kenny. More work to be done, Anderson.

Rolling my shoulders, I pushed back from my desk, half-heartedly accepting that it was time to turn to paperwork, my ever-present nemesis. It worked best to think of paperwork as the evil necessary to do the work I cared about --

counseling. That bit of mental gymnastics allowed me to lean back in and boot up the laptop.

As good fortune would have it, Belinda poked her head in the doorway and interrupted me.

Belinda is sixtyish. She looks fortyish. She is what my dad calls, "a force of nature", and as he also would say, "dresses to the nines." She is the prime candidate for being my mom in the next life. I will have to come back as an African-American, or adopted, to make this happen. Or maybe we'll both come back as Swiss, or dolphins. Anyway, Belinda is efficient, smart, kind, and, best of all, crude. She thinks I'm the cat's meow and covers my disorganized butt on a regular basis.

Since her husband Cal died suddenly several years ago, Belinda has taken an even deeper interest in my life. She considers herself my advisor in all matters professional, personal, and otherwise. Cal and Belinda invested well and she doesn't really need the modest income generated by her job at Anderson & Greenberg. It's a labor of love. She claims to communicate spiritually with my biological mom, Sheila, receiving essential instructions on how to help me avoid having too many irons in the fire at once.

Belinda has spent so many years working for therapists that she's developed her own informal counseling practice in the waiting room. The clients love her. I regularly hurry them into my office before her frankness and compassion cures them, and they don't require my services. It keeps me running on time.

"Your only real deficiency is that swill you call coffee," I said, looking up from the dreaded screen.

"What are you talking about?" Like Phil and Dennis, Belinda often pulls me back to the real world from my internal-dialogue-made-public.

"Nothing," coming back to the moment. "I forgot to leave you a note about Kenny Jensen being referred." I have a knack, at times, for expressing the obvious. "Don't ever retire, my practice would fall apart."

"Yes, it would," she tilted her head in mock pity. "But from the peaceful look on Karen's face, you kicked some serious therapeutic ass today. Take the rest of the day off, hotshot."

"She did the work. I was just there when she was ready."

"False humility is bullshit."

"You're right. I'm f*ing brilliant."

"OK, now reel it in a bit."

Pretending to reel in an imaginary fish was rewarded with a hearty giggle.

A few progress notes later, it was time to shut down for the day. Belinda headed out to make the bank deposit. To our surprise, several insurance companies had correctly reimbursed us for work done in the past several months. We wanted the checks to clear the bank before the companies got bought out by another healthcare conglomerate.

Dennis finished with his last client of the day and left to join his husband Jerry for their weekly Wednesday ritual of soup and coffee. This would be followed by separate 12-Step meetings. Dennis would be hitting his AA home group. Jerry would catch an Al-Anon meeting, the self-help program for loved ones of alcoholics and chemical dependents.

As a gay Jewish man, a recovering alcoholic and a counselor, Dennis helped bring diversity to the recovering community. He loves that. He met Jerry at an Al-Anon conference fourteen years ago, and they'd been together ever since.

Jerry is forever after me to join him at his Al-Anon meeting, "All therapists are co-dependent as hell, Hank!"

Dennis tells him it's co-dependent as hell to keep hassling me about meetings. Jerry says it's because he cares about me. Dennis grumbles that the line between caring and nagging seems a little hazy for Jerry. Jerry ignores him. No one else gets away with ignoring Dennis the way Jerry does.

I admire him for that.

I was invited as always, but tonight there were more important fish to fry. I had a date with the girl of my dreams. Dad time. My daughter, Haley. Eight years old and as iridescent as the comet she is named for.

Haley is the best part of my marriage to Gail. Divorced for two years now, Gail and I had managed to create a cordial, uneasy friendship. It was complicated by the fact that I still thought she was the sexiest woman this side of the Quad Cities. She may know this. My keen therapist assessment skills have often been rendered impotent in the presence of Gail. She's also in the counseling biz. Working with kids in school settings requires an inscrutable visage.

She's my greatest unsolved mystery.

I hurried out the door, taking the stairs to the parking lot. On days when I indulge my passion for a luncheon cheeseburger and there's no time for a bike ride, the stairs beckon. Today, having gone the distance with a Vanilla Coke, I took the stairs double-time.

Rationalization can be a wonderful thing.

Walking into the early evening I breathed in the perfect chill and began letting go of the workday. I inhaled the purple and orange tapestry of the October sky. The song "Shine on Harvest Moon," an homage to autumn that Mom used to sing as she wandered through the house, played in my memory as the sun slowly descended into the other side of the world. Fond memories of my mother helped foster my transition from psychotherapist to dad.

Pumped up and distracted by past and present thoughts, I was caught completely unaware by the sight of the two men in the parking lot, leaning against my midnight blue Jeep Cherokee.

A bit of loose gravel crunched against the silence as I slid to a halt.

The first guy was tall and lean. The other was built like a defensive lineman, or maybe a v-shaped brick wall with the addition of a pillowy beer gut. On the edge of my consciousness, I noted that the lineman didn't look soft anywhere else. JJ Watts with a belly.

The thin man, closest to me, effortlessly pushed himself off the Jeep, keeping his hands in his pants pockets. He had a sallow, scrubbed complexion and close-cropped, military-style flint gray hair. He was dressed completely in black: a wool blend suit, polo shirt buttoned to the neck, tasseled loafers. His look suggested that of a preacher possessed by Satan in a B-horror movie.

I didn't know why a sudden fear hammered me in the chest, but I knew it was the right feeling.

"Doc Anderson." A statement, not a question.

"What do you want?" I asked, hoping the shakiness of my voice was all in my head.

"We came to consult with you on Kenny."

The threat in the man's voice enveloped me from across the lot.

"I don't know who you're referring to and I don't give information in the parking lot. I have someplace else to be."

The tall, thin preacher man grinned, flat and humorless.

"We didn't come to get information, Doc. We came to give it. You see, Kenny's got some very serious problems, much bigger than anything you can help him with. He also has friends who have a strong interest in his wellbeing. We believe it is not in Kenny's best interests to initiate a relationship with a shrink at this point in his life. We hope you understand."

He said this like he didn't care at all if I understood.

"I don't know what you're talking about." The hostility arrived before my brain could tighten the lid on my lips. "Again, I don't make decisions while I'm standing in the parking lot talking to strangers."

That grin again. He turned to the fat JJ look-alike, who was staring off into the distance.

"The Doc's a feisty guy."

No expression or reply from his comrade.

Turning back, Preacher said, "I like guys with big balls, Doc, I really do. My friend Jake, however, likes cooperation. A smart, educated guy like you can probably see that right away."

I looked at the man, who may or may not have been named Jake. Anyone, even someone without the keen observational powers of a trained psychotherapist, could easily grasp Preacher's point.

"I have no problem with you gentlemen. Time for me to leave."

"You bet, Doc. Just keep in mind what I said. You've got a good thing going here. Nice office, fresh air, snappy looking Jeep. Just go back to your worried housewives and husbands who need to bitch about their worried housewives. Forget about Kenny."

An "or else" hung in the air.

Preacher turned toward a generic maroon Plymouth parked a few feet away, in the creeping shadows of the building. Jake stood up straight without any signal, moved one step toward me and locked eyes for what seemed like a long time.

Preacher took his time moving to the passenger's side, opened the car door, stopped, and pointed at the building. "Like they say in the movies, Doc, we know where you live."

He slid into the passenger's seat as Jake strolled to the driver's side. The only hiccup in their well-oiled intimidation routine was the considerable effort required for Jake to secure his bulk behind the wheel. Without another look my way, he cranked the engine, backed out, eased the car past me, and pulled into the traffic on Ingersoll.

I willed the rubber in my legs to carry me to the Jeep, leaning on the hood with both elbows.

Breathe. Holy shit.

They hadn't hurt me. What they had done was project a forewarning of violence so real its after-effects blocked out the meager remaining daylight.

There are people with a hole in their souls; individuals that other kinds of folks should only meet on the opposite side of steel bars.

I knew my recent visitors were such men.

As a connoisseur of fine mystery novels, I have always been frustrated with the fatuous protagonist who has no experience in matters of mystery and mayhem, yet insists on embarking on a solo mission to heroically solve the crime. These folks are a close second on the all-time fool's scale, right behind the person in the slasher movie who says, "We've got to find them. Let's split up."

Based on this idea, I have always believed that common sense would convince any reasonable man or woman drawn into some version of this puzzling quagmire to immediately call 911 and turn matters over to the police.

These assumptions crossed my mind as I carefully punched the remote door opener, commanded my legs to move, and eased myself into the Jeep, hoping my hand would be steady enough to put the key into the ignition.

I could call Phil. I could call Kenny and cancel our next session. I should call Phil and cancel my next session with Kenny. What the hell? I didn't get a license plate number.

Reaching for my cell phone and noticing the time in big numbers on the screen, a dangerous hesitation kicked in.

I'm going to be late again. I'll catch Phil tonight.

A choice I would later regret.

Managing to steady myself just enough to start the Jeep, I drove out of the parking lot and pointed west. The Jeep worked its way past Greenwood Park and the Art Center, turned north, crossed I-235, and headed up Merle Hay Road, beyond the mall.

The Cherokee caught every red light in a not particularly scenic but comfortably familiar drive north, then took the brief jog back east. I hoped the natural calming effect of my approach through the tree-lined boulevard would work its magic and, sure enough, my adrenalin slowly stopped firing off like bottle rockets in a bonfire. By the time I reached our street I was relatively certain I could walk to Gail's door without hitting the pavement face first.

Our street? Gail's door.

Pulling into the sloped concrete driveway I turned the ignition off and stared at the modest, pristine brick home with single-space carport. My mental tumblers shifted and I entered a different mindset, one from a more distant time. These days, this place activates a dull ache – part friend, part enemy – that fills my entire body. The pain reminds me, again, that I love this house and everyone in it. This "Beaverdale Brick", as the locals call the style, used to embody security for me. This was where my bride and I started our life together, where we both came to hide after a tough day. Where my baby slept.

It's not our street anymore.

After two years, I still walk up to Gail's door with confusion about how it stopped being our door. The facts were clear. With the loving confrontation and support of both Dennis and Bob Rathburn, my therapist at the time, it had been established that Gail and I had simply let our intimacy die a slow, mostly civilized death. No screaming. No drunken brawls. No clothes thrown in the street in the middle of the night.

Just way too much avoidance.

My part was repeating the distancing I'd learned growing up in a quietly tense alcoholic family. Gail's part, as others reminded me, was her business, not mine.

How could a man whose life was about communication and resolving conflict allow his marriage to die with barely a whimper? And why was I still pondering that question? Dad would say I was "beating a dead horse." Maybe I was trying to beat the damn horse alive again, hoping he'd answer the question so I could restart my former life.

Feeling the shift from the warmth of my Jeep to the deepening bite of evening, I pushed off thought paralysis for the second time within the hour. I found myself standing on the small concrete porch, both excited and apprehensive. I rang the doorbell. I don't just walk in unannounced.

A squeal came from behind the door, which was yanked open by the combined power of the two prettiest females I'd ever set eyes on, the little one a picture image of the full-size version. The adult had long, blond hair framing a softly tanned face of perfect skin, wonderfully full cheeks, and the kind of naturally generous lips that plastic surgeons are paid big bucks to manufacture. The miniature, mirror-model was wearing blue jeans, an Iowa State Cyclone's red-and-gold sweatshirt, and flashy new black-on-red Reeboks.

As always, I also noticed the significant difference between the two. The grown up one had curves, lots of them. The curves were held barely in check by a high-neck champagne colored silk blouse and a black skirt that stopped just above two excellent knees. I passed on the clever sexual innuendo that popped into my head.

"Daddy!"

Haley burst through the doorway and threw herself into my arms. She quickly let go, took a step back, and put her hands in the place where she would someday have hips. She composed her best attempt at a serious, grown-up look of annoyance and said, "You're late!"

"Sorry, kiddo. Got running a bit behind at the office."

Looking from Haley to Gail, I saw another look of disapproval. On Gail's face. Or, maybe I was just projecting my guilt about being late again. I do that sometimes.

"Well, who cares, you're here now," came Haley's instant forgiveness. "Come look at my room. Mom got me the Cassie Simons poster I just had to have!"

She grabbed my hand and off we went to the back of the house. Relishing the few moments of sitting on her bed - in the bedroom Gail and I had painted sky blue, with white clouds on a wallpaper border - Haley's rapid-fire chatter became beautiful background noise.

These days the walls were plastered with posters of the latest pop diva, Cassie Simons, and a variety of American, English, and Korean boy bands, that prepackaged mix of sensitive, sexy, rebellious, and pseudo-soulful dancers who also happen to sing. I pretended to listen attentively as she told me all about a singer who wasn't even born when I discovered my love for music.

Just as quickly as she'd dashed to her room, Haley grabbed her backpack and jacket, grabbed my hand, and pulled me toward the entryway.

"Let's roll, Dad."

Gail had retreated to the living room.

"We're going Mom!"

Gail peeked around the corner. "Can I check on something with you, Hank?

"Sure," hoping I'd kept the nervousness out of my voice, a different kind of apprehension than the recent parking lot session punching my pulse rate. "Hang tight for a minute, pal."

Haley reluctantly trudged out the door to wait on the porch. She hates to miss out on anything; a second-generation natural born snoop.

Gail came out to the entryway, a furrow of concern across her typically smooth forehead.

"You look tired. Is something wrong?"

"Just a tough day at the practice. It ain't easy bringin' mental health to the masses all day long, ma'am," going for my best southwest Iowa drawl.

"Still covering up with flip humor, Hank." Oh God, another therapist on the prowl.

"Flip humor used to make you laugh."

"You're a therapist, Hank. You know we don't make people laugh. They choose to laugh," giving me what I call a gotcha smile as she emphasized "choose."

"You used to choose to laugh."

"Yes, I did," her nod admitting the past, nothing more. "Anyway, I was just concerned about Haley going with you if you're not feeling well."

"Oh," failing to hide the disappointment in my voice. "Just worried about Haley."

"Well, maybe a little about you." The space between her thumb and index finger was barely visible. Her half-grin qualified as wry.

"By the way," she tapped her forehead. "Just a reminder that Haley and I are going on a quick trip to see my folks after she gets out of school tomorrow. Fall break."

Gail and I had created a flexible, shared custody plan. Some structure. Adapt to special circumstance. Always remember that Haley has two parents that love her to the moon and back.

"Excellent. They'll be happy to see her." I felt the twinge of better times. My former in-laws were great people.

I put on the brave face. "I'll check with you about timing for dropping Haley off at my place when you get back to town."

"Not necessary. I'll call you."

I did my own half-grin, remembering I wasn't the only person in our marriage who liked to be in control.

Humming a bar of *You Can Call Me Al,* by the venerable Paul Simon, elicited a full "you goof-ball" smile that tased my heart.

I wanted to keep going with the snappy repartee, but knew that if I didn't get out of Beaverdale soon, my mouth was likely to say something pathetic. Like "I love you." Like "I messed up and lost you." Like "You look great. How about we give it another go."

I'd gone there before and decided give the horse a break.

"Well, thanks for your concern. We're going to take it easy at my place tonight. Belinda might drop by later. She hasn't seen Haley for a while." Too many words, but no stupid ones.

"That's great. Give Belinda my love. Make sure Haley does her homework."

I wanted to hug her.

No. I wanted to throw her over my shoulder and carry her to the bedroom in an act of caveman love-lust. But, in high heels Gail was an inch taller than me and I only had her by a few pounds.

Instead I saluted, went to the front stoop, grabbed Haley's overnight bag, threw her over my shoulder, and off we went to the Jeep. Haley yelled "Bye" and waved both hands at Gail as we zoomed off toward our house in southwest city.

As we pulled away and pointed homeward, Haley reeled in my wavering attention with her daily report. Mostly it was a life in which watching Ty Thurman laugh so hard during school lunch that milk squirted out of his nose was much more exciting than addictions and thugs and sexy ex- wives.

"Ty's black, Dad."

"Yeah?" I was immediately alert to the potential for diversity training.

"Well, all that white milk coming out his nose. It was cool. He's the funniest guy I know. And cute."

"Funnier than me?" I let "cute" go by, just not ready to know that Haley had noticed boys could be cute.

"Oh, Dad. You're just silly."

I couldn't deny that, so I got quiet and watched her out of the corner of my eye. She carried on and I silently marveled, as I often did, at her ability to live each day as something new and full of possibilities. Haley is my tutor in this. Being her dad has helped me wake up to the moment, something I'd misplaced in my rush to become educated, successful, and important. Haley was impressed with my progress. She had let me know, just before dropping off to sleep last Friday night, that I was a lot more fun lately.

As we motored on, she drifted back into her current obsession, Cassie Simons. I drifted another direction.

What was Kenny Jackson into besides his pornography use? How dangerous were those thugs? How long was it going to take me to let go of Gail? How could I get Gail back?

Realizing that the last question ran in direct conflict with the one just before it, I yanked myself back to the present. "How about Chinese?"

"Good idea, Dad. You know, I get tired of Mom cooking for me all the time." She smiled her mother's smile.

"Oh, a wise guy, eh?" My best old-timey Curly of the Three Stooges voice. "Don't know where you learn this stuff."

Haley did her part. She enthusiastically mugged the Groucho Marx eye roll, as imparted by her Grandpa Anderson.

We had just enough time en route to our favorite joint in Windsor Heights to organize the menu. This process consisted of a plan to "load up on enough food for a small army." No meal of Chinese take-out should ever be eaten in one sitting.

"How ya doin', Kid?" Mr. Liu calls every kid "Kid." "Where have you been lately?"

"My parents have been cooking for me again, Mr. Liu," Haley replied, pasting a crestfallen look on her face.

"Oh, how sad for you," Mr. Liu got right with the program, creasing his substantial eyebrows into a deep frown. "I'll tell Mrs. Liu. We must fix you up with something special," he smiled the smile of ancient Americanized Chinese culinary secrets at Haley.

Twenty minutes later, the Jeep was taken over by a dozen exotic aromas: orange chicken with hot peppers. Sweet and sour shrimp. Vegetable fried rice, Crab Rangoon, and the best egg rolls on the planet. The Lius always put in a little something extra. We're regulars. Tonight's surprise: hot and sour soup.

I pulled into the driveway and punched the garage door opener. I barely noticed a dark Cadillac Seville parked under a massive oak tree down the block. I wouldn't have noticed at all, except it was one of those monstrosities from the early 80s; the mega-sedan with the odd-looking sloped trunk.

People in this neighborhood park cars on the street all the time. Some are teenage boys who may need to make fast getaways from my neighbors' house. Melinda; Ed and Sarah's seventeen-year-old daughter, seems popular with the boys. Ed and Sarah seem careful and protective. Makes sense to me.

I didn't wonder until later if there was anyone in the car. It was too dark to see. I did wonder how many adolescent boys I would be forced to investigate when Haley reached adolescence.

We hit the kitchen through the garage, laden with culinary treasures and ready to chow down. Soon the usually tidy countertop was strewn with cardboard containers and our plates were heaped with happiness. Haley went traditional for her drink, a raspberry juice box. I foraged and found the last Negro Modelo in the fridge.

Chinese food and Mexican beer. What could be better?

We moved out of the small no-more-than-three-people-comfortably-sitting-at-the-counter kitchen and hung a right down the four steps to a sunken living room. This was the largest room in the house. With huge made-in-Iowa Pella windows on two sides, a stone hearth fireplace at the far end, and furnishings of forest green and maroon, this was my haven. Mom had left me a little nest egg from her life insurance policy. As my divorce became inevitable, the nest egg had become a comforting new nest.

I had basically lived in this room for six months after leaving Beaverdale. I'd come home from work on the nights Haley was in Gail's custody, drink a couple of beers, and flop in front of the big screen or the fireplace, depending on whether I had the extra motivation to build a fire. I was mired in a combination of genuine grief and unadulterated self-pity. The nightly pattern was several hours of soundless pain, followed by an uneasy sleep on the sofa. I'd wake early with a taste in my mouth like I'd eaten organic waste the night before and hit the Ground Hog Day button in my brain.

After three months, Dennis got sick of watching me tread water and started showing up at my door with Jerry. Sometimes they'd coax me out of the house for bicycling or shuffleboard. Sometimes I'd just listen to them talk about what I needed to do to get my life in order. Jerry would tell me my decorating tastes were grossly out of style. I would pretend to care.

It helped. I got better. I learned again what friendship is.

"Dad, are you spacing out?"

"Sorry, pal. How's the sweet and sour shrimp?"

"The best. I'd love to have Mr. Liu's secret recipe."

"I'm with you there."

As we were scooping up the last of the sauce with our fried rice, the doorbell rang. That was followed immediately by keys rattling as the front door burst open.

Belinda. I'd given her a key for emergencies. Such as, coming in anytime she wanted.

"Come on in," I shouted.

"Don't be such a smart-ass, Hank," she countered, with another rattle of her keys. "Sorry about the language, baby. Your dad just needs to be set straight sometimes."

"I know what you mean, Belinda." Two fake stern looks.

"Give me some big loving, Haley."

We got up and there were hugs all around before we moved back toward the sofa.

"What'd cha bring me?"

Belinda pulled up short with a look of mock surprise.

"How do you know I brought you anything, girl?"

Haley gave her best fake pout.

"Here you go." Belinda played at begrudgingly pulling a small plastic bag from the pocket of her cashmere jacket. "Go ahead, open it."

The bag flew open to yield a special prize.

"OH, BELINDA! You're the best! Dad, it's the brand-new Cassie Simons CD! How did you find it? Nobody sells CDs anymore!"

A cheap shot from the kid who failed to grasp the risk of robots and online streaming taking over the planet, or at least the music industry.

"Can I play it?" She recovered immediately.

"Sure," we chimed.

Off she went, pounding up the stairs to one of the attic rooms, transformed into a bedroom when the previous owners were with child. In a flash, the pulsating sound of this week's teen sensation exploded from the prehistoric boom box I had passed on to Haley.

"You shouldn't bring her something every time you see her," I said. "Besides, nobody's playing CDs anymore."

"Oh, lighten up, Hank," Belinda lightly punched me in the arm. "I love that girl. The gifts are just for fun."

"Did you see Gail when you picked up Haley?" She switched gears without taking a breath. "Stupidest damn thing you ever did, letting that fine woman get away. For such a smart man, sometimes you are such a fool!"

"Glad you came over, Belinda. Did you say you had to be somewhere?"

"No, I didn't, smart-ass."

"I came to see my baby." She turned and yelled at the staircase, "Haley! Are you going to stay up there all night or come play with Aunt Belinda?"

"Come on up, Belinda. I'll play my CD for you."

"Ha," I pointed to the stairs. "Your treacherous ways come back to haunt you. Now, you get to listen to that drivel. Let me tell you, Mavis Staples she's not."

"Oh my," she quietly grumbled. "Coming babe!"

I took her coat, following her to hang it on the outdated gold-plated coat tree as she headed for Haley's loft.

"By the way," she stopped and turned. "Did you know there's an old-time Caddy with two people in it just down the block? My lights hit them when I drove by. Maybe they're looking to rob somebody or something."

"You've been reading too many crime novels," my mouth suggested, my gut-alarm signaling another possibility.

Belinda went up the stairs and I went to the garage. Keeping the overhead light off, I squeezed past the Jeep and scanned the street through the side window. The Cadillac was gone. I attempted to shrug it off as Belinda's imagination. Still, I was glad it wasn't a big dark Plymouth.

Soon, Belinda had experienced all the musical ecstasy she could stand for one day. Haley dragged her back to the living room. We hunkered down for a serious Cosmic Uno card game. Much like regular Uno, except the stakes are higher. Tonight, we were playing for the title of Uno Champion of the Universe. The champions of the State, Country, World, and Galaxy had already been crowned. In all cases, this was Haley. I'm considering a second career as promoter for a professional Uno league. Haley could become the Serena Williams of Uno.

All this excitement took us right up to bedtime. I called a halt to the carnage.

"All right, Champ, it's time to hit the hay."

"Already?" Heavy sigh. She recovered quickly. "Well, bye Belinda. Love you."

She got a final night's squeeze in the comfort of Belinda's arms, launched herself off the sofa, then skidded to a stop.

"And, thanks for the CD!"

"You're welcome, beautiful. Love you, too."

Haley bolted toward the stairs yelling over her shoulder. "Don't come up until I tell you, Dad."

I looked at Belinda with questions in my eyes. Haley had developed her own secret female bedtime ritual some while back. Privacy and modesty predominated. I now must be called to come forth at bedtime, entering her room only after a knock on the door and permission to cross the threshold. Soon she'd be shopping for makeup. I shuddered at the thought.

"She's growing up, Hank."

"Yeah. I'm not ready."

"Doesn't matter if you're ready. She's going to do fine."

She stood and gave me a look I read as compassion. As she moved toward the door, I trailed along, retrieving her coat, and helping her slip it on.

"By the way, Hank, Haley wants to spend the night with me on Friday, after she gets back from her visit with Gail's folks."

"Sure. That's one of our regular nights, but she loves to stay with you. Girl stuff?"

Belinda managed to look coy. "Well, I was getting to that. Gail and I are going to take her to get her ears pierced."

My words came in a rush.

"Gail hasn't said anything about this. What next? Tattoos and nose rings?"

"Hush." She put her finger to her lips. "I just talked to Gail about this earlier tonight. Haley has been begging both of us."

"She didn't ask me."

"No wonder, the way you're carrying on. My Alisha had her ears pierced when she was 8, and you might remember she's still a good person. Get ahold of yourself," she scolded.

"Is that car gone, Hank?" Subject shift. She was uncanny.

"Yep. Probably the neighbor kids. But we're not done talking about the ear thing."

"Yes, we are. You got any other complaints, take them up with Gail," she instructed. "Friday night still OK?"

"Yeah." My sigh was as close as I could get to acceptance of the inevitable march of time. "The Caddy's gone, but let me walk you to your car."

The street was all clear. Reaching for the door handle of her silver hybrid Lexus, Belinda turned back to me. "And when you see her after she gets her earrings, don't forget to tell her she looks pretty." She smiled a mother's patient smile and patted my cheek.

"It's all good. Love you, too, Hank."

I opened her car door and watched the hybrid start in near-silence, another technological wonder.

Backing into the street, Belinda gave a final wave and headed north.

Maybe I was born in the wrong time. Magic cars. Pierced earrings. Sex on computers. Damn.

I double-checked the locks on the doors and windows. Nothing wrong with being careful, especially with sociopaths on the loose and precious cargo in the house.

I stopped to gaze longingly at my Trek touring bicycle hanging from the hook in the garage ceiling. Being a fair-weather biker, the turning leaves signaled an upcoming end to this season's riding for me. Heat and wind, no problem. Rain or cold, no way. I'd ride my boring indoor trainer through the winter; no competition with a tail wind pushing me the miles to Saylorville Lake on a perfect 80-degree day in June, but much less likely to result in a crash or freezing my nubs off.

Long and slow. That was my biking style. No one except me thought that sounded erotic.

By the time I'd battened down the hatches, Haley shouted down the stairs that I was permitted entrance to her bedroom. I took the steps to the first landing two at a time, now working off the Chinese food.

I love this house, too.

Straight ahead of me was the oak door leading into the attic above the garage. In a stroke of brilliant extravagance, the previous owners had turned this area into a bedroom, well insulated and rustic. With only a skylight into the outside world, some would find the space confining, maybe claustrophobic. I found it comforting, like a treehouse with a view to the heavens. The room held plenty of light oak furniture: a desk, bed, wardrobe. This served as my bedroom and study.

Taking a left at the landing I moved up the steps to what had once been a dusty storage room. This space also had been renovated by the previous occupants, who finally had to leave when the number of children arriving at regular intervals outdistanced the number of rooms that could be converted.

The second attic room had become Haley's private quarters. It was complete with slanted ceiling, two skylights, an oval window, and a walk-in closet. Our joint venture of decorating the room in her brand of elegance had gone a long way toward making this house our home. Pastels and flowers abounded.

We kept the downstairs bedroom for guests – meaning a place to store our junk and put my Dad when he visited – choosing the more exotic upstairs environs for our nighttime digs.

Having been granted an audience, I found Haley had already tucked herself in under the massive down comforter, surrounded by stuffed animals of every ilk.

"Ready to call it a day, pal?"

"Yeah. How about you, Dad?"

"Just going to clean up the kitchen a little and then I'm out for the count."

I resisted crossing my arms in annoyance. "So, I hear you're getting your ears pierced."

Now she looked coy. "Are you mad at me?"

"A little," I felt the heat in my face. "I would have appreciated hearing about it from you, or your mom, not Belinda."

Now she looked worried. "Are you mad at Mom?"

"A little," I took the risk of honesty and then reassured her. "We'll work that out, kiddo."

"Do you still love Mom?" This kid can switch gears and cut to the big questions in a hurry.

"I'll always love Mom. She's the mother of the most beautiful girl in the world." I can step sideways, too.

"That's not what I mean," she rebutted. "I mean LUUUUVVV!" She drew the word out as if she was teasing me on the playground, as in Hankie LUUUVVVS Gaaailll!

"You're nosy. Maybe you'll be a detective someday."

"Or a therapist, like you."

Well played, kiddo.

"Or a therapist, like Mom," I added. Big hug. "Goodnight, Haley. Love you."

"Wait Dad."

"What?"

"We didn't say prayers."

"Right." This was new. "Go ahead."

"God bless Mom and Grandpa and Aunt Belinda and Uncle Dennis and Uncle Jerry and Uncle Phil and all my friends. And a special blessing for my dad. He's having a little bit of a hard time with me growing up."

She looked up from her pillow and winked at me.

"You are number one, kid," was all I could eke out as I patted her comforter and left the room.

I headed for the kitchen to complete my domestic duties, amazed and tired. Clients, crooks, ex-wives. Pierced ears, and a child with wisdom beyond her years who still liked to be tucked in at night. It had been an interesting day and I was looking forward to a retreat into sleep.

THURSDAY

Sometimes dreams are chock-full of colorful characters and abstract symbols. Other times a dream is simple and literal. As a therapist, I believe all dreams are potential roadmaps for understanding our waking life.

I was in a recurring dream, the one about being back in school. I had forgotten to turn in my homework – again – and Miss Bean was having none of the usual "dog ate my paper" excuses. It seemed like a long and very uncomfortable trance, one that had no beginning and no end.

The phone alarm, cleverly set to Dave Brubeck's "Take Five," finally rousted me from my discomfort. It was 6:15 a.m. I hoped to linger a few minutes more, but the after-dream fog of a cajoling Miss Bean morphed quickly into a more immediate meaning.

Haley. Gail. Homework!

Suddenly alert, I hit the floor and bolted to the loft to jostle Haley into early wakeup. This was not our first rodeo. She conveniently forgets to do her homework, and I space out on my promise to Gail to remind her. We get up early and study while breaking out the cereal. So far, it's working out, although I'm aware this ritual could have serious implications in a few years when she brings home Chemistry and Trig instead of grade school science and math.

A worry for another day.

As for this day, Haley threw on her jeans and a clean University of Iowa sweatshirt, choosing the dreaded Hawkeyes where her mom matriculated. She swept a brush through her hair and another across her teeth, then finished grade school Algebra over a hearty breakfast of Captain Crunch and cinnamon toast.

We climbed into the Jeep and headed back to her mom's neighborhood, practicing spelling words much tougher than I'd had in fourth grade. We arrived with the sound of the first bell. I dutifully took my place in the drop-off line with the other last-minute dads and moms.

"Have a good day. Mom will pick you up at three. Road trip to Spenser. Have a great time!"

"Yay! See you soon, Dad." She kissed me on the cheek, grabbed her backpack and dashed off to greet her friends, once again going full speed into the prospect of another awesome day.

Fully awake, I decided to return home for a neighborhood run, followed by a long, hot shower before my workday began.

Against plan, my cell phone intruded.

Damn.

"Morning," I answered grudgingly as I pulled to a red light.

"You better get in here now!" Belinda bypassed my greeting. "The police are here. There was a break-in last night." Her words came out in a rush.

"Whoa, what happened?" I asked, oblivious to the fact that she had just told me what had happened.

"I just told you what the hell happened!" Panic and aggression are synergistic for Belinda. "We got broken into. Somebody robbed us."

"On my way," I sounded official, but she had already hung up.

I pointed the Jeep south, then east, hoping that the cops who set up the speed trap most mornings, just over the rise on Urbandale Avenue, were otherwise occupied today. Perhaps investigating the burglary at my office. No such luck. However, for the first time in my life a road officer listened to my reason for speeding. After confirming the break-in with dispatch, she let me go.

First win of a workday that was strangely picking up where yesterday's left off.

Pulling into the parking lot, I noted a black-and-white police cruiser and the proverbial forest green, unmarked Impala driven by Phil and the other detectives in his division.

Damn. Do homework. Call Phil.

I'd failed at both.

Running on adrenalin, I took the stairs two at a time and hustled into the waiting room. I noticed our standard door lock had been jimmied, the wood frame dented without serious damage.

The driver of the detective car was, in fact, Phil. He was standing in my office in quiet conversation with a uniformed officer. Belinda was at her desk, answering questions from another detective, a hefty, balding guy I'd met before. His name was Goodman and when I visited Phil at the detective bureau, he liked to tell me that psychotherapy was a "crock." He was dressed in a gray, out-of-season silk suit, cut wide in a futile attempt to conceal his substantial girth.

Goodman looked up and took his first shot. "So, Anderson, I guess one of the crazies didn't appreciate your services so much." He looked my unshaven, sweat suit-wearing self up and down with disgust. "Maybe if you cleaned up a little, you'd make a better impression on people."

Be professional. No need to respond. Self-control and positive internal dialogue. It's in all the best self-help books, Hank.

I ignored him.

I had a direct view of Belinda, sitting at her desk.

"Did you get hold of Dennis? Where's the computer?" It all sounded meaningless. Just something to say.

"Dennis was at breakfast with a friend." She surreptitiously pointed at our framed poster of the Twelve-Steps of AA. "He's…"

"I'll be wanting to talk to you, Anderson," Goodman interrupted.

"Hush, you. I'm giving my boss a message," my mom-secretary cut in. Belinda is big on external dialogue, especially the kind where people listen when she talks.

Goodman's face hit what dad calls, "beet red." He clearly was a man used to intimidating people, and didn't much like it when his bully routine didn't work.

"Dennis said he'd come right in," she continued, talking to me but giving Goodman a drop-dead look. "I came in early to catch up on insurance and saw all this. The computer is gone. Don't worry. You know I'm good at protecting the data. Everything's encrypted and backed up. It would take a serious hacker to access our records." She leaned heavy on the word *our*. "I called all of today's clients and told them we had some electrical problems with the building. No sense scaring our folks. Got them all rescheduled."

Belinda's cover of efficiency barely contained the shock her voice revealed. She had walked into this invasion. Alone.

I gave her the A & G secret double thump on my chest sign of respect. "You're a jewel."

"How about we drop the warm and fuzzy moment and get back to the mess, counselor," Goodman demanded.

I turned without responding and went into my office. As I stepped into my home-away-from-home, my stomach turned.

Goodman's word – mess – was an understatement. My sofa had been overturned. The formerly plush cushions of deep green and maroon paisley had been sliced open, their insides strewn throughout the office. My ornate brass lamp, a gift from Gail when Anderson & Greenberg opened, was gone from the decimated cherry end table.

But what ground me to a halt was the graffiti. My legs felt rooted to the floor.

Someone had taken the markers I use to draw ideas and information on my white board and plastered the back wall with the juvenile, inane and terrifying words:

PSYCHOBABBLERS DIE

The intruders had also haphazardly scrawled every profane word I was acquainted with, on all four walls.

"We can immediately establish that the thief wasn't an English major," I said to no one in particular, surveying the room.

"Ohhh," I moaned. "My desk."

My wonderful cherrywood desk with black leather border was the most serious victim of the attack. The drawers had been emptied and smashed into long, jagged splinters. The leather had been sliced with a sharp object, and hammerhead-sized dents dotted the entire top. All manner of desk paraphernalia was strewn about the office.

Phil, already standing in the middle of the room surveying the damage, stepped up, hat in his left hand, an offer to shake his right. "Sorry, Hank. Don't touch anything."

I couldn't lift my arm in response to his gesture.

"What are you doing here, Phil?"

You don't know anything about yesterday.

"I heard the call from dispatch on my way to the station and recognized your address. I got permission to cover with Goodman."

"Yeah, thanks for bringing him along." I could feel the fire of anger creeping into my face. Phil was the safest person nearby to hear it.

"He's a good detective, Hank."

"He's a jerk."

"How about we stay focused on the issue at hand, my friend?"

"OK."

Breathe.

"OK," I repeated. "How's the rest of the office?"

"About the same destruction in Dennis' room."

Something in Phil's expression told me "about" was not exactly the same as "the same."

"We're going to need both of you to inventory what was stolen," he said.

"What do we do right now?"

"When Dennis gets here, do that inventory," he repeated. "Be thorough. Right now, I want you to think of anybody who might have done this to you. Any current or recent cases that have gone badly. Any clients who are operating on the edge. Anybody." He put emphasis on the word. "I'll ask Dennis to do the same."

I couldn't speak. With effort, I ran my hand over my eyes. It didn't work. The assault was still on the walls.

"Could be a dissatisfied client," Phil continued. "Could be somebody you treated who's very disturbed and out on the streets. It appears that nobody else in the building was hit. The graffiti tells us your office was targeted."

I flinched at the cop talk.

"I'd like you to check your files," he moved on, missing my reaction. "See what you come up with."

I regained a measure of composure.

"I can't do that, Phil. You've heard of a little thing called confidentiality."

"Hank, this is not a random B&E; it's serious police business." His tone took on authority. Phil knew the rules as well as I did. "If I'm going to help you, you've got to help yourself."

"Goddammit, Phil." I held both sides of my head to keep my brain from escaping. "I cannot have you guys showing up at my clients' front doors, asking if they've dropped by the office without an appointment to terrorize us."

Anger is just a cover for the fear.

Phil got quiet as he ran his hand around the band of the ever-present fedora.

He leaned down, close to my face.

"I know this situation is a shock, Hank, but please don't use that word with me," his request held both pain and command. "I put up with a lot of offensive language from cops and bad guys; hostile, profane, racist. I hope for something better from friends."

So much for tough talk. I felt like a little boy caught misbehaving in Sunday school. I puffed my cheeks and slowly exhaled. It helped.

As Phil stepped back to restore the equilibrium of our considerable size differential, I remembered that he didn't have to be here.

"Sorry, Phil. Truly. Sorry. I'll talk to Dennis and figure out what information we can give you. And thanks for taking the call."

Goodman walked through the door.

"Should we all have a group hug now or do some damn police work?"

In that moment, Dennis blew in the door. He hugged Belinda, put on a fresh pot of coffee for the police, then assured us all that, client or not, "if we catch the people who did this, they are going down!"

"OK," Phil said, resuming control of the room. "Let's slow down and take some time to understand what might have happened here."

"It's a B&E, Phil," Goodman injected with his normal impatience. "The captain isn't gonna like you going the extra mile just because you got a soft spot for Dr. Demento, here."

Phil barked, "Not helpful, Dale."

Phil rarely raises his voice. He's one of the steadiest men I've ever known. Yet, I also knew from experience that underneath his unique blend of Jesus, Lethal Weapon-era Danny Glover, and Zen Master, there lay an energy that told those who pushed too far into his line of fire to stop, or else. I'd just seen a micro-glimpse of the "or else" by using language that offended him.

"Right," said Goodman, hands up and palms out indicating he also had previous knowledge of Phil on the edge. "Anyway, I don't see a point in dusting for prints. We have no idea who we're looking for."

"Well…" I countered.

The room went silent, and the heat of all eyes turned on me. I felt the burn as I prepared to fill in the blanks.

I gave Phil, Goodman, and Dennis the full narrative of my parking lot meeting with Preacher and his good friend, Jake, if that was his real name. I could sense the collective blood pressure in the room climbing as the story unfolded.

"Why the hell didn't I hear this from you last night?" Dennis was lit.

Without waiting for an answer, he flew right into, "And why the hell didn't you call Phil? You have a release for both of us, Marlowe! The Lone Fucking Ranger rides…"

"You are frickin' kidding me," Goodman piggybacked. "You clowns…"

"Enough!" Belinda stormed into the office and froze us in our tracks. "Phillip. Dennis. Hank. Detective Goodman." For some reason, she gave him a modicum of respect. "I don't know all of what's going on here, but dammit - excuse my language, Phillip - something terrible has happened and no one in this office is the cause of this damage."

Dennis opened his mouth. She silenced him with her eyes and went on.

"We," she said, pointing at Dennis, me, and herself in rotation. "Need you," circling her digit in an arc to Phil and Goodman.

"So, you two mental health professionals," her voice gained sternness as she called out our less than professional conduct. "Cooperate and do what the police tell you to do."

"And you," she ordered those who serve and protect. "Be experts. Do what you do. Find out who violated us this way. Arrest them. Keep us safe."

"And, most of all. Hank."

Her voice softened as she stepped toward me.

"You, Hank, remember that we are in this together and you are not an army of one."

She knows I hate it when she applies the mantra I often use with clients to confront my own irresponsible behavior.

Because she's right. Practice what you teach.

Dumbstruck was the general feeling in the room. We collectively took on the look Dad called, "got your hand caught in the cookie jar."

I touched my ear to let her know I heard her loud and clear.

Phil was the first to reply.

"Yes, ma'am." No modern, gender neutral language. He spoke for all of us.

"Thank you, Phillip."

From an actual height barely beyond my own, she smiled down on each of us, in turn. As if we were all her minions.

"I've got that list of everything they stole from the office." Her demeanor shifted back to business, as if the lecture had not just occurred.

"Can you make a copy for me, please?" Phil asked politely.

"I sure will. Already be done if that man hadn't been wasting my time with foolish questions. Goodman. Huh." She turned heel, but not before giving Dale the look a mutt gets right after being corrected for peeing on the carpet.

Following the requisite awkward pause and a round of embarrassed looks, Goodman stepped up.

"Phil, I still don't see the point of doing prints. Too many people in and out of here, touching stuff. And even idiots wear gloves in a break-in these days."

He looked me in the eye. "Plus, there might be more than one character who frequents this place who's been in our system. Confidentiality issue."

He had a point. "You have a point," I admitted.

"Good call, Dale," Phil said as he nudged me with his elbow.

"Thanks, Goodman." I got the non-verbal message and managed honest gratitude.

"Just doing my job. It doesn't make us pals."

Balance restored, Phil sent Goodman to gather the list from Belinda, "without any side comments, Dale."

"How about I go assess the damage in my office and then make nice with Belinda," Dennis offered, moving to the door. He sounded conciliatory, but his final look at me was stone.

"Sounds great, Dennis," Phil encouraged.

So, there we were, freshly dressed down and alone again.

"Doggone, I'd hate to have her really mad at me," Phil said.

"You have no idea," I verified. "And Phil, please don't use that kind of language around me."

Phil managed the gift of a lean, patient smile.

Shortly, we got to the business of learning from Belinda what else had been stolen. It turned out that the only other missing item of value was a beautiful walnut wall clock with the Serenity Prayer engraved on a small, gold-plated plaque at the bottom. After that, it was just a bunch of pens and paper. General office supplies.

"They just took what they could carry," was Goodman's pronouncement.

The clock had been a gift to Dennis from the treatment center staff when he left to open the practice with me:

GOD GRANT ME THE SERENITY TO ACCEPT
THE THINGS I CANNOT CHANGE, THE
COURAGE TO CHANGE THE THINGS I CAN,
AND THE WISDOM TO KNOW THE
DIFFERENCE.

Seemed like it was going to be a good day to invoke that prayer.

The thieves had also done a number on Dennis' office, dumping his Ficus tree and grinding potting soil into the carpet. His walls were graffiti-filled with the kind of words designed to cause heart palpitations in Midwestern grandmothers, but common to Dennis' everyday language. He repeated most of them, as he took in the disaster and transformed his devastation into high volume anger.

Cutting through the noise, I took in something else: what Phil had meant when he said the offices were "about the same."

"There's no threat."

My voice sounded odd to me. Out-of-body. Like the soft monotone of the Vietnam vet who years ago told me the story of finding his sergeant dead in a Saigon brothel.

"No, there's not." Phil kept his voice soft and casual too, but the look on his face betrayed a deep concern that only certain observers would notice. Observers like me.

"Maybe it was those two bad guys you just told us about. Or, maybe this is some kid whose parents dragged him in to see you; who came back with buddies for the stuff they could hock. Maybe they vandalized the place because it's their idea of a good time."

"But you doubt the 'it might have been a kid' story."

Phil dodged my reply.

"First order of business, find Kenny." His glare anchored me to the floor. "That would be the *police* finding him, Hank. Not you."

"Then, we'll track the guys that braced you in the parking lot. We can put a description of them, and their car, out to departments all over, locally and throughout the state. Lots of bad guys pop up in other districts. We'll send a description of your computer to all the pawn shops. We monitor sites that sell potentially stolen equipment. I'll find out if this fits any other break-ins in the city."

"There are no security cameras in this building, so we don't have any on-site help," he concluded.

Phil was covering all the bases, but it was clear he believed the burglary was connected to Kenny.

"What I won't do is ask why you waited this long to tell me what's going on. No, I won't," he shook his head, as if trying to convince himself.

After a nanosecond of interminable silence, he looked out the window and shuffled his size twelves. Another sign of immense agitation for the big man.

"And I won't tell you how far out of your league you are, or remind you that when Dennis calls you Marlowe it is simply a term of endearment." He opened his chocolate brown camel hair sport coat and pointed at the gold shield on his belt, to drive home the point.

"No." His oversized hands looked like they were holding an imaginary basketball, or maybe getting ready to squeeze my head like a vise. "I'm not going to ask what you'd be telling me if you caught me doing amateur psychotherapy at the station during my free time."

He paused for effect.

"I'm just going to ask you to give me your professional opinion about this guy Kenny, and then we'll move forward." He gave me his best blank, stoic cop look, with a glint of menace in his eyes. I knew he had spoken the truth. And I knew he was stung by what he perceived as my lack of trust.

"I think this kid is into something deep, much bigger than whatever you arrested him for, Phil," naming the obvious.

"Now that is something we can agree on."

Among my growing list of people who walk away, only to turn for their closing moment, Phil headed for the outer door, and stopped. He took a 180 look around to include Belinda, Dennis, and me. Then he ticked off the points of his parting instructions on his fingers, needing both hands.

"This was an easy building to get into. The lock on the door to the lobby was simple to beat. Talk to your landlord about security cameras. Get a locksmith in and have better locks put on your doors. Other people work late in this building; inform your neighbors. Don't work after hours unless both therapists are here. Keep your phones close. Don't go to the parking lot alone after the light fades. Don't let Belinda work late and make sure you walk her to her car."

His tone became what could only be heard as gracious. "Thank you for your help, Belinda."

Then he looked just at me.

"Walk me out, Hank."

My mouth went dry.

He pointed Goodman and the uniformed officer, who had silently held vigil in the waiting room throughout the drama, toward the door, motioning me to follow.

I couldn't wait, grabbing Phil on the arm as we moved into the hall. "What?"

He stopped and waved his team ahead.

"I just had one more very important thought." He tapped my chest with his hat. "You need to give Gail a heads-up."

My throat constricted.

Yeah. I thought of that.

"I know."

"Just a precaution." Phil was lousy at pre-packaged sincerity. "We don't know who did this. The graffiti suggests you could be the primary focus."

Suggests.

I stared at my clenched fists as I tried that lie on for size.

"There is good news," I said.

And we could use some.

"Gail's taking Haley to visit her parents. They'll be out-of-town until Friday."

"Still," he pressed. "Better to alert her sooner than later."

I nodded mechanically, already playing out the call to Gail in my head.

"And promise me this."

"Anything, Phil."

He reached into the inner pocket of his sport coat and held up his phone.

"If you hear from Kenny, your first call is to me."

"Absolutely."

He replaced his phone, centered the fedora on his head, and extended his hand one more time. I responded from reflex.

After watching Phil march to the elevator, I drifted to the end of the hall, trying to find my sea legs. I leaned back and slid down the wall, feeling the weight of the morning merge with the uncertainty yet to come.

Do it now.

I dragged my phone from my pocket and hit speed dial.

The call went straight to Gail's mailbox.

Sound calm.

"Gail. It's Hank. I need to check in with you about something?"

I decided vague was better than scaring the hell out her by voicemail.

"Give me a call as soon as you can."

Yeah, cryptic messages aren't scary all, Anderson.

Grasping for anything that would ground me, I pushed to my feet and drifted back to my office. I righted my desk chair – low-back, soft, cushy, burgundy leather, on rollers. Adjustable height, allowing someone of my modest stature to reach the floor. Purchased for far more than I could afford as an office-warming gift to myself when Anderson & Greenberg first opened our doors.

I was startled by the condition of the chair. The arms, the swivel, the rocking mechanisms. Everything worked. The leather was intact. My chair had escaped unscathed.

I sat down and closed my eyes, enveloped by something intact and familiar. Sinking deeper into the chair, I was torn between waiting for Gail's callback and the overwhelming hope that if I refused to move, or speak to anyone, this disaster would magically pass.

Open your eyes. Look up.

The graphic language burned into me.

Stand up.

I stood up.

What next?

Growing up in an alcoholic family and years of work as a therapist, I had certainly learned how to move through a crisis. I used both hands to brush the imaginary malaise off my torso and out of my head. At a time like this, 12-Step recovery folks would say *One Day at A Time...Easy Does It.* If need be, one hour or one minute at a time.

How are we going to do business surrounded by this rubble?

Dennis and Belinda and I were unharmed. Phil was angry, but still on our side. I had my skills and my chair. A couple more chairs and we were back in business. Therapists travel light.

Heading for the coffee pot, I found Dennis and Belinda sitting at her desk. They had been talking in uncharacteristically quiet tones as I zombied about. I stopped and made immediate amends for the danger I had exposed us to. They gently chastised me, having some previous experience with forgiving me. I listened. All were aware that I did not promise to never be impulsive again. Then we moved on to making plans to get the office back to functional.

I would notify the other tenants of the break-in. I would also talk to Kensington & Associates and arrange to sublet their extra office space for a few days.

Kensington was a big-time practice with plenty of room. They had attempted on several occasions to lure A & G into their fold. We didn't play well enough with others to risk giving up our autonomy for bigger offices and a myriad of managed care contracts, and so had respectfully declined. We'd received a cordial, "if you ever change your minds, let us know," from the partners of the practice.

I was sure they would help.

Dennis would go to the paint store and acquire the supplies to re-paint the offices as soon as possible, then call our local computer guru to order a new machine for Belinda.

Belinda would contact our insurance carrier to arrange for a damage estimate. She would call in a locksmith and a carpet cleaner, then hit the furniture stores with the company credit card in hand. Her mission, restore us to comfort. She also would get bids from security companies who could wire us up and send in the cavalry, in the event of further night invaders.

As we each prepared to set off on our appointed rounds, Dennis said, "Hey, Marlowe, if you need to, you can stay with Jerry and me until Phil sorts through this disaster. We have plenty of room for you. And Haley. And Gail."

He hadn't said it directly, but his somber nod toward the threat on my office wall spoke volumes.

"Gail and Haley are heading out to see her folks after school; so, we're good there," I said. "And I'd rather be at home."

He looked at Belinda and shook his head.

"I left Gail a voicemail and I'll bring her up to speed when she calls me back."

Silence from them both.

"And I'll stay alert and promise to call Phil immediately if anything untoward is in the wind." I went for a pinky swear.

Belinda gave the official nod of approval and Dennis settled his hand over mine. "We'll settle for that."

"Oh, you therapists with all that damn touchy, feely stuff." Belinda's imitation of Goodman didn't match the nurturing glow on her face. "Let's get busy."

Within several hours, we had temporary space with Kensington, a time that the insurance adjustor would come by that afternoon, and a comfort-call from Phil. He reassured us he was on the job, but had no new information.

I asked Belinda to call Phil back and let him know I had decided to go on a short road trip. If he needed me, he could reach me on the cell.

As I gathered my gear, Belinda, hands on hips, blocked my exit.

"What Dennis said, Hank," she stressed. "I've got plenty of room."

"I'll call you after I talk to Gail."

She let me pass.

It was time to visit the Sage.

By three that afternoon, I was standing at the grill, deep in a reverie of intense heat provided by a beautiful three-by-five-foot stainless steel flattop grill and two bubbling deep fat fryers. The singular smell of super-heated peanut oil enveloped me, creating a barrier between this cloistered space and the multi-fragrant world beyond the kitchen.

I felt the reassuring sense of an ordered universe, supplied by the sesame seed hamburger buns aligned neatly parallel to the grill. Each held its own special condiments, as ordered by customers on one of the speaker phones attached to menu stands in the perfectly angled parking spaces placed side-by-side, perpendicular to the sidewalk, extending from the front door into the endless Earth might be flat after-all horizon.

No computers, no headsets. This was the real deal.

If I had grown up in Fairfield, Iowa, perhaps this day would have led me to join the folks on the campus of Maharishi University to find peace and tranquility through Transcendental Meditation. Before my time and its current incarnation, the school had been Parsons College, one of the most infamous party schools around and a last stop for the truly academically challenged. The eventual uncommon-law marriage of a southeastern Iowa burg and a university built on principles of Eastern culture was an amazing story. There have been challenges. For the most part, it seemed to work.

However, my formative years were spent not in southeast Iowa, but in the southwest part of the state. A more conventional small-town upbringing. My sacred meditation had become, "Order up." I spent much of my childhood hanging out with, and eventually serving up, fast food delights in the very root beer stand where I now stood.

When adulthood overwhelms me, I am still drawn back to this Mecca of simple pleasures and cholesterol.

"I see we have a new kid at the grill." The diminutive white-haired man dressed in a tan cotton short-sleeved button-down shirt and dark brown Dockers smiled at the young manager working the french fry and onion ring corner. "Think he'll work out, Luis?"

"He's a little slow. Seems like a hard worker, though," the young man replied without breaking his rhythm.

"SLOW," I countered. "I've only been here an hour and the customers are already spreading the word that the King of the Grill is back in town."

That got a smile from these two fast food marauders.

"Well, is there room for an old man to play backup to the King? How about I do bun prep and order set-up. The after-school rush is about to hit and some of these kids aren't much interested in the salad bar in the dining room. Although that new veggie burger is doing pretty well."

"If you are, in fact, J.R. the legendary restauranteur I've heard so much about, it would be an honor."

Luis graced us with a bit of gentle, "I've heard this routine a hundred times" laughter.

Now, most folks are completely ignorant of the secret world of the individual franchise food business. Those of us in the know will tell you we live and die by "the rush" – those times of day when customers better be coming fast and furious if the restaurant is going to stay in the black. In pockets of small-town America – where the fight against the oily clutches of the soulless corporate food conglomerate rages on – the lunch, after-school, dinner, post-game, Saturday-night-bars-just-closed, and Sunday after-church rushes are the lifeblood of the rural restaurateur.

In the town where I grew up, that person is J.R. Anderson. My father.

Dad is a local legend. It's been said that if you cut him, he bleeds root beer. He and I know that is especially true over the past fifteen years, since he decided to stop bleeding Canadian whiskey.

My liking for nicknames had led me to dub him, The Sage. The gifts of listening and quiet wisdom go hand in hand for dad; talents that seldom leaked through the deluge of amber liquid during his years of drinking.

"Nice surprise, coming in and seeing you holding the spatula, son."

"You can take the boy out of the greasy spoon, but you can't take the greasy spoon out of the boy."

With that, the order board up front began to sound off with a series of familiar dings and light up like a mysterious alien slot machine. All attention turned to the river of pickup trucks, foreign compacts, junkers, and the occasional rebuilt muscle car, packed with adolescent carnivores, pulling into the parking lot from the area schools, ready to replenish their beef and pork reserves. From that point on there was little conversation other than the repetitive, "Order up!"

Cheryl, the front room person, took the orders on paper, hung them on the wheel, then set up completed feasts with drinks as fast as the two day-time waiters; Randy and Francine, could haul trays and make change. Luis, Dad, and I fell into a familiar cadence: burgers, hand-cut fries, homemade onion rings.

And, of course, the famous Iowa pork tenderloin. Not some little bit of over-tenderized, sautéed piglet on a decorated plate like the art nouveau stuff they serve in the faux class joints in the city. When the waiter brings my entree in those places, I look at the plate and wonder when they're going to bring me dinner.

No, we're talking a breaded pork loin the size of a small Frisbee. On a beautiful white or wheat hamburger bun. You know it's a good sandwich when you need to work through the edges of the meat to get to that bun.

We moved fast and in unison for about forty-five minutes, completely focused, without any distraction from the crises beyond the kitchen walls. Mindfulness by sandwich.

As the rush began to slow, the children of this fine community satiated on our old-school cuisine for one more day, I stepped back from the grill. Hot, smelly, and content.

"Guess we still got it, champ," I grinned at my dad.

"Better than therapy, kid," he grinned back. "You could probably make it in this business."

He rested against the counter and cast an eye over his domain. "How about we taste some of our own creations?"

"Absolutely."

"So, you drop by for the fun and I do the cleanup?" Luis had been here before.

"Sorry." Kind of.

"No problem." He picked up an elongated stainless-steel spatula in each hand, waving them in harmony, as only a culinary ninja could. "I've got staff coming in for the after-football practice and dinner crowds. It's good to see you, Hank."

Dad dropped a couple of the largest tenderloins we could fry up onto buns with ketchup, pickles, and onion, then we headed off through the back room, where the ancient cauldron sized tanks of root beer syrup mixed with sugar and water. The weathered feeder lines that ran to the front taps still pumped, the only concession to modern times being a rig for the sugar-free version of our beloved sassafras concoction.

We ambled through the pristine backroom, past the walk-in cooler and into Dad's tiny office. Using his battered, gray metal desk for a dinner table, and sitting in equally battered aqua colored vinyl armchairs, we each tore into the best sandwich on the planet.

"My doctor says I have to pace myself with these babies." He held the sandwich at eye level. "No booze, cut down on fried food, no cigars. What's left?" He shrugged and took a serious bite.

"There's always sex," I suggested, in mid-chew.

He held a finger up to give pause to the conversation.

"That's a great sandwich," he approved. "Sex," he continued. "Too complicated. Speaking of complicated, how's Gail? And how's my grandbaby?"

"Both full of life, as always. Come see them."

"I will. Soon." He brushed stray crumbs into the ancient army green metal trash can. "Luis is the best manager I've had since that Anderson kid. I'll take a few days off and come on up."

We ate quietly for a few minutes, savoring the taste of the food and the comfort of our connection.

"So," J.R. broke the silence. "What's going on?"

The Sage knew I hadn't just dropped by for a free tenderloin.

I gave him the skeleton of the story, explaining that I'd received a police referral, then shortly thereafter was treated with the visit from Preacher and Fat JJ, followed by the break-in. I added my well-established longing for Gail and my fear for my family. As usual – since he got sober – Dad listened without interruption, looking me straight in the eye through the entire monologue.

"So, what do you think?" I asked.

"You didn't immediately tell Phil about the guys in the parking lot." Just the facts.

"No, I didn't tell him about my longing for Gail either." Resistance covered by sarcasm.

"Nope." He didn't take the bait. "How about giving me a ride? I walked to work. We can shower up. I have your extra clothes in the guest bedroom. Want to catch a meeting?"

I admit that I take some perverse pleasure in maintaining my 12-Step anonymity with Jerry, thus enabling his ongoing harassment about attending meetings. I am certain that Dennis takes an immense amount of perverse pleasure in maintaining my anonymity with Jerry.

In truth, I had been going to Al-Anon since falling under Dennis' tutelage some years ago. I didn't start attending when Dad got sober. Like many family members of alcoholics, I believed for years that the drinking was his problem, not mine. I was confident, if he would just get it together and quit drinking, there would be peace in my world. Admitting that my life was interwoven with Dad's alcoholism was more than I could cop to as a younger man.

It has been said that therapists are called to their work by a desire to save the world. Dennis taught me the truth. Most of us are trying to understand our families, and ourselves. Then save the world.

"Can you guess how much better your work will be if you deal with your own co-dependency, Anderson?" He hadn't arrived at affectionately calling me Marlowe yet. "If you're going to hang out with me, go to Al-Anon."

And so, I did. For the most part I went back to the scene of the crime for the beginnings of my recovery process – home.

The Anonymous part of Al-Anon is tough to come by in a town of less than 6,000, not counting livestock, cats, and dogs. The Catholic Church is jam-packed with the same natives who come to the restaurant for Coney Dog Night every Thursday. AA meetings upstairs in the Sunday School Annex. Al-Anon in Fellowship Hall. Everybody knows everybody. And their parents. And siblings. And cousins. Hell, a lot of us are family.

What I lose in anonymity, however, is more than made up for by Mabel, who all these years later still tells me what a fine person my mother was. And Carl, who tells me at every meeting that he doesn't believe in counseling and then tries to finagle ten minutes of free services as we go out the door. And all the other people that remind me of who I am and where I come from. These people understand alcoholism, and they help me understand my addiction to trying to fix other people's messes, sometimes at the expense of my own health and wellbeing.

I still make plenty of mistakes. Gail comes to mind. There have also been some wonderful results: Dad is my friend. Haley thinks I'm improving. And Dennis believes I've become a good therapist.

As the meeting opened, I listened to the Step 10 reading: "Continued to take personal inventory and when we were wrong, promptly admitted it."

That fit.

Some nights I have a lot to say. Tonight, I just wanted to be in the company of these people, some of whom had known me since birth. When the discussion came around the table to me, I passed.

Mabel talked about her struggle, even after a decade of healing, to ask for help when she needs it.

"I just have to tell myself I don't have to do everything on my own, and there are people better at some things than me. Hell, after seven years of sobriety, even my husband has learned some good shit that I need to listen to." There was genuine loving laughter from the group.

Dad would say, "It felt like she was talking about my life."

As we filed out the side door of Fellowship Hall, uniformly leaning into a light wind that reminded us of the icy rain and blizzards to come in the next turn of seasons, some found their own special recovering alcoholic drifting to the parking lot. Some headed for the "meeting after the meeting," coffee and conversation at Dad's place, served by the evening shift. Others drove home to the heartache of loving someone who still drinks and drugs. I gave Carl a hug and a quick, "Catch you next time."

My guy was waiting in the lot. We climbed into the Jeep. I checked my phone.

No message from Gail. No problem. She only calls me right back when Haley is at my house. She said she'd call when they got back to Des Moines.

The mind trick almost eased my anxiety.

I cranked the engine and headed for Dad's ranch-style just off the town square.

"How was the meeting?" He wasn't intruding, just interested.

"Great."

"Get something useful?"

"Yeah. It's a good idea to ask for help and admit my limitations."

"Helpful reminders." He managed to say that without expectation.

I pulled into his driveway. What used to be his and Mom's driveway.

He understands loss.

"Coffee?"

"Getting late. I'd better head back."

"Let me know if you need anything." He put one hand on my knee as he opened the Jeep door, looking me straight in the eyes. "I mean anything."

I can't say for certain, but I believe Dad's eyes got teary for a moment. Maybe it was just the funny way the light danced in the shadows of the streetlamp on the corner of 4th and State.

Heading past the city limits, I pointed the Jeep north into the night. I cruised by dimly lit early-to-bed farmhouses, gravel side roads, the coal black sheen of farm ponds, and the flattened, uneven fields of a corn harvest. Lost in thought, muscle memory took me back to I-80 East.

I was cautiously optimistic. I had Dad, Belinda, Dennis, and a more informed Phil in my corner. My daughter and a great Al-Anon group loved me.

Gail. You haven't talked to Gail, yet.

I was optimistic, not overconfident.

Knowing I couldn't will the phone to ring, I flipped to speculating about culprits from my past who could be responsible for the office invasion. Ten minutes on the dashboard clock yielded no one more remote than my newest client.

"Time for a distraction," I informed myself.

I went back to before-my-time musical roots and cued up Santana's best album, Caravanserai. I was momentarily reminded of the horrifying notion that automobile CD players are headed for extinction as I listened to his guitar talk to God, adding my steering wheel percussion to the band's driving beat.

With almost no traffic and the Hunter's Moon, no irony intended, as my compass point, I hit the exit east just as Carlos was winding down. I moved on to The Man, Marvin Gaye, then to his heir apparent, Leon Bridges. Mired in spirit, soul, and sadness, I brought it all together with a new discovery, Black Pumas: a little Latin and a lot of soul.

Just about the time I was fading into the night, I re-energized for the final leg into the beckoning lights of the city by singing along, in weary falsetto, with the Queen.

Aretha took me home.

No cars at the curb as I hit our street. That meant I was safe, or my neighbor's daughter was doing her homework. Either way it was a good thing for somebody.

Shuffling into the kitchen, I leaned heavily on the counter, feeling the full weight of the past several days. The kind of tired that sleep alone would not fix. Emotional miles, not the drive, had used me up.

Now what?

I reached into the pocket of my old-school tan suede jacket.

"Where's your phone, Hank?" I chastised myself, yanked back from lethargy and headed for the garage.

Relax. In the console tray. It's right where you left it after the meeting.

The blue message light was blinking aggressively.

Gail?

Checking my recent call list, I saw four messages in rapid succession. None of them Gail. I punched through the list.

Belinda: "Oh, baby, you've got to love credit. I found some beautiful furniture, Hank. Call me."

Dennis: "We've got paint. And Jerry wants you to know he's so worried about us that he might need an extra Al-Anon meeting this week. Call if you need anything, Marlowe."

Phil: "Nothing new on the break-in, Hank. Sorry. Give me a call soon." Pause. "Or, immediately if needed. Take care."

Belinda, again: "Hank, Gail may call you. I decided to call her and let her know we're all safe. I thought she should know about the break-in. In case it's on the news. Now don't give me any trouble about that mister. We're all family. Like I said, you think you can handle any damn thing on your own." Click.

One of the great things about Belinda is that she doesn't require my physical presence to argue with me, or dress me down. Saves wear and tear on my voice.

I started to speculate on the connection between Belinda's call to Gail, and no return call from Gail to me. Standing slump shouldered staring at the blank screen, the answer was clear.

If she wanted to talk to me, there would have been a fifth message. Now what?

Minutes later, I was engulfed by the living room sofa, breathing calm in and the calamity of the day out. The softly cinematic "Explosions in the Sky," was providing backup on vinyl, cued up on my recently rediscovered turntable.

Millennials were driving a return to the smooth clarity of LPs.

Yay Millennials!

FRIDAY

Seven hours later, I woke somewhat invigorated, in my clothes and a light sweat, the turntable arm long since returned to its resting place, and a robust morning sun powering in through the glass patio doors. The cheery daylight suggested warmth to the day, in contrast with the metallic frost coating my lawn, brilliantly shining a warning of the sometimes beautiful, sometimes brutal Iowa winter that was on the horizon.

I'd been dreaming that a blinking blue pulse with massive fangs was chasing me. A bit frightening, but truly lacking in imagination. Maybe as my waking life became more chaotic, my dream life was becoming increasingly pedantic. Some neuro-psych PhD student could probably find a journal article in that, maybe even write a research grant.

What next?

The question was apparently not going away until I got off the couch. I decided to reboot my plan from the post-B&E morning: make coffee, go for a run, and take a near scalding shower. I pulled on a garish ISU Cyclones sweat suit and stocking cap, setting off to follow my breath as it escaped my lungs and hit the morning chill. Two hours later I was fully awake, clean and - reluctantly - on the phone.

A call to Belinda confirmed the delivery date of our new furniture for the following Monday. I told her I had left Gail a message and not heard back. I managed to end the call before launching into speculation that she might be avoiding me. It was early, so Belinda let me go without incident.

Now what?

My new favorite question was like a stereo needle stuck on a scratched record.

Call Dennis. I was on a roll. Hank Anderson, man of action.

"Hey, partner, did you get some sleep?" Dennis answered the phone already knowing it was me. Caller ID – technology for control freaks.

"I did. I caught a meeting in the hinterlands. Slept. Went for a run. Now I'm following Haley's advice and energizing myself for the possibilities of a new day."

"We should all be listening to your daughter," he agreed. "We've got paint."

"As your message said. We've also got furniture. Monday."

"Well, I guess we know how we're going to be spending our weekend. Jerry is a wiz with a paintbrush. We'll have the place looking like its old self in no time."

"Aren't we too important or rich or famous or something to be painting our own offices?"

"Painting is good for the soul. It's blue-collar labor. It has a beginning and an end. You can see the beauty of the finished product."

"Well, with all those clichés in place, how can I resist?"

"Exactly." He did what he does best and pivoted right into teaching mode.

"It's also a good way to make amends for your most recent bonehead play. Steps 8, 9 and 10 all rolled into one."

"Sure," I allowed. "Accountability by paint, it is. You're absolutely right, which makes your day."

He ignored my gibe.

"It's those words that will still be sitting under the paint that scare the hell out of me," he said, a tremble in his voice that I'd rarely heard from my usually fearless friend. "What is going on here?"

"I'd like to believe that one of your upscale, urban sprawl West of I-35 clients is involved in some exotic white-collar insurance scam, and that the amateurish nature of the break-in was just a smoke-screen by a team of techno-espionage dweebs trying to gain access to our computer files to determine whether the feds have turned him, and you are covertly operating as a field contact for a deep cover sting operation. Perhaps the graffiti was just a lame attempt to cover their tracks."

"Bad timing, Marlowe," he said. "This is serious shit."

I winced at the truth.

"Yeah," I admitted. "I'm scared too, Dennis. For you and Belinda. And if this is related to my work with Kenny, anyone close to me. If this is not related to Kenny," I went on, "I'm drawing a blank. And it's not for lack of rumination."

The distress in my voice must have been up-front.

"And, how about your safety?" He tempered the sandpaper in his voice as he circled back. "You've taught me that when you forget about Hank, you can be pretty reckless."

We gave that a moment of silence.

"So, we don't know for sure what's going on," he allowed.

"Right."

"But you have a best guess, Marlowe." An old technique given to Dennis by his mentor to help clients move toward insight.

"I've only got one," I said. "As I told Phil, my new client might be into something real nasty, and it isn't just the wholesale porn business."

The fear and confusion in that thought was palpable.

"All the more reason you should have immediately brought Phil into the discussion."

Like any good therapist, he brought us back to his earlier imperative.

"That ground has been covered." I moved on. "I went to talk to Dad. Went to the meeting for help figuring out what to do next."

"And...?"

"I decided to call you, and with the counsel and support of my partner, come up with a sure-fire strategy for both protecting my client, if this is about him, and not getting the people I care most about seriously hurt by several major bad asses." I caught myself. "Along with keeping in mind the safety of the guy that shaves my face in the morning."

More silence.

"It isn't every day that two guys straight out of a Martin Scorcese movie step into our lives," I added.

"So now it's our lives, is it?"

He kept talking.

"This is my day to run the consultation group at the treatment center. Let me know if you hear anything more from Phil."

Before I could reply, he took the pop out of his voice.

"I know how focused you get once a person asks for your help. It's a blessing and a curse, Marlowe. So, I guess we have to figure this shit out."

He said 'we.'

He hung up before I could respond. Small victory for him, considering the size of the mess.

I arrived at Kensington & Associates in time to meet my first client of the day. The practice manager had led me to a loaner office, which was impressively furnished in red oak desks, smoked glass tables and leather chairs. It was luxurious, but I missed my Dr. Seuss print, another precious object oddly undamaged in the assault on our space.

After the session, I checked Dennis' schedule and called Phil at the station. He was out on a call. I left a message on his voicemail, letting him know I had reached out to Gail, but not heard back from her. I asked him to meet for an update with Anderson & Greenberg at five that evening; donuts and coffee obviously on me. He only needed to call me back if five didn't work, a technique that saves me a lot of back and forth.

Surroundings and distractions being as they were, I still managed to muscle through a pretty good afternoon of psychotherapy, including one of my all-time favs, Malcolm.

Malcolm had survived numerous childhood beatings before his rageaholic father abandoned the family. He was the owner of a great family restaurant in the city, the loving father of three adult children, and a volunteer mentor for boys whose fathers had disappeared from their lives.

Amidst restaurant talk, we had managed to do some important work together over the past several years. Malcolm had become a man at peace with who he was, and a loving warrior for disadvantaged children. He was finished with his ongoing therapy and had just stopped in for a "tune-up" appointment, wanting to talk through a conflict he was having with his amazing wife and business partner, Betty. Betty had been talking about early retirement from several decades of working side by side. She was "tired of the smell of meatloaf every morning."

Malcolm talked. I listened. He was a pro at this. In short order, so to speak, it became apparent to Malcolm that one of Betty's concerns was that he was still working too much and didn't have enough time for her. They were not as young as they used to be, and she wanted both quality and quantity in their time together.

"I've got to make a plan before things get bad again, Hank. I almost lost her when I pushed my depression down all those years, working seven days a week. I found out it's easier to prevent troubles with her than clean them up. Maybe it is time to begin thinking about retirement."

He decided it was important to invite Betty to tell him more about her worries. He said he would listen as closely to her as I had listened to him during our time together. I suggested they return to a regular date night, a time-tested recommendation in the world of couples' therapy. Perhaps something slightly more romantic than a visit to a competitor's restaurant.

After Malcolm left, I checked my schedule for the last appointment of the day. My old friend, the stomach butterfly, flapped his wings.

Kenny Jensen.

I was conflicted. I wanted to help Kenny extricate himself from whatever bear trap he had bumbled his way into. The break-in, coming on the heels of my encounter with Preacher and Jake, had given me information crucial to something more basic than his emotional health; it might be vital to his continuing to walk upright. Even more important than my client. I needed to keep my family and friends safe, an imperative that intersected with my commitment to drop the mental health action hero routine and become a team player.

I tapped on my forehead, hoping there was a hidden Brilliant Solutions Button connected to my frontal cortex.

Call Kenny. Guide him into Phil's hands. Safe Kenny. Safe family. Time for the detective and his department of qualified professionals to untangle this puzzle.

That would require a trip downstairs to the A & G offices to grab his phone number from the file. Camping out at Kensington had cramped Belinda's efficient style of having my schedule for the day's sessions on my desk first thing in the morning. That was made even more difficult by that formerly beautiful desk having been reduced to kindling.

Or. Let Kenny see the sign on the A & G door that we are redecorating and clients should migrate to Kensington for sessions. Grease the wheels of his honesty by telling him about Preacher and Jake. Guide him into Phil's hands. Safe Kenny. Safe family. Time for the detective and his department of qualified professionals to untangle the rest of this puzzle.

Rationalizations don't have to be rational; they just need to work. I waited for Kenny's arrival.

As Dad would say, "What little the plan had going for it went south in a hurry."

The clock ticked over to start time. No Kenny. He forgot. He blew off the appointment on a gorgeous, crisp fall day to go hiking, or sleep in. He got the time confused. The usual reasons most clients miss sessions.

It looked like I was going to get that walk downstairs after all.

Arriving at the office door, I was greeted by Ted the locksmith. The main door was newly replete with shiny gold-plated mega-locks. Ted was on his knees, surrounded by implements of installation: drill, cordless screwdriver, and assorted other tools I didn't recognize. The earthy smell of sawdust was floating through the air. An equal amount of wood shavings had landed on both the hallway carpet and our local locksmith.

Ted is a burly man with coarse, hair the color of rusted sheet-metal, a roadmap of freckles and a barrel chest. His stovepipe Popeye biceps are, regardless of weather, stuffed into a chambray work shirt rolled to his elbows. When I envision the stereotype of what a good locksmith should look like, Ted was he.

Ted and I are old friends from the pre-garage code and keyless entry days, what with my historical tendency to lock myself out of cars, buildings, homes, and such. That went well with Ted's need to make a living. He also let me know years back that he respected the work of Anderson & Greenberg. He was a "Friend of Bill W's," code for AA attendance and an homage to one of its founders, Bill Wilson.

Ted bounced to his feet with an ease that was inconsistent with his mass.

"Sorry for the sawdust, Mr. Anderson. Just finished installing the deadbolt. Belinda came by early and let me in. I gave you the best. Keys are on Belinda's desk."

He gathered tools as he continued his report. Ted steadfastly refuses my offer to be called Hank, and he is always in a hurry.

"No worries, Ted. Carpet cleaners are next on the agenda."

"That sure saves me some time on cleanup, Mr. Anderson. Appreciate it."

He slipped on his jean jacket and easily hefted a toolbox big enough for me to use as a spare bedroom.

"I'll bill you." He shook my hand and hoofed it toward the elevator. "Take care. Gotta get to the next job."

"Thanks," I called after him. "Easy does it." Without a hitch in his step, Ted smiled over his shoulder at the familiar AA slogan.

James, the technician from Day and Night Security was also at work, just inside the waiting room. I knew he was James from Day and Night because that's what the patch on the left pocket of his blue jean shirt told me. He was preparing to install our spanking new security system.

"State of the art, Mr. Anderson," assured the tech. Looking up from his stash of mysterious technology, he pushed his Buddy Holly, Elvis Costello, or Rivers Cuomo glasses, depending on your musical tastes, up the bridge of his nose. They seemed slightly out of place on a tanned, pretty boy face framed by a perfectly unruly mass of jet-black hair.

If Paul McCartney's mother had married Buddy's father, James would have been their love child.

I gave him a thumbs up.

"Call me Hank. And you can do any high-tech thing you desire to secure this entrance as long as you promise not to explain it to me."

James looked a bit confused. "Sure. I just don't get why you wouldn't want to know how this stuff works. It's awesome."

"Let's say that I'm a bit slow on adjusting to all this fancy modern machinery," I explained. "Just take Ted's lead. He gave us the best equipment available and the minimum amount of instruction necessary."

"No problem." James pretended to understand. He was clearly a very agreeable guy.

I had to ask. "James, are you aware that you bear a striking resemblance to not one, but two, rock stars?"

"Yes, sir, uh, Hank," he confirmed, his cheeks reddening with obvious embarrassment at the compliment. "Sir Paul and Buddy. In fact, I am a musician. This is my day job. Maybe you've heard of my band, *Slippery When Wet.*"

This he said with obvious pride.

"Sorry. I don't get to the clubs much."

"No problem. We've only been playing out a few months. We're the only racially diverse classic rock ska band in Des Moines. I'm lead vocals and guitar. You haven't lived until you've heard 'Maybe I'm Amazed' and 'Not Fade Away' played up-tempo."

"I can imagine." I really couldn't, but I was interested. "Do you play any Santana?"

"Yes sir." He launched without reserve into a uniquely altered, but recognizable fast reggae chorus of "Everything's Coming My Way." He had a good, clean tenor voice with just a bit of sandpaper on the edges, for soul.

"Excellent," I applauded. "Anybody who does Carlos is aces with me."

Aces?

"We do originals, too. We're going to record our own album. I'm working on a ballad. The master plan is to release it online. Maybe you'll come see us sometime, down on Court Street or in the East Village."

"Must be great to have two passions." I immediately liked this young fellow.

"Music and security, man," he grinned a perfectly brilliant white-toothed front man grin. "It's a good life."

James went on to say he would get the system in today. It was simple enough. Being on the sixth floor with no window access, we only needed the door equipped to thwart invaders. News of our break-in had spread quickly, and the building owner had also instructed Day and Night to install an upgraded front door system, along with security cameras in the lobby, elevator, stairwell, and parking lot.

"My next stop, Hank." James would move from our offices to the lobby. "That will take a day or two."

He said he'd have us connected to central dispatch by the end of the workday. When complete, any attempt to break into the building or our offices would send an alert to Dennis, me, the owner and, if not cancelled, the police.

"It's wireless and..." he caught himself mid-sentence, honoring his commitment to leave out the details. "Sorry. Force of habit, Hank."

"No worries, James."

I was encouraged by the progress in restoring the office to order, and moved to optimism by this young man who was living his dream.

Ignoring the disaster being held at bay behind my closed office door, I went to Belinda's desk and saw that her phone was another of the items that had escaped calamity. I checked the voicemail. I had a call from Amir; he and his wife, Lila, needed to reschedule their couple's therapy appointment. Their babysitter was sick.

Several other clients had called to check on appointment times. Dennis had a new referral, a guy returning to town from forty-five sober days of high-priced addictions treatment in Arizona.

From Kenny, nothing. There was no message saying, "My car broke down and I can't make it today."

Wishful thinking.

More of an update from my end for Phil than I had planned on.

I left Dennis a message to catch him up and make sure he was aware of the five p.m. with Phil, then unlocked the metal credenza where we keep intake files. I found Kenny's folder lying at the top of Belinda's work-to-be-done stack. His face sheet had yet to be stapled to the folder's inside cover, but I found it mixed in with the various consent forms.

Belinda's slipping a little.

I secretly enjoyed finding the occasional error by our black Mary Poppins of office efficiency. My own sins in the area of paperwork were legendary.

I found Kenny's number on the face sheet and dialed him up. Three rings and, "You've reached the man, leave your message and I'll get back to you when I'm not having so much fun." Rather pathetic, but in keeping with my early impression of his style.

"Kenny. This is Hank Anderson. We had an appointment scheduled for today. It's important to follow through. You can call and speak to Belinda or me to reschedule."

I didn't threaten him with a report of non-compliance to Phil. This was his first no-show and maybe he had a good reason, like Preacher and Jake were holding him hostage in some backwoods shed outside of Altoona or Grimes. I groaned to myself at the thought of Kenny coming to harm.

It was time to make good on a promise and report to the detective.

Phil and Dennis were already waiting at the donut shop when I arrived, sitting in what was euphemistically called a booth: a hard plastic and metal joke, perhaps perpetrated by design engineers of my stature at the expense of people of Phil's stature. They turned as I walked in, fixing me with matching looks reminiscent of my parents and the bad-grade-card days of my youth. Apparently, all was not forgotten.

Three large coffees got us started.

I announced Kenny as a no-show for his appointment. The chair, not Phil, groaned as he sat back as well as he could and blew out a deep, slow breath from the depths of his frustration. He sipped his coffee as punctuation.

"Well, that fits. Dale and I went to his apartment. No answer. The door was unlocked. Under the assumption Kenny might be in danger, we went in. It looked like a tornado had touched down in his living room. No blood. No signs of a struggle. No Kenny."

My usually smooth coffee tasted acidic at the thought of Kenny gone missing.

"So, Detective," Dennis posed. "What does this mean?"

"It means somebody has broken into Kenny's place since we arrested him," Phil's impatience for stating the obvious leaking through. "His apartment was immaculate when we took him in."

"Which means our break-in and Kenny's situation are connected," Dennis said. He sounded as if he'd solved the case.

"Hold on," I said. "There's something else. I couldn't quite grasp what it was when I was looking for Kenny's phone number today..." My mind went blank.

Both detective and counselor waited for my wheels to turn. I perused the donut rack to clear my thoughts.

Yeah.

I pulled out my phone and dialed Belinda, raising a finger to signal Dennis and Phil to hold their silence.

"What's wrong?" Again, she was not wasting time on a greeting.

"We're fine," I reassured.

"I guess I'm over-reacting these days."

"We all are. Question. Did you organize Kenny's file yet?"

"Of course. Same as always: face sheet on the inside cover, financial form, consents, correspondence. All that stuff. Why?"

Either someone had decided to check Kenny's file without an invitation, or the gremlins that moved my car keys at home had also invaded the office. I went with the former.

"I think somebody got into his file. He didn't show for his appointment and things were out of order in his folder when I went looking for his number."

"Somebody's been in the files?" The horror of someone raiding her domain vibrated through the phone. "But how? Everything was locked up when I got in."

"I'm with Phil and Dennis. I'll get back to you."

"You be careful." I heard Mama Lion, loud and clear.

"Absolutely." I left no doubt in my tone. "You, too."

I hung up, staring at the screen, wishing the phone had offered a less troublesome answer.

"Seems like our intruders had a specific agenda. They got into Kenny's file. They managed to open and relock the cabinet without causing any damage. We missed it when we were looking for what was stolen."

"Those cheap locks can be easily sprung and pushed in to relock," Phil explained.

Dennis sat up straight and crossed his arms. "Someone was looking for a written summary," he pronounced, nodding in my direction. "They wanted to know what he told you."

Phil's hands engulfed his cup. "They found nothing important and decided you must keep your records on a computer so they stole Belinda's."

I gripped my cup to keep from recoiling.

No need to be a detective or a clinician to put Preacher and Fat JJ into this version of the story.

"We've got to find Kenny," I urged Phil.

"I," he diverted from the plural, pointing at his barrel chest. "I have to find him. I'll update the

Captain. I'll talk to his former employer, see if anyone from work has had any contact with him. I'll reach out to that relative of his. I'll talk to anyone we can identify who might know where Kenny could be."

"What you do next." Phil leaned in, consuming the space between us. "What you and you do," pointing his trigger finger at Dennis, then me. "Is repaint your office. Do counseling. Mind your own business. And one more time for effect, keep me updated on anything new."

He didn't wait for a response. The table quivered as Phil swiveled out of his chair, pushed upright with both palms, retrieved his fedora from the table, and put it in place.

"Like Dennis, I know how much you care about the people you serve, Hank. And I'm genuinely sorry for putting you in this situation."

He looked through the shop window, as if searching for a time machine and a pre-Kenny do over.

"That being said," he continued. "Let me do my job. Thanks for the coffee."

Straight out of noir central, he tipped his hat and moved out the door.

Dennis' dark frown mirrored my sense of helplessness. I looked at the shelves of freshly made donuts and felt nauseous.

Not a good sign.

The phone rang as I walked into the kitchen. My pulse quickened as *Gail* lit up the screen.

I tapped the green answer button, going for casual.

"Hi. Thanks for calling back."

She went on offense.

"The message Belinda left me had a bit more in it than the one I got from you," nudging me with an accusing tone. "What are you into this time, Hank."

Damn it, Belinda.

"We had a break-in and vandalism at the office."

"I know that much. What else?"

"Phil thinks it might be something bigger, something about a client of mine."

"Phil thinks?" She was relentless. "Another one of those cases, Hank?"

Say it.

"We all think this might be something bigger and directly related to me."

My honesty shocked her into temporary silence.

I relaxed the coils in my shoulders and dove into the deep end. As I replayed Preacher, Jake and the graffiti, the story seemed other-worldly, and I was living it. I finished by revealing my delay in informing Phil.

"So," I stammered, losing my momentum. "It would be a good idea if I didn't have Haley overnight for a few days, until this gets sorted out."

Nothing.

I kept the defensiveness out of my voice. "I'm being careful for our daughter's sake."

"No, Hank." The frost filtered through the phone. "Careful is teaching her to wear a seatbelt and look both ways before crossing the street. This is *you* being *careless* and going back to cover your tracks. Not the first time."

Her disapproval was visceral, like a slap through the phone. I decided not to let guilt for past blunders derail my message, rolling on before the former 3-A debate champ of Spenser High could pick me apart.

"You might be right," I admitted. "You'll be pleased to know that Dennis and Phil agree with you. I'm sorry this is happening, and taking shots at me won't fix anything. So, while you're all busy being right, I'm telling you that it would be a good idea for Haley to have a few extra nights with you. OK?"

"Not OK," she muttered. "Yeah. I get it."

As Dad would say: in for a penny, in for a pound.

"One more thing."

"What!"

"Maybe you ought to stay in Spenser until this all blows over." I closed my eyes as if that would protect me from the verbal blast that would likely come next.

Just more ice.

"No one is going to chase me from my house, Hank. We're coming home tomorrow."

"This is *you* being careless, to make a point, Gail."

If such a thing as an angry chuckle exists, Gail invented it.

"As they say, be careful what you ask for, you might get it," she said. "I may need some time getting used to the new and improved honest Hank."

"Alright. I'll talk with Belinda," she said, going for closure. "Haley was already doing an overnight on Friday. I'm sure we can both bunk with her for a couple of days. I'll tell Haley it's a fall vacation bonus. Grandparents and Belinda."

"She's really excited about going to Belinda's." No response from her. "For the ear piercing." I went for broke. "I'm embarrassed and ticked off that I had to find out from Belinda."

"It's a mom-daughter thing, Hank," she responded with an edge, then stopped to take a breath. "My turn to apologize. She'd be so disappointed if we changed our minds now."

"I'm not talking about changing our minds. I already got what-for from Belinda on that. When we were together, I would have gotten angry about this and kept quiet. Ignored you for a day or two. We'd pretend it would just go away. How many times did you tell me to follow the advice I give clients and get honest with you? Two-way street, Gail."

I grabbed for air. That was a long speech in the annals of Hank-Gail communication.

"Again, my apology."

"Forgiven. I am a man of infinite patience for those I love."

Damn.

"Well, I gotta go."

"Sure."

Enough honesty for one day.

"Time for me to head in to the office, too. Give my love to the Haley."

"I will. And you take care, Hank. I mean that." And then she was gone.

I stared at the diminishing brightness of the phone screen.

Not bad. Except for the brief romantic nose-dive. Change is sometimes a slow journey, with concessions made for the occasional bump in the road.

My Al-Anon buddies would say, "Progress not perfection."

Following Phil's orders, Friday afternoon became Friday night and I was standing in my office, paintbrush in hand. A current fav, Lord Huron, and an old love, Kate Bush, were cued up on Jerry's, modern mega-corporate Bluetooth player. Manual labor always benefits from high-energy tunes.

I loathed to admit how good the sound was.

I was decked out in a '90s vintage UNI Panther's sweatshirt, my guilty wardrobe pleasure of blue jean bib overalls, and black well-beaten Converse high-tops. Converse or Chuck Taylors, the dream shoes of every early '60s kid, well before my time. They'd had a resurgence, in keeping with my theory that if I never throw any article of clothing away, it will eventually come back into style.

I imagined I looked like an undersized Scandinavian country rock musician. Rock 'n' roll.

Dennis and Jerry, on the other hand, were dressed as spectators at a Martha Stewart paint-off: khakis, navy Polo mock turtlenecks, slightly weathered Topsiders.

"You guys encourage stereotypes," I chided. "I don't want any squealing or other histrionics if you splatter paint on those duds."

"Just because we're from Iowa, doesn't mean we're country people." Jerry made the label sound vile as he sneered at my bibs. Jerry likes to remind us that he isn't from these parts, having been recruited out of an urban Chicago high school by Drake University. Shooting guard. All-conference. Twice. "I came for the hoops and stayed for the love," is his claim.

The Mason brothers, a couple of former linebackers for Des Moines Dowling High School who had morphed into very successful commercial movers, had quickly removed our furniture disaster, so we had plenty of room to paint. The carpets had been cleaned so we laid out heavy-duty drop cloths. All we had to worry about was making sure we hit the walls. We attacked both war-torn offices with primer in a united attempt to hide the venom, then circled back to my space.

As a big picture kind of guy, I took the roller in hand and began covering the wall in wide swatches of power beige. Jerry, obviously the most meticulous of our little troupe, was working the edger along the doors, ceiling, and floorboards. Dennis, of course, provided supervision.

And Dennis' lecture about the value of manual labor was on the mark. After the chaos of the past several days, the controlled repetition of dip, roll, rest, dip, roll, rest was a welcome activity. Unlike most of the work of psychotherapy, this job really did have a beginning and an end.

We were quickly turning my office from a raging profanity project into my home away from home again. Still, I wondered how long it would take before I could look at the walls and not visualize the malice that lurked underneath. We were covering the ugly, but it seemed as if the words were alive, the hate oozing through.

It will take more than One Coat Guaranteed Paint to heal this assault.

"Knock, Knock." A friendly woman's voice interrupted my silent reverie. I peeked around the corner of my office doorway.

Gail. No phone call.

"Uh, hi." I was dumbstruck. Our last communication did not suggest a forthcoming family gathering.

She was dressed in an oversized Hawkeyes sweat suit, black jogging pants, and pristine white Nikes with black and gold trim. She managed to look elegant.

Jerry saved the day.

"Oh, Gail. Come in. I'm so glad you're here," he gushed. "These animals are working me to death." He looked at Dennis and me with mock recrimination. "You look fabulous! Who but you could make a sweat suit look like a fashion statement?"

"You're too sweet," Gail hugged on Jerry, gave Dennis a squeeze and, then, offered me her smile.

"Well, it's break time. I have someone waiting in the hall with Belinda who'd love to see all of you. I wanted to check first to see if the walls were presentable."

I recovered from my shock and managed to sweep a hand in grand gesture around the room.

"Coming right along. It looks almost the same as before," she sighed. "That's good."

"Daddy!" Haley came strutting through the waiting area and into my office, ears on full display.

Belinda was right behind her, a bit breathless from the jog down the hall. "She just couldn't wait."

Using my keen therapist's third eye, I immediately noticed both Gail and Belinda warning me with wordless stares that could only be interpreted as, "Don't screw this up."

"Kiddo, I didn't expect you tonight! This is great." Time with my daughter was a highlight for any day.

"Wait a second." I stopped, pasting a quizzical look on my face. "Step back a bit." I tapped my temple with a finger. "A little more."

She backed into the waiting room.

"Right there. Stop. There's something different about you, but I can't make out what it is? A new hairdo?"

"No, DAD!"

"Huh. Let's see. You've been tanning?"

"NOOO!"

"Geez." I scratched my head. Doing my best wide eyes, I went for silly.

"Oh, yeah! Look at those ears! There's jewelry sticking out of them. Gold hearts! I've never seen anything like that. Is this some strange new Des Moines custom? It's so beautiful, so glamorous, so festive."

"Do you really like them?" The hope in her voice overcame any resistance I was harboring.

"Absolutely," I said. "You look wonderful."

She ran into my arms. "It hardly hurt. I was really brave."

Looking over her shoulder I gave Gail my famous winning smile and received her famous wry grin that might have been saying, "You overplayed it a bit, but you get points for that one, Anderson."

Take your victories where you can get them.

Haley stepped back into the office and said, "We came to help you paint, Dad. Mom said you're redecorating and Belinda told us you'd need our help."

Clever and uncharacteristically subtle.

Belinda was conveniently staring at the floor.

Haley stopped and scanned the newly painted walls. "It looks almost the same," she said. "Except no furniture."

"Just a little fresh paint before new furniture comes. And we can use all the help we can get, kiddo."

At that, Gail produced three large, weathered cotton shirts with the Drake logo from an old Yonkers bag she'd carried in. "We'll just duck into the bathroom down the hall and put on our knock around clothes."

To my credit, I didn't offer to help Gail change. Instead, looking at Haley, I said, "I'll head downstairs and get the sodas. Number One rule of work detail and daughters; stay hydrated."

"Thank God you're here, Haley," Jerry moaned and sank into my covered chair, forearm draped dramatically across his forehead. "We haven't been allowed any liquids all night."

That got a giggle from the whole crowd.

I headed for the door just as Dennis and Jerry began to moon over Haley's new ears.

"You look beautiful, Haley."

"I think you ought to go for gold hoops, girl."

"No, I'm thinking diamonds."

"Yes, talk to your dad about diamonds, Haley. You'll be stunning."

Walking down the hall, as the voices faded, I smiled to myself. In therapy, we sometimes talk about Family of Origin: Dad and Haley were the folks with my family blood in their veins. And then we talk about Family of Choice: Gail, Belinda, Dennis, Jerry. The special people we pick up, or allow to pick us up, along the way. Despite many bumps in the road and errors in judgment over the years, tonight I was feeling pretty blessed on all accounts.

It occurred to me that Kenny was gravely disappointed in his Family of Origin. What little I knew indicated he didn't have much in the way of Family of Choice, either. I found myself hoping we would have the chance to find remedies for some of that loss.

Hitting the stairwell and taking the steps two at a time, I headed for the soda machine in the lobby. As I pushed through the door to the first floor, the air was sucked out of my happy place.

A familiar form was standing at the glassed-in front door of the building, eyes squinted, looking in. Shaved head glowing in the fragile lighting of the outer doorway. I didn't need tape from a security camera to know who it was.

Kenny.

"Let me in, Doc." His muffled voice had a memorable end-of-first-session urgency as it leaked through the glass door. "I need to talk to you. Now!"

Hearing Phil's voice in my head, I reached into the right pocket of my overalls and held tightly to the keys.

Call me first.

I listened to his voice in my head. Listened. Understood. Agreed. I reached into my left pocket for my phone.

Belinda's desk. Where I left it.

I pulled the keys out of my pocket and unlocked the door.

Kenny didn't wait for the door to completely open, squeezing inside and hustling past me into the cover created by the careful overhead lighting in the atrium.

"Thanks, Doc. The life you saved may be my own."

Weak stabs at humor were emerging as a pattern of communication in my brief time with Kenny.

He had replaced his uniform with a dark sweatshirt, jeans, and an out-of-style pale-blue Members Only jacket.

"What are you doing here, Kenny? And what do you mean? Where were you? We had an appointment scheduled for today."

They teach us in big time therapy school to ask one question at a time. They just hadn't prepared me for Kenny.

"I've been driving around. I was sitting in your parking lot for a while. I didn't know where else to go." His voice was strained, just short of panic. "I saw Belinda come in with some woman and a kid, but she locked the door. The lights were on in your window. I was hoping it was you."

He saw Gail and Haley!

"It is me." My voice oscillated between fear and frustration. Was he followed? Had my daughter and her mother been drawn closer to the fire of this man's foolishness? The stakes had changed. It was time for some answers to this craziness.

"So, we're both here, Kenny," exasperation bleeding into my words. "Now what?"

"I don't know!" He slapped the wall, then hugged himself, shifting back-and-forth like an anxious kid in a rocking chair. Except he was standing.

"All I know is I went out this morning. Just walking around with nothing to do. I came home to get ready for my appointment with you and somebody had broken in to my place."

He was almost panting with fear.

"Man, it was a disaster. They tore my apartment up. I got out right then. Like I said, I've been driving around all day."

Crisis response. You know what to do. Get him up to the Kensington offices. Find a phone. Keep him away from friends and family.

I injected calm into my response.

"So, you came to a safe place. This is a safe place," I repeated, reminding both of us.

Call Phil.

"Here's what we're going to do, Kenny. We're going to call Phil Evans. He'll know how to protect you."

"No cops, Doc," Kenny went rigid and looked toward the door.

"Wait." The softness in my pitch didn't match the speed of my pulse. "Then tell me what this trouble is about."

"Like I said, Doc, you really don't want to know."

"Kenny." I added a protective parent to my tone. "You came to me for help. You don't want cops and you don't want to tell me the truth. How can I help you?"

Gentle pressure applied.

"I don't know." He shrunk deeper into the shadows. "I just didn't have any place else to go."

"You're here now. Safe," I repeated for the third time. "You can't just keep driving around, hoping this will go away by itself. Let's find a phone and get reinforcements from the good guys."

More careful pressure. I took a step toward him and was pounded by a deluge of words, along with a rush of tears.

"It's drugs, Doc! They pay me. They said I could keep everything I stole, that I wouldn't get caught. Just make the deliveries and keep my mouth shut. Now they're going to kill me!"

Aw, Kenny.

"Who's they?"

"I don't know," he screeched. "Two guys! They found me on my route a couple of months ago. Showed me a bunch of money. They knew about me. Somehow, they knew I'd been stealing the porn. They said they could make sure nothing bad happened to me. Or make sure something really bad did."

He squeezed himself tighter. Comfort from the coming storm.

It hadn't occurred to Kenny that "they" were the bad that already was happening. Out of fear and greed, he'd apparently taken a big step up in the crime world. Thief to drug runner. Career advancement for those with a low street I.Q.

As the mystery was finally beginning to unwind, I found a deeper level of calm.

One more time. "What guys, Kenny?"

"I don't know," he whined. "One was fat. Big muscles. Mean. The other one looked like a vampire."

Not much detail, but enough to rattle in my skull. Fat JJ and Preacher.

Time for the cavalry.

"Here's what we're going to do. Now." I stepped forward. "I'm taking you up to the offices we're using on a temporary basis. I'm having my office painted." No need for the real, scary truth. "We'll figure this out."

"No!" He waved me off. "I got to go, Doc. There's nothing you can do. It was crazy to even come here."

Kenny began backing toward the door. Following his movements, I looked over his shoulder and saw a car, slowly cruising into the parking lot. In the haze between the dark night and the lighting of the lot, I couldn't tell who it was. The way things were going, it seemed a good idea to assume the worst.

"Kenny, come upstairs. Right now!" I attempted to command his attention as I edged to relock the door. "You can't deal with this alone. Who could? We need to sit down, calm down, and think this through."

"OK. OK. OK." His rocking slowed as he rapid-fired his compliance. "I can't go back out there," he mumbled to himself.

Kenny half-turned and gestured toward the parking lot. The car stopped and idled, headlights staring us down. His conclusion was immediate.

"Oh, God! It's them." He flew past me and exploded out the door with a speed and power that only terror inspires. He darted to the right and vanished into nightfall. I dashed out the door behind him. Too late. Kenny was a rocket ship fueled by panic. He cut through the lawn behind the building, sprinting full speed toward Grand Avenue.

I froze, startled by the sound of a car door opening and aware how vulnerable I'd just become. The dark sedan had found a parking spot next to my Jeep, under the light pole. A single man stepped out. Taller than Preacher. No beer gut. A silhouette against the fading sky.

Phil.

I wavered, leaned to the left of the door, and found a wall to hold me up. So much for calm.

Phil jogged over as I managed to point and gasp, "Kenny Jensen."

Phil spun on his heels, running off in the direction of Kenny's retreat and disappearing into the gloom. I gingerly settled onto the wrought iron bench near the entrance, the one usually reserved for smokers and vapors.

I took a minute to recount my blessings, particularly the one about the car that contained Phil, not Fat JJ and Preacher. Using a breathing exercise designed to restore composure, I managed to decompress enough to relocate my keys as Phil wandered back into the illumination cast from the lobby.

"No Kenny. He must have had his car parked somewhere close. We know his make, model, and license. I called it in. Are you OK?" I couldn't see his face well, but I could hear his concern.

I assumed he couldn't see mine either. If it had been daylight, my face would, no doubt, have been even more pale than usual.

"As Dad used to say, looks like I'm gonna live."

"The question is, why did seeing my car bring on that reaction?"

"We couldn't tell who it was. We both thought you were the guy who may or may not be Jake, and Preacher."

He nodded.

"Well, I'm glad it was only me."

I rested my elbows on my knees and breathed through my fingers.

"For sure."

"Now that I've chased Kenny into the night, fill in the blanks?"

I looked up.

"Reflex test. Your department hired me as a consultant to study detectives in quick-response crisis situations. Run now, get the story later. You passed with flying colors." I did my best imitation of a smile.

"You are even less funny at this moment than all the other times you are not funny." Phil put on a credible scowl for a fundamentally good guy. Years of practice interviewing and unnerving crooks. "What really happened?"

"I was heading to the soda machine."

I revived enough to sit up straight, then stand.

"He just showed up at the door. I let him in. He told me he's been making drug deliveries from his truck. They knew about his stealing. They're blackmailing him. He's terrified, Phil. I tried to get him to come upstairs to the Kensington offices, so we could call you. When he saw the car, he bolted."

"Let's go inside, you're shivering. We're going to run some patrols around the neighborhood and check out his home address again. He's probably long gone by now."

"OK, but let's keep this low-key. The whole gang is upstairs painting, including Haley."

"Low-key. Sure."

"Hey," it suddenly dawned on me; Phil was standing before me in weathered blue jeans sans fedora. "What are you doing here, this time of night?"

Phil pulled a paintbrush out of his back pocket. "Paint detail."

He stood erect and saluted. "Belinda called and encouraged me to help out. Catherine and the kids are visiting her sister in Centerville. No secondary job tonight. So, here I am."

As we retreated into the lobby, I regained my equilibrium and remembered to fetch the items promised just a few minutes past. Go for sodas. Return with Phil and sodas. Nothing odd. Nothing out of the ordinary.

Other than the dull ache in my chest for Kenny and the nagging question of how we were going to help him out of this corner he had painted himself into.

Paint metaphor. Geez.

Back in the office, Phil and I and the sodas were welcomed with open arms. Everyone assumed my errand had taken longer due to Phil's appearance in the lobby. We said nothing to suggest otherwise.

"Alright, you goldbricks," I said in mock drill-sergeant-ease. "Let's see what you've accomplished while I've been out buying supplies. Those that worked receive liquid replenishment."

On cue, the whole group groaned.

There was no discussion of the unscheduled visit from Kenny as we moved on to Dennis' office and knuckled down to finish the painting. With Belinda in-house to supervise, Dennis was returned to the labor force. I knew Gail to be a credible painter of walls. Phil, as always, was a hard worker, stopping to take one phone call, his subtle grimace letting me know the police had found no sign of Kenny.

Haley mostly wandered around holding a roller and catching everyone up on the details of her amazing life.

"Impressive, team," Jerry crowed as we put the final touches on his partner's walls.

"How did schmucks like us ever end up with so many wonderful and talented people who love us?" I queried, putting my arm around Dennis' shoulders.

He ruffled my sandy hair like a long-suffering and loving parent, then turned to Haley.

"Malts for anyone? Dad's buying!"

"Absolutely," she beamed. "This painting stuff has worn me out, Dad. Like Grandpa would say, I need to refill the tank." Laughs all around.

"It's getting a bit late," Gail balked. "Maybe we ought to be getting…"

"Nonsense," Jerry cut her off. "It's in our contract. Malts are guaranteed at the completion of the job. I negotiated it myself."

"It's decided then," I said, a bit overeager. "Let's go."

Phil begged off, and I let him. He had taken time out of his already break-neck schedule to help us out. He had crooks to catch and a Sunday night Bible study class to prepare for, co-led with his ever patient and oft-waiting wife, Catherine.

As Dennis secured the new and improved building lock behind us, I walked Phil to his car, fully expecting to receive another round of his "don't pretend you're a cop" lecture.

I was not disappointed.

"You're deep into something here, Hank," he said. "I don't know all of it yet, and I'm sorry for getting you involved. But the more we know, the worse it gets."

His face was granite.

"I'm also worried because, as previously noted, you can be impulsive."

His candor stung.

"You are not a police officer. You are smart and I have learned a lot from you about people's pain and how they heal. You also have a serious problem when it comes to knowing when it's time to keep your nose out of their business."

"I really appreciate everything you're trying to do, but what do you expect of me, Phil?"

My dialed-up volume registered annoyance, not appreciation.

"I'm in this. Kenny picked me as his confidant. I don't just sign off because the work gets difficult. You refer to me because you know that's true, and then you lecture me because you know that's true."

"A friend once told me during a tough time in my life that committed and reckless are two different ways of being. I'm just returning the favor," he reminded, in a gentler voice.

I put my hands in my pockets, fighting the rawness of memories past. I was the friend, and Phil was a different kind of cop, then, caught in the middle of a nightmare case.

"I remember. Which reminds us both that this is not our first rodeo together."

"Acknowledged." Phil humbly admitted to his own past impulses.

I released the tension in my jaw and gave him the grace he so often gave to me.

"First, I'll continue to be careful. Second, I'll remember I have a family that needs me. Third, I'll keep my eyes and ears open, and call you if anything – I mean anything – strange happens. Good enough?"

"You keep saying all that. And it keeps not happening. You had my back, Hank. Now, I have yours."

"You're right, again. And for the record, I was headed for a phone with Kenny when you showed up tonight."

"I'll give you that one. Last thing," he added. "Revisit this with Gail. Things are even more hinky after tonight."

He opened his ebony leather jacket and did the old badge on the belt tapping thing again.

"Just until I get a handle on everything."

Kenny had seen my daughter and her mom tonight. This was one step closer to the criminals that were, without a doubt, tracking him. Phil was increasingly worried this insanity could touch my family. Directly.

"Hank, if those bad guys are looking for Kenny and they think you can help them find him, they might just come back at you. And the people closest to you. Pay attention. Head up. Give me a few days to get on top of this."

Something he'd tell other cops before they went out on patrol.

"I will."

One gift Phil brings to my life is that he, unlike Dennis and Belinda, sometimes lets me have the last word. He reached out and squeezed my shoulder, then folded himself into the Impala and pointed it toward the modest security of his home in Clive.

I turned and looked over the remnants of my odd little paint crew, clothing splattered and waiting eagerly by the vehicles. These were not people I could allow to sit in the line of fire with me if Preacher and Jake did come back.

Carry your phone, Anderson. And put Phil on speed dial.

We all made our way to the closest ice cream shop, a caravan of three suburban vehicles on pilgrimage to a traditional, time-honored institution of better-than-decent malts. After we all found near nirvana in a round of frosty treats, Dennis, Jerry, and Belinda yawned in unison.

"It's late," Jerry said. "I'll be in the office for a bit of weekend work tomorrow and this grumpy man of mine needs his beauty rest." He winked at me.

"That's right," Belinda parroted. "My car is loaded with the fruits of our shopping trip. Hank, you get the little one and her momma to my place."

So obvious.

"Kisses all around," she said, enveloping Gail and Haley in her protective arms before any protest could be issued by Gail or myself. "You drive them safe now, Hank."

Belinda gave me a big smile and she winked, too. My god, the paint crew was transmuting into a winking, smiling, meddling matchmakers' convention. To his credit, Dennis kept a poker face as he gave hugs all around. He climbed into Jerry's sensible, yet sporty white Infinity sedan, and they headed for home. Belinda started up the hybrid and silently drifted back onto the main drag, pointing west.

That left Gail, a sleepy Haley, and me. I couldn't remember the last time I had been out on the town with my daughter and her mother. I liked it, and it was damned uncomfortable.

Gail opened the passenger side rear door and buckled Haley into the Jeep, as if she still completed that motion every day. Haley mumbled something unintelligible and was asleep before I cleared the parking lot. Other than Haley's tranquil sleep noises, there was a conspicuous silence.

It's quiet. Too quiet.

"You can drop us at the front door of Belinda's building."

"Sure."

We lapsed back into silence.

Unlike the therapy room, where I have learned the value of waiting for the other person to speak, my tension rose and I broke the hush with, "Well, this is a bit awkward."

"What do you mean? It's not like we're on a date, Hank."

I felt the jab. She appeared to have read my mind, which all therapists know is impossible.

"I would definitely tell a client at this point, do not say 'I wish it was a date.'"

In the glow of the dashboard I could feel the disbelief in Gail's gaze on the side of my face.

"That's part of what makes you a great therapist, Hank. You always know what landmines to steer your clients away from. And you know that only a fool would say those things to his ex."

"Yep, only a fool." More awkward than before. "Anyway, thanks for coming out to help tonight."

"It was Belinda's idea and Haley loved it."

Maybe I hid the flinch from the second hit, but I felt her looking at me again. She lightly touched my hand on the steering wheel.

"And it's important to me to be here, when friends need me."

Now my hand felt hot.

Friends.

It didn't feel great. It hurt.

Better than a sharp stick in the eye.

Knowing when to quit for a change, I retreated into another ten minutes of uneasy quiet, using the time for a gut check. I knew I needed to tell her about my last conversation with Phil and our deep concern for the safety of my inner circle.

I pulled into the 15-minute parking in front of Belinda's condo building.

"How about I carry her in," I asked?

"Thanks."

I gently unhooked Haley from the seat belt and lifted her to my shoulder, rewarded with a brief, bleary-eyed smile as she nuzzled in.

Doorman Don, as Haley called him, was on nights. He had been alerted to our arrival and buzzed us in. Carrying fragile goods, to the elevator and up to Belinda's floor, I enjoyed the warm, limp weight of my daughter. Gail had a key. The muted light in the hallway led us directly to the smaller guest room Haley had occupied on many sleepovers. It was dark, but I had the path to the bed committed to memory.

Gail turned the switch on a nightlight, pulled back the covers, and I gently laid Haley on the flannel sheet. Gail pulled off her tennis shoes. Haley snuggled her face deep into the pillow. Gail and I communicated silently as we stood side-by-side, our eyes deciding, as we had many times in another life, to let her sleep in her comfy clothes rather than wrestling with pajamas.

For a moment, in the one dance where Gail and I had almost always been in sync, I felt at home. On impulse, I gently put my hand on her back. She turned into me and, as we kissed, I could feel the chocolate warmth of her breath. Sliding my hand under her shirt, I touched the softness of her back in a way that never, even in our troubled times, failed to excite us both.

Haley rolled to her side with a soft growl of sleepy pleasure.

Gail stepped back, quickly readjusting the chambray with a sweep of her hands. I stepped back.

"Let's talk in the kitchen," she whispered. "We don't want to wake up Haley."

The kitchen. Talk. Deep breath. Let go. Damn. OK.

We moved out of the bedroom, past the stillness of Belinda's closed bedroom door, to the kitchen. It only took a few steps to talk myself into going for noble, pretending that what just happened, didn't.

"Hey, thanks again for coming over to the office tonight," I said, before Gail could decide to discount our moment of intimacy. "Really appreciate it."

She played along.

"I'm glad we could help. I hope they find whoever did this soon." Gail was closing out the evening.

I wanted to hold her. I wanted to run to the bedroom and scoop my daughter into my arms. I wanted to escape with them to some remote cabin in the mountains until the whole world was a safe place.

Suck it up.

"One more thing."

She leaded back against the counter and crossed her arms.

"There's been another development. Phil will let us know when he's sure it's safe for you and Haley to go home."

I felt her withdrawal wash through me like anesthesia. She looked through me.

"I need you to go now."

Moving to the door, I kept as much space between us as possible. "I'll let myself out."

Driving home, I had one inescapable thought: Gail, Dennis and Phil were all correct in their judgments. I could project blame onto Phil for referring Kenny. I could blame Kenny for being a thief and a drug mule. Maybe I could go all the way back and fault Dad for drinking, leading me into a life of co-dependency and an addiction to excitement.

Bottom line, though, I had decided to take us all down this road when I didn't tell Phil about Preacher and Jake as soon as they appeared.

As I pulled into the drive and punched the garage door opener, I had the presence of mind to look up and down the street. No one. I thought back to the Cadillac sitting along the curb, less willing to dismiss its presence than I had been two nights ago.

My cell rang as I walked in the door. Belinda. Against my better judgment, a quality that was seriously in question these days, I answered.

"I thought you were sleeping."

"How did it go, Big Shot?"

"My dad always said a gentleman never kisses and tells, Belinda."

"Blew it again, huh."

"That's an understatement," drearily replaying my latest fiasco with Gail.

"You never should have let that fine woman go, Hank."

"She's your friend. Has it occurred to you that she wanted to divorce me? Maybe *you* ought to let go."

I was tired.

"I didn't mean to anger you, Hank. Get some sleep. You sound tired." The woman was amazing.

"Good idea. And I'm sorry I barked at you. I'm not angry at you. You're the best."

"Yes, I am," she confirmed. "Haley and Gail can stay here as long as you need them to, so stop kicking yourself. You're a fine young man who occasionally doesn't see the shit before he steps in it. It isn't like the rest of us are perfect. We all care about you, too. Don't forget that. Goodnight."

As usual, she hung up before I could respond. I felt the proverbial lump in my throat. Love, guilt, frustration, worry. My heart was not a tidy place tonight.

"A modern man who knows how to get in touch with his feelings," I said to the empty room. "Yippee."

I hit the button to re-engage the alarm and trudged up the stairs to my bedroom, eager for a soft pillow and cool sheets.

I stopped on the first landing, a powerful thread to my heart pulling me to keep moving past my bedroom until I found myself standing in the middle of Haley's room. The man-in-the-moon, could be woman-in-the-moon, shined through the skylights, casting hazy images against the walls. I grinned at the pale green aura of neon Glow Stars that Haley and I had pasted to her ceiling in a fit of frivolous interior decorating.

The combination of faint natural illumination along with the plastic glimmer of the stars was oddly soothing. I crossed the room and let myself down onto Haley's bed, a guy with tired bones and an exhausted mind.

I'll just rest a bit and think good thoughts about my best girl.

It seemed like seconds later when I woke, disoriented, the moon person staring me in the eyes through the skylight. My pulse was throbbing to the beat of another unwanted reoccurring dream. Once again, Mom had come to me in dreamtime, as she had in real time throughout my childhood.

"Hank, be careful," she warned me. "You'll be the death of me. You take too many chances." Mini-bikes and ATVs, tree climbing, school skipping, blowing through curfew. I'd really put Mom through her paces. As if she didn't have enough to deal with, given Dad's regular after-closing time drinking binges.

Mom did die, only 58 years old, but with many miles of life on her. She'd worked hard at the restaurant, worked hard trying to manage Dad's alcoholism, and often forgot to work on taking care of herself. She did get to enjoy six years of his sobriety and five in Al-Anon. After time with Bob Rathburn and lots of my own Al-Anon, I'd let go of blaming Dad for her early death. I had mostly let go of blaming myself, too.

"It was a stroke, Hank." Bob's velvet hammer of truth snuck into my head. "Was it stress? Yes. Were you a difficult kid? Sometimes. It was also genetics and years of unhealthy eating. Until she got around to her own recovery program, she took better care of everyone she loved than she did herself."

"You learned some unhealthy stuff," he'd pushed on. "You were also loved."

I lay still, aware of my soft breathing and trying to quiet the rehashed clatter in my head. So motionless that I imagined a familiar creaking sound floating up the stairs.

Haley's on the way up to bed.

Not possible.

The cold night groaning into my old hardwood floors.

I was chalking up the noise to a dream hangover when I heard a second distinguishable squeak. Not just the sounds of the inching shift in temperature. This was weight coming down on the ever-present warp in the floorboards, just inside the front door. The third and sixth planks. I'd been making that sound every time I came through the entryway and turned toward the stairs or kitchen since day one of my move.

Is somebody here, or is this a dream within a dream?

I rubbed my eyes and blinked.

Awake. Not alone.

I sat up, fear thundering into my ears and delivering energy to my legs. I stepped onto the carpet and rushed toward the open doorway of Haley's room; dread had not yet translated into caution. The thick pile consumed the noise of my steps. I slid against the wall next to the doorway and strained to listen through an urge to scream.

Who!?

A dull thud of soft-soled shoes echoed through the darkness. My mind made its best, and worst, guess: Preacher or Jake. Preacher *and* Jake.

Sound carried up these steps like the restored Boonville steam locomotive roaring into a mountain tunnel.

Without waking me, he or she or them had beaten the lock, not knowing the planks were a secondary alarm system.

A bit too late, the intruder heard it, too. An awkward attempt at stealth called me back from frantic. The well-travelled wooden stairs were another percussive alarm system, unknown to the feet moving my way. I counted squeaks in my head. One-two-three-four-five-six-seven-eight-nine-ten. The prowler had reached the first landing and the doorway to my room.

Silence. The carpet of my bedroom.

Gathering some semblance of focus, it hit me that standing in the dark while the attacker found an empty room, then continued to climb, wasn't a viable plan.

Think!

I'd probably been seen coming home by a less obvious stakeout than an ugly Cadillac. Whoever was creeping through the house knew I was here and saw the lights go out.

I grabbed at the pockets of my jeans. No phone.

On the bed!

Another groan of heft hit the stairs. The stalker had found me missing from my bed and was back on the landing, moving this way. Next was Haley's room. If they'd been watching my movements and knew my schedule, they would assume Haley had been in the back seat, and settled in here for the night. Whoever this was planned on coming to her room to find me, or us, or…Haley.

Coming for Haley!

Too late for the phone. No way to get down the stairs through the creeper. If it was Jake, he'd fill the whole stairwell. If it was Preacher, he'd just look at me and I'd have a heart attack. I desperately looked around the room for anything resembling protection.

The hammering of my heart was intensified by a compressed explosion in my head. I looked around the room again, no less terrified but with a monstrous rage possessing my body.

Fight. With what?!

Weapon.

Shrinking further from the door, I backed into Haley's dresser and nudged the hard plastic of her portable CD player sitting on top. Probably still loaded with the hot, new Cassie Simons CD.

Something. I can hit the Play button. Maybe the music will drive him away.

Bordering on silent hysteria, I grabbed the handle. It wasn't much but there were no other choices. I reached behind the player and disconnected the cord from the back panel. As I lifted the player, the cord slipped from my hand and I heard the faint, sickening clunk of the plug knocking on wood, bouncing off the dresser and settling onto the carpet.

It wasn't a big sound. Just enough to cause a hesitation on the steps, followed by accelerated footsteps and the hazy cast of a cell phone flashlight increasing in strength as it led the prowler up our stairs.

In retrospect, I saw Jake's stomach come through the door before I saw the rest of him, his paunch and the handgun with a funny barrel extension poking through the portal.

Bracing my feet at shoulder width, I hefted the CD player with both hands, aimed for what I hoped was the middle of his body, and swung left to right with every ounce of electric energy my frame could muster.

"Uuuhhhh!" I nailed him square in the chest as he stepped into the room. He staggered backward; his light released into the night. The gun went off.

The pistol made a quieter sound than I'd expected, as a bullet embedded itself somewhere in the slanted ceiling.

I pivoted into the doorway as Jake stumbled backwards. His heel must have caught on the edge of the stairs; my blow alone could not have shifted his massive bulk. Without a word, arms pinwheeling, he catapulted onto his back and bounced violently down to the first landing.

Jake was stunned, flailing like a giant overturned tortoise, his girth making it difficult to maneuver in the tight space. I hoped his head had knocked on wood on each step; it was too dark to tell. He was, however, a professional, a Neanderthal and surprisingly fast for an overweight turtle. Almost immediately, he fought to regain his feet.

I rushed down the stairs, as Jake was finding his sea legs. He staggered upright and lurched toward me. The gun was gone from his hand. It didn't matter. If this animal got a grip on me, he'd simply crush my spine.

The stairwell didn't allow for a full swing of the CD player. In full lizard brain, I threw myself from the steps with the machine right in front of me, like a battering ram, smashing Jake square in the face as he raised his head. With the grotesque squishing noise of hard plastic on flesh and another muted grunt, Jake spun to his left, grasping at air as he was launched backwards down the remaining stairs. My feet hit the landing; something in my left ankle gave way. Not being a man with a lifetime of experience giving and receiving pain, I screamed, stumbled, pitched to the right, and followed Jake down the stairwell to the first floor. The makeshift weapon flew from my hands. I arrived at the bottom crosswise, on top of my assailant, his ample torso a partial cushion for the crash.

My eyes slammed closed as my head pounded the hardwood.

It took painful effort to force them to reopen.

Through a cascade of nausea and blurred vision, I was staring directly into Jake's face. His eyes, also open, were blank and unblinking. I noticed that his nose was pushed sideways, bloodied, flattened by the blow. His head tilted at an odd angle. He looked as if he was considering a question for which there was no answer.

I had no previous experience with this sort of thing, but guessed he was dead.

I rolled off the body and landed with a soft thud on the unyielding oak.

"Damn." My head was spinning. Everything hurt. I did the sensible thing and closed my eyes again.

"You amaze me, Doc."

My brain barely registered the sudden awareness that the speaker could not be Jake. I forced my eyes open a second time.

Preacher.

He stood in the entryway, shaking his head, shifting his gaze from his ex-partner to me.

I lay completely still. No fear left. Just pain.

"I'd get a real doctor to check out those injuries, Doc," he monotoned. "You came down real hard." He knelt, checked Jake's neck for a pulse, then picked up the gun that had managed to careen its way down to his feet. "I'll just take this with me, if you don't mind."

He stood, leaned over, picked up the coat rack - an apparent casualty of the battle - and set it upright in the exact correct position. Then he took in the entire scene once more and shook his head again, in apparent disbelief. He stepped slowly backwards, gingerly leap-frogging the offending creaky boards, turned the door handle and stepped into the night, gently closing the door behind him.

At some point, I pulled myself to my knees and, head in a firestorm, crawled up the stairs to retrieve my cell phone.

Later, I wouldn't remember dialing 911, or how I got back down the steps.

An EMT whose nametag read Jeff told me later that I was holding vigil on the third step when the ambulance and street officers arrived. He said I initially refused to take my glassy-eyed stare off Jake or to relinquish the bloodied CD player that I had somehow recovered.

Apparently, I insisted they call Phil. Since I appeared to know a highly regarded police detective, they humored me. With no blood escaping my body, they allowed me to sit unquestioned and untouched as we waited for him to arrive.

I refused to leave the stairwell, remaining on guard as if I believed my attacker would stand again and, with his vacant stare, resume the fight to reach my daughter. At some point, I heard the third and sixth floorboards creak again. Pinballs ricocheted in my brain when I jerked my head up in reflex to the sound.

"Hank," Phil began softly. "Hank." A little stronger. His latex-gloved hands reached out gently to take the musical weapon from my hands. "You're safe. It's me, Phil," he said, in his most reassuring tone. "We've got to get you looked at by the EMT's, buddy. You're injured."

I looked at Phil as if meeting him for the first time.

"I think I hurt my ankle. Then I killed him." I gave the first explanation as if one was a prerequisite for the other.

"Don't explain anything else yet, Hank." Phil shut the conversation down. "You're in shock. Let's get you looked at, and then we'll talk."

Motioning to the EMTs to block my view of the deceased thug as they checked my head and ankle, Phil dialed his cell phone. I vaguely heard Dennis' name as he began speaking.

The EMTs fit my ankle with one of those contraptions that looks like a black spongy mukluk. They asked a bunch of mental status questions and I passed – I knew who I was, where I was, and was kind of in the ballpark about who they were. They also determined that my head hurt, using the phrase "possible concussion" and labeled my vital signs "stable."

Phil had returned. "These good people are going to take you to the hospital to X-ray that ankle and check for other injuries, Hank. I'll be over shortly and we'll talk." He carefully laid his baseball mitt sized hand on my shoulder. "Dennis will be there. I called and he's on the way."

I looked up.

"Is Jake dead? My ankle hurts. My head hurts." I couldn't fully grasp the connections.

Phil let the question go. He stepped aside as the EMTs assisted me onto the rolling gurney, my neck secured in a protective collar. "Just a precautionary measure, Mr. Anderson," Jeff assured me.

As they wheeled me toward the door, I suddenly became aware of the buzz of activity, people in various types of uniforms flowing in and out.

That answered the question. Jake was dead.

I was not.

"Preacher was here, too," I spoke to wherever Phil stood, as my thoughts began to clear. "He told me to get myself taken care of. Then he left. He took the gun."

Phil didn't answer. He just pulled a notepad and pen from his pocket and wrote something down. Then, he gave the ambulance crew a look that sent us out the door.

I slowly became aware of the welcome sound of Dennis in protection mode.

"He doesn't need a psych referral. He's got us."

I pried my eyes open and mechanically watched a nervous young man scurry out through the privacy curtain. Probably an ER social worker, wondering why he hadn't listened to his parents and become a CPA.

I guessed that I'd made it to the hospital. In my somewhat restricted position, I noticed the bed was surrounded: Dennis, Phil, and a woman, about my age. She had porcelain skin, nearly translucent. She was either a new acquaintance or the most beautiful angel of death I could imagine. Soft, shoulder length red hair. Dressed in a simple black tea-length evening dress that showed excellent cleavage. All of which, even in this debilitated state, commanded my attention.

She looks much better in black than Preacher does.

Attempting to lift my head, I winced and collapsed back.

"Gee, you're beautiful," my voice croaked, "But I just don't think I'm up to dancing tonight."

The woman smiled and looked at Dennis. "You didn't tell me he was funny."

I shifted my eyes to Dennis.

"I like her already. Who is she?"

"I'm your attorney, Jill Bennett," she answered for him. "So, be quiet and speak only when I tell you to. OK?"

It wasn't really a question.

Phil cut in, "I'll need a statement from you, Hank."

Before I could even begin to open my mouth again, my new champion spoke.

"My client has just been through a horrifying experience. He's in shock and he may have a concussion, Detective. As I just said, he's not talking to anyone yet."

"He talked to you just fine, Ms. Bennett." Phil had some experience with this type of situation. "He's not under arrest. I'm not going to read him his rights. He's a victim who has been assaulted and we need the details. There's another bad guy out there. For the safety of your client and others, we need to know what happened."

I flashed back to Jake and me, lying there with Preacher looking down on us. He didn't kill me. He just walked away. I had no idea why.

I had taken a life. Two killers, yet I was alive. It was a defective puzzle.

The curtain parted and in rushed pale-blue clad catalytic energy, with attitude. She was short, stout, with gray-flecked midnight hair. Her nametag said Juanita.

"None of you have any business talking to this man right now," she informed Phil and my new attorney. "This is an emergency room and you'll all go sit in the waiting area until the doctor has cleared Mr. Anderson for visitors."

Everyone just looked at her.

"I said move, people. Out, out, out!" She scowled at Phil and Dennis, but I think I noticed a quick smile for Jill.

It was the best part of an awful day to see these powerful, pushy people tuck their tails and shuffle off to the waiting room. My smile found a direct line to the pain in my head.

"You're one tough customer, Juanita. Those folks don't scare easy."

Juanita matched me with a stern look that showed victory.

"You've got to keep a tight rein on things around here, honey. Twenty-three years tells me that." She talked, checked my IV and scanned the vital signs monitor simultaneously.

"We'll just give that no-nonsense attorney of yours time to work her magic on the good officer. Make sure this turns out right."

"What happened?" I was foggy about the trip from home to the ER.

"The EMTs wheeled you in about forty-five minutes ago. They tried to keep you awake in the event you have a concussion, but you were tapped out. The ER doctor checked you out immediately. He'll be back in a few minutes to tell you what's what. Just between you and me, you're going to be fine."

"Fine is relative, Juanita." I looked at her, deciding from our three minutes together that I could trust her. The words gushed out of me. "They were going to kill me, or my little girl. They didn't know she wasn't home."

My horror and shock melted like an ice cube in a blast furnace. I cried. The pain tightened like a vise grip around my head, but I couldn't stop.

Juanita took my hand. She was quiet while I wept, my brain threatening to detonate and my breath coming in short rasps for air. I don't know how long I cried, trying to wash away the agony of my personal horror movie.

Finally, I took a deep breath and exhaled slowly, immediately grateful for the presence of this natural counselor.

Juanita took her cue. "Young man, I've seen a lot of pain of all kinds, inside and outside pain. Your outside will heal just fine. Inside takes time. But you already know that. I hear you're a very good therapist."

She looked me right in the eyes, the way I do when it's time for a client to pay real close attention.

"I read the admission note. You were protecting yourself and yours, honey. You're alive, your baby's alive. That's what's most important. A bad man died and there's tragedy in that. But you're still here and that's joyful."

It would take a while to get to joy.

The curtains parted again, and a harried looking caramel-colored man with dark Albert Einstein hair, dressed in a white hospital coat, hurried in. He barely looked old enough to play doctor, let alone be one. He didn't introduce himself.

"Well Mr. Anderson, how are you feeling?" His manner was abrupt, like a guy who had already seen too much in his young life.

"Better." I smiled at Juanita. "My ankle is throbbing and my head hurts like hell."

"I believe your ankle is just a bad sprain, but we're going to re-check the X-rays to make sure."

He took a penlight out of his coat pocket and shined it in each of my eyes.

"Nausea?"

"A little. That happens when I kill people."

The doctor flinched at my perceived callousness. I immediately wished I could suck that remark back into my mouth.

"A mild concussion and shock," he said. "We're going to do a CT scan to be on the safe side."

He stepped back. "I've ordered a psych referral. You've been through a lot and I want you to talk to someone." Not an invitation, doctor's orders.

"The social worker has come and gone. I have people to talk to. I'm a psychotherapist, myself."

"Oh, is this something common to your work, Mr. Anderson?"

He immediately cringed at his own callousness and I saw the heat of embarrassment rise in his face.

He was young, he was tired. He'd made a mistake and he knew it.

"We'll get you into radiology as soon as possible. I'm sorry for your difficult evening."

He hurried out. It wasn't an apology, but it was something.

"He's a very good young doctor," Juanita offered in his defense. "He's had a long night, too."

I didn't respond. No doubt, she was right. I just didn't have anything left for the good doctor this night.

SATURDAY

Between the late hour and the various tests, I'd been kept overnight for observation. It was a private room. Good insurance buys better accommodations in the profitable world of non-profit medical care.

Or maybe they didn't trust me in a room with another human, dangerous hombre that I had proven to be.

I woke from the limited sleep one can squeeze in when recuperating in the hospital. Looking across the room, I was greeted by the concerned visages of Dennis and my father. Dad looked exhausted, no doubt from having driven to Des Moines in the middle of the night, followed by not sleeping another wink.

"Dad, if I look as bad as you do, let's go home and get some serious rest." I was reminded that smiling caused the sensation of a ball peen hammer trying to escape from the inside of my skull.

J.R. rose from the awkward gray vinyl visitor's chair and simply laid his hand on top of mine.

"A badly sprained ankle and a mild concussion," Dennis confirmed the doctor's diagnosis. "It looks like you can go home today."

I recalled that Juanita had moved things along nicely and given me a hug before having the transport guy roll me away to my room. It had taken much of the night to poke, prod and photograph me in all the right places.

I'd had enough time on my hands, and enough residual internal juice, to call Phil and Jill Bennett back in and make a full statement of my first home invasion, as best my wounded memory could recall. With my permission, Phil had recorded the whole thing. The catharsis with Juanita helped me leave out some of the emotional color commentary, but as we finished, I could feel myself beginning to pull away and shut down.

Come back…

Jill said, "I'll do all the talking with media."

"Media?"

It hadn't occurred to me that this night could become the next round of my Andy Warhol fifteen minutes of fame.

"You'll make the local TV news and maybe the *Register*."

"Oh, my God," I groused. "Not again." Some time back, Phil and I had made the papers over another unique case. It wasn't fun. The person who said any publicity is good publicity was either a liar, or way too hungry for attention.

"Not to worry," she waved all concern aside. "It will be reported, with help from yours truly and a certain unnamed detective, as a basic home break-in gone bad. Nothing will be said about your involvement other than the victim was knocked unconscious in the B&E and will fully recover."

"You're hired."

"Sign this," she demanded, putting a release in front of me and clicking the pen.

"It gives me power to act on your behalf. Only answer your phone for numbers you recognize. I'll have my office manager get you a cell phone just for family and friends to call. Belinda -- whom I like a lot -- already knows not to give out information to anyone who calls your office."

"I love it when you're strict."

She laughed a great, full-throated laugh. It hurt my head, but I wanted more. I couldn't remember the last time I had flirted with any women other than Gail.

"Just rest up and let me be your attorney."

"Like she said," Phil dittoed. "Rest up."

"One last question, Detective."

"One, Hank," he held up one digit. "You need rest."

"How did they get in my house?"

"Just like the office, you have crummy locks and an alarm system that probably makes a loud annoying noise, but isn't connected to anyone. They easily disabled it. And using the street number of your office as your home code wasn't very original. These men are pros. Think deadbolt and a better security system at home too, my friend. I should have known to remind you of that."

I eased sincerity into my face.

"A second last question, please."

He rubbed the back of his neck and I realized he looked drained. He raised one more finger.

"Any word on Kenny?" I'd had a bit of time between tests and tears to hope he had been found. Safe.

"Sorry." He brushed imaginary lint off the brim of his hat. "No sign of him, yet."

The unspoken upside was, we both knew that Jake and Preacher wouldn't have come to my home if they'd found Kenny. Neither of us said it. The downside was that Preacher was still out there.

I attempted a real smile.

"Thanks. Now, you kids go get some rest. You've had a long night, too."

"The detective and I are creatures of the night," Jill cut in, pulling on a waist length leather jacket. "We don't get tired, we get mean."

Phil offered a courtesy nod in acknowledgement of the backhanded compliment. It appeared that his obvious concern for my wellbeing had taken the lawyer vs. cop edge out of Jill's demeanor. The two had established a tentative peace.

Dad reached over and touched my forehead, as if feeling for fever.

"The doctor told us you could check out as soon as you woke up. He wrote the discharge order, son."

"How about we go to my house," Dennis offered. "Jerry would love to take care of you for a couple of days." He often puts it off on Jerry when he wants to help.

I wanted to reclaim my home as soon as possible.

"No, thanks. I'll head home with The Sage," I said, nodding toward Dad.

"Let me call the nurse then." Dad didn't argue, although his face held doubt.

"No time like the present."

My pronouncement had more spring to it than my body felt.

A couple of hours and a pile of paperwork later, I gingerly slipped into the clean boxers and the Luther College sweats that Dad had retrieved from the house for my trip home. The grunt that escaped my lips when I tried to bend over suggested my running shoes could go untied for the time being.

I was deposited via wheelchair into the backseat of Dad's recent Buick upgrade – a zippy, deep-red LaCrosse. He still lamented the demise of his beloved LeSabre. With Dad driving and Dennis riding shotgun, we set out for the scene of the crime.

I left a thank you note for Juanita and promised myself to send a copy up the ladder to the Director of Nursing and the CEO of the hospital. Exceptional people don't hear often enough just how good they are.

Nobody talked much on the way home. Dennis has too much clinical experience to push me right away and Dad simply knows how to wait.

He pulled into the drive. I cautiously stepped out of the car, with Dennis' help, stopping to look down the street to the spot where I suspected Jake and Preacher had waited for me to settle in the previous night. Shivering through my clothes, I hobbled through the side door, assisted by my ankle support and a handsome aluminum cane, both supplied by the hospital at a fee that would probably bring some insurance underwriter to tears.

"How about setting me up on my old friend, the sofa," I said to no one in particular.

I one-stepped it down to the living room, diverting my eyes from the front door and carefully avoiding the creaky floorboards. Phil had made sure someone tidied up after the crime scene work was done. No remnants of police or ambulance presence staring me in the face. No blood. Nothing broken. No obvious impact.

Dennis fetched pillows and a blanket. He reminded me to keep my head elevated because of the concussion. Once I'd deposited myself on the couch, I noticed he was eyeing me with a combination of sympathy and annoyance. I could read his questions like they were running across his forehead like unedited closed-captioning.

"OK, Doctor Doom. Here's the scoop. I'm exhausted and my body hurts all over. I cried a lot last night in the ER, but I still can't quite reach the idea that a man is dead because of me."

"He's dead because of himself, Hank," Dennis corrected with a wagging finger. "He was a man

184

who hurt people for a pastime, maybe for a living. Still tragic. But what else could you have done?" Rhetorical. "It was him or you."

"I get that logic, Dennis. I also get that I hit him, he fell, and he's dead."

The surge of emotion was unwelcome. I was angry. Not with Dennis, just angry. The internal counselor dialogue told me this was part of the trauma. A louder voice just wanted everything to go away.

"Gotta get some sleep," I announced, retreating into myself.

My dad spoke for the first time since coming through the door. "Excellent plan. Just lay back carefully, son."

He opened a medication bottle. "Here's a little something for the headache. I'm right here and I'm not going anywhere. Luis can handle the restaurant for as long as it takes you to get back on your feet."

He sat down on the stone hearth of the fireplace. "We'll rest when you rest."

"Yeah," Dennis said, pointing at my father. "What J.R. said." He sat across the room in Haley's favorite recliner.

Looking at my father and my best friend, I felt tears well up one more time.

"Damn. Sherlock never cried over the death of a crook," I protested.

"Yeah, but he had that cocaine thing going for him," Dennis responded. "He just numbed out."

So, I cried again. Dad and Dennis simply "held space," as we say in the biz. Quiet, concerned, and protective.

Then I slept for a long time.

SUNDAY

The sound of soft voices and the exquisite aroma of hazelnut coffee drifted out of the kitchen, drawing me back into the waking world. I'd slept from light to light.

I moved a leg, attempting to find some leverage to get off the sofa and, instead gasped loudly. Every muscle in my body felt bruised. Alerted by my pain, Dad came out of the kitchen.

"Stay there, son. I'll bring you a cup of coffee."

"Who's here, Dad?"

Like a line of ants called to a single breadcrumb, the kitchen quickly emptied of more people than it could reasonably hold. The living room filled with most of my known loved ones: Dad, Dennis, Gail, Belinda, and my new advocate, Jill. One and all carried coffee and looks of grave concern.

I wondered where Haley was.

"Gee, you scheduled a game of how many bummed-out looking people can be jammed into a kitchen, and you didn't invite me."

"Ha!" Jill's frown turned upside down with a small chuckle.

Gail turned and gave her a look I was all too accustomed to – disapproval.

"Hey, what can I say? He's funny," she offered back to Gail, perhaps recognizing the glare from a previous relationship in her life.

After a brief, uncomfortable moment, Jill stepped forward. "I need to speak with my client. Alone."

Gail shot another stern look.

If it didn't hurt to move, I'd be scratching my head. What gives?

Dad caught the direction of where things were heading. He gently took Gail by the elbow and said, "Let's put on some more coffee, dear. You can catch me up on everything that incredible granddaughter of mine has been up to."

Gail saw right through the ruse, but she's never been able to resist my Dad's charms. Something he apparently neglected to pass along in the Anderson DNA process.

"All right, J.R.," she said with mock gruffness. "Don't push." Gail's eyes were on me, but her message seemed more for Jill.

Even in my weakened condition, I kind of liked the tension between these two lovely women, both concerned about my wellbeing. It was a bit confusing. Wasn't I still in love with Gail?

I decided to chalk it up to my current emotional and physical vulnerability. I also decided I might be bullshitting myself.

The whole gang – except Jill – exited back to the kitchen. She was dressed in what I believe is called "business casual," a phrase that was probably coined by the same goofball who came up with the terms "thinking outside of the box," "transparency," and "boots on the ground." She wore a pants suit of soft, brushed navy-blue material with a white scoop-necked blouse, stopping just short of provocative.

As Dad would say, "this woman could look good in a burlap bag."

She noticed I was noticing.

"Are you intimidated by strong, successful women?" Her grin included dimples.

"Regularly. But I still prefer them."

She gave me another smile. The room brightened considerably.

Trying to pull myself to a full sitting position again caused my brain to collide with my skull. I moved more slowly, careful not to let my head roll off my shoulders. Jill took a seat at the far end of the sofa.

"I'd keep my distance, if I were you. Morning breath. Slept in my clothes, which is becoming a disturbing habit. I'm not really at my best."

She disregarded my protest and moved on.

"Hank, here's the good news. Phil informed me early this morning that the police aren't interested in causing you any trouble. You were defending yourself and your home against an intruder who probably has a long and colorful criminal history. I should be able to talk to the City Attorney's office and make this all go away. It doesn't hurt to have a detective and an ace criminal defense attorney in your corner."

A big breath of air escaped from my lungs. "I've been so busy replaying what happened that it never occurred to me I could be in trouble."

"Good, one less thing to upset you. This part will be over before it starts."

"So. What's the bad news?"

"Only that Phil has a few more questions. He wants to fill in some blanks."

"I'm a little foggy on what happened at the hospital."

"I was there. I reviewed the transcription of the tape." She produced a printed copy of my statement.

I slowly read what I had remembered from the nightmare, as if reviewing the case history of a client. Clinical distance with an aching head.

"Yeah. I still don't remember things like how I got back downstairs or retrieved the CD player." Guessing those would be among Phil's questions.

I lapsed into therapist mode. "After some time, as a person moves through their trauma, additional details of the incident may resurface. Or, they may not, especially when there's been head injury."

"Well, Phil wants to hear that from you."

"When?"

"Whenever you feel up to it."

"How about later today."

She looked unsure, given my condition, but said, "I'll schedule it. I'll be there to make sure everything goes according to plan. My plan."

"Don't you have someplace else to be on a Sunday?"

What am I fishing for?

"Special circumstance," she replied.

Jill stood to retrieve the gang from the other room. "You have a lot of people who care about you, Hank. Cop, dad, office manager mom, ex-wife. This is not your everyday situation. Use them."

She was so right.

"Jill." She stopped halfway across the room. "Thanks for running interference for me."

"Dennis is an old friend...of Bill W's, if you know what I mean. I didn't always look this good."

That told me she was a recovering addict of some sort. Perhaps this was part of Step Twelve for her.

She smiled once more. "And, as they say, you haven't seen my bill yet, big fella."

Big fella. Don't hear that much.

Everyone filed back into the room.

"Time to get on down the road. I don't sleep well away from home." Dennis stood, looking very tired. "I must say, this has been a very stimulating and weird gathering."

He locked eyes with me.

"And I'm damn glad you're still here, partner." No sarcasm. No Marlowe.

"I can't find the right words to thank you," I replied.

"No, you can't. Call me for anything. Anytime. Now I need to roll. Jerry won't be happy until he hears the whole story."

Dennis patted my arm in a weary "please don't get into any more trouble" kind of way. He hugged Dad and Gail, linked arms with Jill and headed for the door, stepping right on the spot where Jake had died. I was sure that was no accident. At some point, I would have to reclaim my home from the horrible intrusion and shattering violence, or find a new home. I didn't know how I would get to that decision. Yet.

As I watched them leave, I found myself enjoying Jill's retreat much more than that of my friend. That seemed like progress of some sort.

Belinda had been uncharacteristically quiet. She gently hugged me with a promise to reschedule my next several days of appointments.

"You need a break. No argument," she said firmly.

She squeezed my hand, about the only place on my body that didn't hurt.

"I'll tell folks you're under the weather and going to be just fine."

"Gail, honey," she instructed. "You keep an eye on this young fool. He clearly needs some watching. And don't roll your eyes at me."

Gail halted in pre-eye-roll.

I was left with Gail and Dad. She started first.

"I don't know quite how to say this. Hank. I know I get on you about…uh, I know I haven't always been easy to deal with. I…"

She came to me, kneeled at the edge of the couch, and gently took my tender face in her hands.

Tears were welling in her eyes. "They thought Haley was home. With you. You stopped him, or them, or whoever."

She was rambling in a most uncharacteristic way.

"I'm so sorry this happened," she said, quickly composing herself and standing. "So. I'd better go. I need to pick up Haley from the Madison's. She spent the night. Fortunately, we made a deal to limit TV during the school year. We rarely watch the news and I don't get *The Register* at the house."

She did a panoramic wave of her hands. "Maybe she'll miss the whole thing."

Gail gave J.R. a quick "Love you, Gramps" and hurried toward the door, as if she'd said too much and had to escape.

"Oh." She turned at the edge of the room. "I'll check in on you. Wouldn't want to get in trouble with Belinda."

A person needs to be mighty fast to get out of range before my mouth kicks into gear. She was gone before I could say a word.

J.R. and I just stared at the closed door.

"You have an interesting way with women, son," Dad mused. "Now, how about Tylenol and decaf. Sorry. Doctor's orders. No caffeine for mild concussions. And maybe some breakfast."

Dad milled around the kitchen, in his element. I took my coffee in one hand, cane in the other, and shuffled toward the shower, staring at the cup of decaf, the enemy of all real coffee. As I passed the place where Jake had taken his last breath, I forced myself to look. No physical change. The dull, dark, hardwood finish was just as it had been two nights ago. No blood. No indentation from the weight of two men crashing down the stairs.

The only imprint was etched inside of me.

I circled around the spot and made my way to the downstairs guest room, complete with two-person shower stall. I sometimes wondered if the previous owner had made good use of the multi-person shower situation, since this originally was the master bedroom.

My thoughts turned back to Jill and Gail in rapid succession, and in that order. The pounding of the shower almost disguised the heat of my guilt.

What the hell's wrong with me? Guilt? I'm divorced.

And then…

Gail still loves you, too. As a friend. As Haley's dad. That's all.

As the near-scalding water pounded on, I let my brain continue to work on something other than Kenny.

What about the kiss?

I knew the answer.

Everybody is scared and vulnerable. This is a strange time. Hold on to the familiar.

I could follow the thread from there.

Jill's been invited into the room in a big way, taking up some of the space that has always belonged to Gail. It's hard for her.

My thoughts topic jumped.

Does Hankie like Jill? Maybe I just liked the attention. Maybe falling on my head brought me to a new level of acceptance of my failed marriage.

Realizing that my relationships with certain women might not be the most pressing mystery in my life; I called myself back to the moment. By the time I stepped out of the shower, my muscle pain had melted considerably. The headache had decreased to a small sledgehammer level and my thoughts were running short of overdrive.

I put on a favorite home uniform - khakis, buttoned-down blue jean shirt, untucked, suede loafers – and went to investigate the results of Dad's kitchen efforts.

Veggie omelets, hash browns with onions, English muffins and another cup of fake coffee made me feel almost human again. Our conversation drifted to the varying merits of women in business casual versus comfortable dress, and whether it was wishful thinking or astute observation that a bit of a turf war had occurred between Gail and Jill this morning.

"You are the King of the Kitchen," I said, wiping the last bit of everything off my plate with a final bite of muffin and popping it into my mouth.

Dad gave me a still-worried smile. "I'll do the dishes."

I sat in silence as he completed his task by hand. No dishwasher for him. The ritual was comforting, full of his easy presence.

What a difference a day brings.

As the time closed in for me to head over to Phil's place of business, I got busy reassuring Dad that I could drive an automatic transmission Jeep with a left ankle injury. It was time for me to venture forth on my own.

"I'm not real comfortable with that plan, but I'm not going to push, son." That was Dad's version of pushing.

So, why was I was sitting there minutes later, garage door open, hands on the wheel, unable to stop them from shaking long enough to start the damn vehicle?

Absent the sound of a purring engine, J.R. poked his head out the door, stepped into the garage and opened the passenger side.

"You'd be doing me a big favor if you'd get me out of the house and let me drive. You know I'm not one for sitting around."

"Well, if it would help you, Dad…"

We arrived at the station, and Phil's office, with time to spare. Early is on-time to Dad, even in the days of massive hangovers. Comes from years of fielding complaints from hungry people "screaming for their ice cream." That was a trait he and I shared.

Phil was even earlier, waiting by the entrance. He escorted us through the front desk security area, then led us back to a Sunday-quiet detective bureau. Perhaps even criminals sleep in, after the insanity of the weekend. We left Dad in the waiting area with a cup of cop coffee supplied by a stout sergeant who looked both grizzled and battle-worn, just as one imagines a desk jockey should look. I followed Phil to his office.

Adding a little spice to the day, the next face I saw was Dale Goodman, sitting on the far side of Phil's desk.

"I didn't think you had it in you, Anderson," he said. "Had you pegged for one of those hardcore pacifists."

"Thank god you're here, Goodman," I countered, trying to stare him down. "All the compassion and sympathy that's been coming my way has begun to get under my skin." Pregnant pause. "And I know I can count on you to be an asshole."

"I'm here for you, Anderson." Goodman was having a good time.

Jill Bennett walked in just as Goodman and I were winding up our snappy patter. She gave me a fist bump. Phil waved us to the department issued uncomfortable chairs in front of his desk.

"Everybody's here." Phil, as usual, played referee. "Let's get this done as quickly and easily as possible."

A half hour or so later, Phil had again walked me through the past evening with as much finesse as he could muster. He seemed satisfied there was nothing much I could add that would assist the investigation. Jill was mostly quiet, just there to again make sure things were done by the plan. Her plan.

They were. So far.

"That's all the questions, Hank."

"Not quite, Phil," I said. "I've got a couple. Who was this Jake? Was that even his name? What about Preacher? Where is he? What happens when he comes back for us? What am I in the middle of?"

I leaned in too quickly for my headache. Resting my elbows on his desk, with head in hands worked better.

"And," finishing with the clincher, "Where's Kenny?"

I had discharged some of the recent past and was beginning to worry about the future.

"Well..." Phil sounded cautious. "We're going to talk about that now, Hank. Turn the recorder off, Dale."

Damn.

"I'm not going to like this part of the discussion any better than what we just covered," I guessed aloud.

"It's kind of good news in a way, isn't it, Detective Goodman," he said, turning to his partner.

"Yeah, good news, Detective Evans." If Phil was looking to Goodman for positive validation, we were in deep shit.

I attempted a look of calm that my body didn't feel.

"We got out of a meeting with the Captain, right after he got out of a meeting with a bunch of other people, just before you got here, Hank," said Phil. "This information is for your ears only." He looked at Jill. "And your attorney, of course."

"What!?" I was fraying at the edges.

"Jake was what the folks on TV call 'imported muscle'."

Phil reached into his center drawer and set a baggy on the desk top. Android phone with a cracked screen.

"He had a glove on his gun hand, but not on the hand he used for the cell phone light. Preacher took the gun, but he missed the phone. We found it on your stairs."

"With this case going all the way up the ladder," he continued, "we were able to run his prints in a hurry. He wasn't from around here. No connections in Iowa. No family anywhere that we've been able to locate yet. But his face and prints were in the system. A very bad man with a record of arrests in Kansas City, St. Louis, Chicago, and New Orleans. He did time at Statesville in Joliet. Armed violence for hire."

"Consistent to the end," Goodman chimed in.

Phil nodded.

"The guy you call Preacher is one of the good guys, though," Phil reported. "Well, kind of."

"One of *what* good guys?" I massaged my temples, unable to digest the leap from Jake to Preacher in my current state.

"He's with the DEA. Undercover informant." As Goodman jumped back in, Phil closed his eyes and sat back in his chair.

"What the hell does that mean, Phil?" A roadmap of confusion must have been etched across my face.

"It means that -- for some reason unknown to the Captain, Dale and myself -- this guy has been working with the DEA. Maybe he was in trouble himself and made a plea deal. We don't have that information. Anyway, he's out on the streets posing as a dealer, or thug, or both. Kenny told you – he's mixed up in a drug trafficking operation. Preacher's working on the inside."

Jill caught on more swiftly than I did.

"So, this good guy," she said as she stood, barely tall enough to look down on Phil sitting erect in his chair. "This good guy was there when a monster came to kill my client and his child, and he did nothing!"

"We don't know anything of the sort, Counselor," Goodman cut in. "Maybe he knew they were just going to scare Anderson. Maybe Jake decided to go off the rails on his own. There are a lot of possibilities."

"One of which is that you have a guy out there who was willing to jeopardize the safety of my client and his family to cover his ass," Jill shot back.

"Hold on." Phil halted to debate. "First of all," he said, glaring at Goodman, "he's not our guy. He's some guy who has infiltrated the local drug trade. Second, we're telling you this now to let you know that Preacher will not be coming after you or your family, Hank."

"He already came for me, Phil!" Pain like an ice cream brain freeze shot through my frontal lobe, shoving me back in the chair.

It was the wrong day for turning up my voice volume. Phil waited. I coughed and waved him on.

"The first time in the parking lot, he probably came to warn you off, hoping to scare you away from Kenny."

"He came back," I modulated.

"He was probably looking for a way to stop the other guy from hurting you without giving himself away."

"That's too many probablys, Detective," Jill said. "Not reassuring in the least."

"I've been getting background." Goodman tried to take things in another direction. "This goon, Jake Sizemore, was working for people cooking a lot of meth out in the countryside and bringing it into Polk County. This Preacher guy is on the inside, trying to find out who and where. He's being run by someone from the DEA, who says his man's close to finding the power behind the street level dealers."

Jill looked Phil, not Goodman, in the eyes, her voice laced in sarcasm, her ferocity matching his physicality. "Nice spin. But the truth is, you've got a very dangerous man out there taking very big chances with your friends." She punctuated by poking her pen at Phil, just short of threatening.

Apparently, the truce between my attorney and my pal, the detective, was officially over.

"How could this happen, Phil?" Resting my chin in my palms didn't quiet the throbbing confusion. "I got the case from you."

It was crazy, but an image of the many cups of coffee Phil was going to owe me for this madness flashed through my muddled cognition.

"We didn't know that the two cases were connected." He turned to Jill. "As I said, he's not our guy and the DEA doesn't see fit to share details on every case they have going. Turns out Kenny had some shirttail relative who knows somebody who knows somebody. The judge was cutting the kid a break. We had no idea he was somehow hooked in to the other investigation." Phil turned to me. "I'm really sorry, Hank."

Before Jill could go on the attack, I jumped in. "I know you are, Phil."

"So, call him in." She was undeterred. "Now!"

"I can't call him anywhere, Counselor," Phil's formality had an uncommon hint of frustration. "As I said, he's not working for us."

"So, tell the DEA to call him in," Jill ordered.

"Believe me, I will be having that conversation with my boss in the immediate future. From what I understand, though, these people keep plenty of space between themselves and anyone who might jeopardize their cover. And the Feds, no doubt, have invested weeks, maybe months, of time in their man getting this deep. He's been given a lot of leeway to make a lot of tough decisions."

"None of this can leave this room," Goodman yanked us back. "The DEA's got a man out there in a very sketchy situation."

Before Jill could attack, I turned on him.

"Well, there's another man out there in a very sketchy situation. Kenny." I carefully stood up to my full five-foot-seven. "He's running from some very nasty people, one of those being an undercover something-or-other taking big risks with other peoples' lives."

I scanned both cops, resting my hands on the desk.

"So, you just told me what we're not going to do, gentlemen," I said. "What the hell *are* we going to do?"

"You're going to go home and get healthy, Hank."

It was Phil's turn to stand. Using his command voice, he ate up a lot of space.

"I'm going home to my lovely, if slightly annoyed, wife who reminded me as I was leaving that this is the Lord's Day. We – the police, that is – are going to continue to do our best to find Kenny and hustle to learn more about this guy you call Preacher."

Not good enough, but there it was.

Phil again requested that Jill and I keep the information about Preacher confidential; the man's life might depend on it. We agreed, in principle. Understanding the limits of his power, it went without saying that Phil knew I would talk to J.R. and Dennis.

Jill ended the meeting with a brief but impassioned discourse to both detectives on all the terrible things she was going to do to the PD if I, or my family, suffered any further pain as a result of this situation. To his credit, Goodman kept his mouth shut, albeit after being eyeballed by Phil.

Phil offered his hand. "Again, I'm truly sorry, Hank."

So much for my plan to storm indignantly out of the office.

"I know," I said, reaching back to my friend.

Jill was not so forgiving. She issued Phil her most scathing defense attorney scowl, grabbed her briefcase, and stormed out of the office for both of us. Phil refused to take the bait, sending her off with an expression of etched granite.

I hobbled out the door and down the hall, where Jill was already retrieving my dad with a comment that ended with, "…couldn't find their asses with both hands and a flashlight." Belinda would love that one.

J.R. took us both by the arms and led us past the sergeant's desk, toward the exit. By the time we had reached the parking lot, Jill was fully under his spell and had calmed considerably.

"I'll get the car while you wind things up with your attorney, son. Thanks for all your fine work on behalf of my family, young lady." He shook her hand and ambled toward the Jeep.

"If anyone else addressed me that way I'd be deeply offended," she sighed at J.R.'s retreat.

"He is smooth. Of course, I'm a younger, faster version. Same charm, more stamina."

She raised a very attractive eyebrow. "Were it not for our current professional relationship, I might be interested in testing that claim."
Damn.

"I hired you. I could fire you."

"No, you didn't. And you couldn't," she countered. "I'm just too competent, and you're not in any shape to have this conversation right now. Anyway, I'd have to deal with the wrath of Dennis. You wouldn't want to put me through that, would you?" She smiled a smile that warmed the distant sun.

As Jill turned and moved through the parking lot toward a silver Prius, I noticed I was becoming quite fond of her exits.

Easily distracted. Modern evolved man that I am. Right.

Waiting for Dad to pull to the curb, it struck me that no one had offered up Preacher's real name.

Maybe it was better not to know.

On the ride home, I gave my father the details of the meeting.

"Friends like Phil are hard to come by," was his comment.

"I know, Dad."

"But it seems like pretty women are growing on trees." He didn't even smirk, but I got the sense that dad was getting some vicarious pleasure out of this aspect of my predicament.

"I'm a little out of practice."

"Like riding a bike, which you're good at," he assured. "Let's get you home for some rest. You've had another long day."

Once in the door, I returned to the sofa and closed my eyes. I immediately conjured up pictures of Jake: leaning on the car, poking through the bedroom door, laying inert in the entryway. Each time I was able to erase him from my head, the image was replaced by one of Kenny running from Phil, off into the night.

"Having trouble winding down, son?" Dad wandered into the living room with his ever-present cup of black coffee. "It's like I can see the name of that young man running across the worry wrinkles in your forehead."

"I didn't get your alcoholism, Dad, but this may be worse. I got think-aholism. Can't shut it down."

"Makes me tired just watching you," he agreed.

"Well, it has its upside, too."

"And that is?"

"Sometimes I actually come upon a worthwhile idea."

"Did you just have one?"

"Well, I told Dennis after my first session with Kenny that something didn't fit."

"Like what?"

"I can't quite hang my hat on it, as you would say."

"Yet...."

"Yeah. I can't hang my hat on it...yet. I remember telling Dennis that it all went too easy. All those secrets for all those years, and he just walked in and laid them on the table."

"You and I have both seen that happen before. A guy comes to an AA meeting. He's tired of the pain, and the war stories just come pouring out."

Another statement I'd made to Dennis dropped through the fog in my head. "That's what Dennis said and that's part of it, Dad. But there wasn't much pain. It was like he was talking about somebody else's life. Then he just shut down."

"You've told me before that some folks do that," Dad said, playing devil's advocate.

"Still, something didn't fit." I could almost see it through the haze. "Maybe it was a canned story, tailor made to fit his denial."

"Denial? Of what?"

"If I knew, I couldn't tell you, Dad."

"Don't tell me son. I'll ask the questions; you keep the answers for yourself."

I let my thoughts drift back to Dad's question. The one time that Kenny's emotion seemed real was when he talked about his father's alcoholism. It was safe to guess that his father was a center-point of suppressed rage.

"He's carrying deep, deep bitterness for somebody real important." I looked at Dad and saw the sad memories of another father's addiction – his own – briefly flash in his eyes. There was a time when I would have ended any conversation about alcoholism right there, an unspoken agreement between J.R. and myself to take care of one another's discomfort.

I'll help you avoid your guilt if you help me avoid my anger.

This time, instead: "This is the work I do, Dad. I'm no detective, like Phil, but sometimes I can figure a puzzle out and light a path for someone."

"I know. And I'm proud of you. Keep going."

We'd come a long way.

Maybe Kenny is deeper into this mess with drugs than he admitted to me. After all, like father like son is a common unfortunate inheritance in chemical dependency. It follows families for generation upon generation. Stealing porn from IP for his own personal use. Stealing drugs from the bad guys, for his own personal use. Not the first person to lie to me about drug abuse. He said his dad had been out of his life for as long as he could remember...

"So, there's more to the story," Dad unintentionally interrupted my method of wandering to the truth.

"There often is."

"You're just not sure what it is. Yet," he repeated.

"Yet."

"Well, as we say in the country, it's nothin' a good night's sleep can't help."

"It's late afternoon."

"I'm plenty tired. How about you?" He stood. "Let me put a little food together. Then, maybe we'll both feel like giving our thoughts a rest. Sometimes the best ideas come when we're not trying to find them."

Damn, he was good.

Dad fixed us a dynamite salad of greens, mandarin oranges, cranberries, and almond slivers, and tossed it with dressing made from ingredients he cobbled together from my pantry. We munched lettuce, sipped on cans of Doc Brown's Crème Soda, and made conversation that purposefully avoided subjects like drugs and dead leg-breakers.

By six, the prospect of dusk demanded we light the floor lamp standing guard in the corner of the room. With a bit of supervision, Dad started a nice little fire. I was fading fast, the safety of Dad's company and the strain of the day colluding to bring on system shutdown.

Just as I was about to stretch out on the sofa, the shrill ring of the new cell phone Jill had provided grabbed me from its resting spot on the end table.

"This is Hank."

"Daddy, are you OK?" Haley's worried voice came through the line and touched me.

What does she know?

"Sure. Tip-top. What's up, honey?"

"Mom and Belinda said you slipped on the stairs and hurt your leg. I'm checking on you through your special work phone." There was a nurturing pride in her small voice.

"Oh, yeah," I recovered quickly. "I'm just a little under the weather, kiddo. The doctor wants me to rest up for a couple of days. Stay off my feet, and avoid excitement."

Like crazed DEA operatives following me.

"Grandpa came to visit and he's taking good care of me," I added.

"Grandpa! When can I see him?" Her worries faded rapidly in the face of a visit from J.R.

I pulled the phone away and turned to Dad. "It's Haley. She wants to know when you're going to see her "

"Tell her I'll talk to her momma tomorrow and figure out a time to come by after school."

"I heard that," Haley said as I put the phone back to my ear. "Tell Grandpa J.R. I love him and I'll see him tomorrow."

She caught herself, remembering the original reason for the call. "Oh, Dad, I hope you feel all better real soon. Love you. Bye."

I gave her a "love you, too," smiling at the phone screen as she clicked off.

"Now, how about that sleep, son."

Based on the call, I decided – for reasons totally irrational but perfectly acceptable to Dad – to sleep in Haley's bed again tonight. Dad had fetched me an old Drake Bulldogs sweatshirt and gym shorts for night gear. "I'll set up in the guest room. If you need anything, I'm right here."

We verified that both of us had fully charged cell phones that would be placed at bedside and I slowly pushed myself up the stairs, ankle, and all. Propping myself up in Haley's bed, I felt close to her, knowing she was safe. I slept immediately and soundly.

Sinking into dreamtime, I was attacked by a vision of Jake, staring at me with bottomless eyes devoid of any humanity. The night movie jarred me awake to a gloomy, silent house, anchored to the bed.

As I lay calming the ache, it struck me that in our brief and violent relationship, I had not heard Jake utter a single word. I had killed a man who grunted twice, then quit breathing.

"Good thing Jake came in first, Doc." The soft voice sliced through the chill. "Nothing like a lumbering fool to give a guy a fighting chance."

I bolted upright, almost passing out from the jolt to my concussed brainpan. I had no air to scream.

In the doorway was Preacher, standing in the milky aura cast by the moon and stars easing through the skylight.

"Didn't hurt knowing about the squeaky floor before I came in this time," he added.

I could sense, more than see, the vaporous smile on his face. I tried to speak.

"Now, don't try to talk yet, Doc. You've had a rough couple of days and I'm truly sorry for coming in on you this way." He didn't sound sorry. "But I need some answers. Dropping by to chat during daylight hours might prematurely unite me with the local law."

Dad.

"I wouldn't recommend yelling for your dad." Preacher appeared to be clairvoyant. "He's sleeping peacefully and everybody's safe. Up to this point," he emphasized. "Let's keep it that way."

My lungs exploded and the words poured out as softly as I could control them.

"He..." I stammered, not able to say Jake's name. "He was going to kill us and you did nothing."

"You make it sound like I should have done something," he mused. "Somebody's been telling you stories about me."

He peered into the skylight, as if considering what would happen next.

"Maybe you already know, then." He decided on honesty. "I'm DEA. This is way bigger than you and your bleeding heart, Doc. This train wreck is about drugs, lots of drugs. Crystal meth made in labs, somewhere in the boonies."

My memory speed-shifted, locking on to the newspaper headline I'd seen just days ago.

I'm no expert on methamphetamine, but anybody in my line of work knows it's a rural epidemic of death: cheap, easy to make, and amazingly potent. There were small-time home-cooking shops dotting the countryside, often made up of young, dead-end white folks consuming as much brew as they sold. Frying their brains, neglecting their kids, and then dying.

The local pharmacies had taken to locking up Sudafed some time back, the ephedrine in nonprescription cold remedies being a central element in the deadly potion. Farmers had become better at securing their multi-use anhydrous ammonia, another key ingredient. Addicts were finding substitutes. They were persevering in their pursuit of drugs in ways they had never pursued life, just as addicts had all the way back to Prohibition.

Consumable toxic waste from God's country.

Preacher called me back to the room. "Who'd a thought that fertilizer from Ol' McDonald and a pile of cold pills could have started this shitstorm?"

I noticed a change in Preacher's voice, from monotone to quiet urgency. He was beginning to sound like he looked – a real fire-and-brimstone preacher, building momentum as he railed against the evils of sin.

"Here's a long story short, Doc." He'd quickly regained control. "Jake found me after I ingratiated myself to certain unsavory people, and I've been working on the inside ever since."

"Inside?" My radar sparked with the curiosity that had been fed by Phil's earlier disclosure.

"Layers, Doc. Lots of layers," he explained. "This is not just a bunch of high-forehead, corn-fed inbreds cooking up moonshine in the back forty. Jake and I were collections agents. Middle-men for the lowlifes selling on the street. Kenny was my first break. Believe it or not, he's one step up on the food chain, from cooker to transport. He might lead me to whoever's running this, dare I say, organization."

He went on like a kindergarten teacher walking a five-year-old through a simple lesson.

"He's been loading the meth in his delivery truck and making drops to select street dealers. Kind of like a multi-level marketing company, except it's crank, not beauty products."

My disgust pushed through the night air.

"So, you're putting this kid's life in danger to track the drugs."

Preacher's shrug was almost imperceptible.

"I'm the best chance he's got in this circus, Doc."

I sat up slowly, working to shove my anger into a compartment.

Why is he telling me this?

"Must be lonely out there, Preacher. All those bad guys and you."

"Preacher?"

I'd let his assigned nickname slip.

"Just a name I gave you when I didn't have one. When you came by my office to terrorize me, you and Jake neglected to introduce yourselves."

His smile was back, nothing behind it. "Hey, I kind of like that, Doc. A nickname. I'll keep it."

"So, Preacher," I stayed with our newfound connection. "Why did you trash my office?"

"Don't know what you're talking about." I heard what might be doubt in his voice for the first time.

"Maybe." Or maybe Preacher was lying. A talent he would have perfected in his current employment.

"So, here we are, Doc, both looking for answers."

"Why come to me now?" I made it sound like a demand, but this was the only question of the night that I already had the answer to.

"Upping the stakes to scare you a second time was a mistake, Doc. My mistake." He tapped his chest. "Kenny talked to you. He came to you when he was scared. Maybe he told you something important."

"And you didn't find anything useful when you broke in and went through his file."

"I told you." The threat in his voice cut through my accusation. "We didn't do any break-in."

"Maybe Jake was flying solo that night," I offered another theory.

No response. I could hear my heart pounding in my ears. I made myself wait.

Let's see what this jerk does with silence.

He blinked first. "What did Kenny tell you?"

"As I said before. It's confidential."

He stepped closer to me, but also deeper into the shadows. The menace was unmistakable. "You see, Doc, I've been out here a while and I can smell the finish line. Tell me exactly what you know."

He emphasized 'exactly' with another step toward the bed. Then *he* tried silence.

I shivered and recoiled against the headboard, remembering another recent night visitor and my limited options.

I had no idea what had brought Preacher to this crazy life. Whatever his motivations, I realized he was committed enough to his cause that he had taken a chance with the lives of Haley and me to protect himself and complete his mission.

And it was a mission for him. He was a zealot. His current religion was busting meth labs. Whoever he had been before going underground, Preacher had since joined the special fraternity of lost souls who live by the credo, "the ends justify the means." It was safe to assume he wasn't going to take a simple 'no' for an answer. I needed to give him something to go with, something that would not result in additional harm to me, or my family.

What the hell. I'm in way over my head anyway. I'll try the truth.

"There's nothing he told me that would lead you anywhere." I tried to wave off the disaster. "All I got was that you and Jake recruited him. He was frightened and closed off. Just like you, he tried to warn me off."

"Gee, Doc. I would hope you'd give me a little more credit," he said. "A smart guy like you could come up with a better story than that."

Checking option one off the list, I stretched my fingertips under the blanket and grasped the cold aluminum cane I'd taken as my bed partner tonight, both for walking assistance and a sense of safety. I'd pretty much always been all field, no hit, on the medical league softball team. Still, prior to this week, I never would have expected to protect myself with a loaded CD player.

"It's so lame, it has to be the truth," I proposed, as I got a stronger grip on the hard rubber handle in my right hand and took hold of the top edge of the blanket with my left.

"Jake was stupid. I'm not..." He left the end of the sentence hanging as he moved another slow step forward, the skylight illuminating his transition from phantom to hard, cold reality.

As he came just within reach, I threw back the covers and awkwardly waved the cane with one arm. He pulled in at the abdomen, the just better than feeble blow catching him in the rib cage.

To my surprise, he grinned, rocked on his heels, and gingerly rubbed his side. "I'm getting to like you more all the time, Doc. A cane. Really."

I gripped the handle with both hands quivering and held it out in front of me.

His monotone left behind that flash of humanity. "Just hoping to scare a little real honesty out of you."

"I've been scared for three days," my voice shook. "And I already gave you all I got, you son-of-a-bitch."

His face was untouched by my rage.

"Maybe so, Doc, maybe so." He blended back into shadow. "I'm hoping so, for your sake."

A handgun somehow had appeared in his hand. "You see, my courageous and foolish friend, you'd be unlikely to win this fight twice."

"And this isn't just about you, Doc." He pointed the gun toward the stairs. And Dad. "There's your family and friends."

I slumped back into the pillows and lowered the cane.

The gun disappeared as quickly as it had materialized. Hands in pockets, Preacher backed toward the open door and gave me another of his parting stares.

"Nothing more?"

He moved as if to leave, stopping as he had in the parking lot.

"You see, Doc. I know where you live."

MONDAY

I couldn't will my legs to move after Preacher left, but I could reach the phone resting on the nightstand. As I stared at the screen, it seemed as if calling the police for help was both unnecessary and beyond me. Preacher was gone. I let Dad sleep and held the phone for comfort.

The weakness in my body clashed with the buzz of my racing, tangential thoughts. I couldn't sleep, but I couldn't seem to get out of bed, either.

All the bad guys I know about have already been here, so I guess we're weirdly safe. Preacher is ready to trip over the edge. How can he believe he's the best chance Kenny has? Where the hell is Kenny? OK. Breathe. Dad slept right through this. You're alive. Again.

Fortunately, it wasn't all that long, in relation to my recent penchant for unwanted nightlife, before another cloudless dawn crept through the skylights. By that time, I was able to relax my muscles. I lightened my grip on the cane, then the phone, massaged my aching fingers, unglued myself from the bed, and limped downstairs to the kitchen.

By the time Dad shuffled into the room in his in flannel pj's, I had already called Day and Night – several days and nights too late – to set up a high-tech security system for the house. I was also cheating on the doctor's orders with my second cup of real deal coffee, the caffeine losing the battle against my exhaustion.

"As they say, the early bird gets the fresh coffee, son." He reached for a coffee cup. "Is caffeine a good idea yet?"

"I've been up for a while. I had another late-night case conference."

Dad stopped in mid pour; for him, a gesture of great surprise and concern.

"Preacher let himself in. He was looking for information on Kenny."

"Oh, my God!" This was Dad's version of hitting the roof.

"He didn't hurt me, and he could have," I said. "I'm hoping he was convinced that I just don't know anything that would help him."

I proceeded to tell Dad the story of my latest midnight rendezvous with this very disturbed and dangerous man.

"Jack Daniels, I understand," Dad responded. "I hear about meth at AA meetings, but this stuff is just beyond me."

"It's beyond lots of people, Dad. It's zero to a hundred miles an hour overnight for a lot of these sad folks. Apparently, that's where creatures like Preacher come in."

"Now what?" Dad always moved quickly from problem to solution.

"I already followed Preacher's earlier advice and called about a new security system. Now, for a change, I'll do what I've been told to do. Call Phil."

This time, Phil came to us, within the hour. I assumed he had other work to do besides being my personal police detective, but, as always, he was there for me. At my request, he left Goodman back at the house. He sat down over coffee with Dad and me, listening to the story of my night visitor without interruption, although his constant cup swirling made me wonder what strong emotions lurked beneath his calm.

"I wish you would have called 911 right away, Hank," he admonished.

"And your fellow officers would have done what, Phil?"

It seemed like we'd been pushing each other a lot the past few days.

He sighed. "Yeah. There's probably nothing they could have done. This guy's like a ghost." Another sigh. "I have to take this to the Captain, Hank."

"As they used to say, Phillip, somebody needs to put a net over this fellow." Phil and I both registered surprise at the anger in Dad's voice.

"I agree, Mr. Anderson."

"When can we expect to hear back from you about this, Phillip?" J.R. was in rare form.

"As soon as possible, sir," Phil promised. He looked at me. "You need to get your locks and security system upgraded."

"Funny, that's what Preacher said."

"I thought this fellow was on the good side of the law, Phillip." The man was unstoppable this morning.

"In a way, he is, sir. It's just that sometimes these guys get lost in character. Too much time pretending to be someone else. And at constant risk of being found out."

Dad just kept going. "Shouldn't your compatriots in the DEA be providing you with some details on this situation?"

"As I've told Hank, Mr. Anderson, collaboration is often not an exact science." He stared into his cup. "I'm working on it, sir."

"I called the company that revamped the office about a home security system before you got here," I injected, as much to settle Dad down as to reassure Phil.

"Thank you," Phil said, nodding his approval.

"No disrespect intended, Phil." Dad returned to the familiar. "I'm just feeling more than a little protective of my family. And no need to call me Mr. Anderson. I'm J.R. to my friends." He nodded my way. "And, sometimes my family."

"No problem, J.R. I'd feel the same way," Phil pointed his cup at dad. "I want you to know that Hank and his family are very special to me. As they say, I'm on the job. I'll call as soon as I know more."

He retrieved his hat from the table and pulled himself up with the effort of a man burdened by too many worries. We finished with a round of handshakes and, once again, Phil left us with, "Be smart. Be safe." If this continued, Phil soon would rival Dad as Master of Slogans.

"You got pretty heated up there, partner," I chided Dad, after Phil was out the door.

"No offense intended, son," J.R. reddened, a bit. "Just concerned."

We both got quiet. Dad broke the silence. "What's on for today?"

"It's time to get back on the horse." I sounded more certain than I felt. "I'm going to work for a while."

"Is that a good idea? Belinda rescheduled your clients. You didn't get much sleep."

"Just sitting here could be detrimental to my safety. Bad people keep showing up. I'd be better off wandering around the office, rather than sitting here, stuck in my head. And I need to tell Belinda and Dennis that Preacher dropped by again. The security guys won't be here until the afternoon. I'll just work for a couple of hours and be back in time to let them in."

"If that's what you think. Promise me you'll take it slow."

"I promise I'll take it slow," I parroted, taking in the deep concern on his face. "Promise, Dad," I committed, with more seriousness. "How about you? Don't you have a business to run?"

I was concerned about his safety, too, and figured the best place for him was a couple of hundred miles down the road, back at his hometown restaurant.

"If you don't mind an old controlling recovering alcoholic hanging around a bit longer, I'd like to stay. Luis can continue to hold down the fort. And I made a promise. I have to spend some time with my granddaughter."

He and I both knew the truth. Dad was going to stick around to keep an eye on me and his other loved ones. Some ancient, hyper-masculine part of me said I should resist the offer. I was, after all, a grown man.

And he was an old man.

"Sounds great. Stay as long as you like."
Dad decided he'd call Gail and offer to pick Haley up for a little Grandpa J.R. spoiling time right after school. She answered and was thrilled with the idea. Off he went to buy unnecessary gifts for his granddaughter, the privilege of grandparents everywhere. We agreed to meet back at the ranch at seven for a late dinner.

I called Belinda and we argued about whether I was ready to come in to work. She insisted I wait until the following day, clearly taking advantage of my weakened condition to overcome any argument presented. I finally relented and agreed to go in tomorrow to catch up on phone calls. I would ease my way into seeing clients again after an excruciating eight days from the time this roller coaster ride had begun.

Shuffling from the kitchen, I circled back to the sofa. I wasn't sure what to do with all the peace and quiet, other than think dark thoughts. Sitting down seemed like a good place to start.

I'll just close my eyes for a bit.

Phil, Dad, Gail, and Haley are on the front stoop. They are just outside the solid oak door, unable to push through and enter the house. One by one, they gaze longingly through the small paned window. Haley is held up by Gail, identical twin urgency and fear etched on their faces.

Jake is on the floor, still dead. A part of me floats up from the sofa. My essence separates from my physical form, which sleeps on.

I watch as Jake's vacant reptilian eyes snap open.

He's alive!

As he begins to breath, the air is slowly being sucked from my lungs. With each breath he takes, I am pulled toward him, reeled in by some invisible lariat. I open my mouth to scream for help, but have no voice. I gasp for oxygen, claw at the invisible cord, aware now that Jake is not coming back to life. He is, in fact, stealing my life and drawing me toward his death.

I wave frantically, gesturing my friends and family to come inside. They mournfully beckon me to them, but I can't break free of Jake's vortex.

Dennis appears, magically flowing through door, onto the threshold, over Jake's body. He stands in the center of the entry. He rotates 360 degrees. Surveys the entire scene.

He's in teaching mode. "Hank. This is some pretty obvious stuff." Dennis has that know-it-all look I hate. "Jake stands between you and the people you love," he lectures on. "You want to let them in, but you want to keep them at a safe distance, physically and emotionally. They can't get to you. The life is being drawn out of your...what? Your essence," he laughs in a sarcastic tone. "Geez, this is the stuff of a Way Off-Broadway dream sequence. How about a little more creativity?"

With that, Jake's eyes slam shut and suddenly, I can breathe.

My eyes popped open and I was panting like an overworked racehorse. Squeezing my eyelids closed and open, I risked a look over the sofa. Just to make sure.

No Jake. Nobody. I'm alone.

Sitting up, I looked at my watch to reorient myself. In what had seemed like minutes, I'd slept away another morning. The living room was shadow dancing as the afternoon sun passed over the house. There was a hollow nip in the air, but I was sweating post-traumatic fear and guilt.

Damn.

The doorbell rang. My startle reflex ignited, the jolt reminding me to go slow. I Frankenstein walked to the door, with the addition of growing skill with the cane for balance. I diverted my eyes away from the floor. Given my daymare, I nervous about looking through the window in the door.

I was oddly pleased to see the face of my new friend, James, standing on the porch, his Day and Night van parked on the street, right in front of the house.

"Come on in."

He hesitated, eyeballing my cane. "Sorry. Is this a bad time, Hank?"

"Recovering from a slight sprain. Just woke up from a nap. Perfect timing."

"Good to see you again." James, the ever cheerful. "For a guy who doesn't like technology, you're investing in a big way these days."

"All it took was an office B&E to change my mind," I explained, deciding not to mention my more recent visitation by Preacher.

"Sure. Well, I'm here to serve. Usually, they send a sales person first to give you all the options and pricing. But since we already met, I volunteered to review the whole package with you." His face lit up like this was a bonus in an already good day.

I led James into the living room. He had no problem stepping on the offending boards.

"Cool house, Hank."

A return to decaf, neither of us needing additional nervous energy, and the minimum amount of necessary information later, we had a plan. James made several of his best attempts to describe my choices. He wanted to talk about a Smart Home. I just kept asking for his simplest and sturdiest recommendations and saying yes.

"If it's OK, I can save you a call to your regular lock guy. I'll redo the locks right now, Hank. Then tomorrow I'll bring help and we'll wire the windows and set up the connection to your phone and dispatch. We're going with good coverage of elevated cameras. None of these doorbell cameras for you."

"I'd prefer if you did all the work yourself, James. Even if it takes longer. I'm a bit short on trust these days."

"Not a problem," he assured. "I'll fix you up in no time."

A tall order.

James went to his truck to tell his boss he'd be with me for the rest of the day. Leaving him to his work, I retreated to my bedroom to read, going for the last Laurie R. King mystery, rather than the latest Sue Johnson book on couples' therapy.

Enveloped by my cushy grandfather's chair, I immersed myself in someone else's whodunit. Next thing I knew, James' tenor drifted up the stairs. My fatigue had managed to overcome the intrigue of the novel and I'd slipped off to sleep again. No dreams, just the refuge of solitude.

I guess J.R. and Belinda were right.

"Done for now, Hank."

I stretched and made my way downstairs. James was waiting with two sets of keys for the latest in hardcore lock systems and a promise to return in the morning to continue his work. As he walked toward the company truck, I heard him hum "Love Is All We Have Left" by U2. This guy really knew the good stuff.

But does he do Motown?

Shortly after James pulled away, I was called back by a series of frantic knocks at the door.

"Son? You home? I can't get the garage open. You OK?"

I opened the door to a very worried-looking J.R.

"I'm so sorry Dad. James, the fellow from the security company, was here to install locks and we put a new code into the opener. I completely forgot you wouldn't be able to get in."

J.R. touched his chest and stepped in.

"I thought something terrible had happened."

"Because the garage opener didn't work?"

"Hey, that wouldn't have been anywhere close to the strangest thing that's happened around here lately."

"Point taken, pal." I put my arm around his shoulder. It was my turn to offer comfort.

"You'd be happy to know, I never made it to the office," I added. "Slept the morning and most of the afternoon away."

"Seems like just what the doctor ordered." He returned to his usual composure. "Work can wait one more day. You must be hungry," he added with the assurance of a man who had devoted his life to full bellies. The rumbling in my stomach reminded me that I'd slept through lunch.

"I could eat."

Dad reached back onto the front stoop, and latched onto a large brown grocery bag that gave off the delicious scent of Mr. and Mrs. Lui's house of plenty. He was visibly excited, food being both his livelihood and his passion.

"Man cannot live by salads alone," Dad fussed. "Let me get some plates and chopsticks."

We removed the treasured containers of beef broccoli, sesame chicken, and cold garlic noodles from the bag, grabbed plates, and retired to the sofa.

"How's my best girl," I asked?

"I picked Haley up from school and we went to Water Works Park for a walk."

Passing cartons back and forth, we attacked the food with decent chopstick dexterity.

"Then we went across to the lake. They've really turned that into a beautiful place. She told me about school and pierced ears and some singer named Cathie something and a bunch of other things I didn't understand. That girl can really talk." He smiled and shook his head.

"Then we got french fries and sodas at the enemy's lair."

"International fast-food franchise?"

"Only for my granddaughter."

"So. It was perfect."

"Exactly. She asked when you were going to feel better enough for her to come over. I told her in a few days you'd be rested and more able to get around." He got quiet.

"What else."

"She knows more, Hank. You think you can protect her by not letting her watch TV. But people talk. There's social media. Babies have cell phones. Several kids at school asked her about the excitement of having a man break into your house."

I lost my taste for the noodles.

"How is she?"

"She's mostly concerned about you. That, and annoyed that the adults tried to sneak one past her with the sprained ankle story. I told her, on my honor, that you were OK. Jill and the detective kept the details out of the news, so, she doesn't know anybody died."

He smiled a tender grin.

"And then, out of the blue, she asked me how I was doing. She wonders how I'm getting along all these years without her Grandma Sheila," his smile carried years of sadness. "Her exact words. How are you getting along all these years, Grandpa?"

I waited.

"I told her I miss her Grandma every day."

He tapped the plate with his chopsticks. Discomfort showing the depth of his pain.

"Then she said that even though she didn't really remember her Grandma Anderson, she missed her every day, too." Tears began to trickle down his cheeks. "She said that seeing me helped with her sadness. Exact words."

"Wow."

"Yeh. Wow. Then," he shook his head. "Then, she gave me a big hug and instructed me to drop her off a little early so I could get back here and keep an eye on you."

He looked up at me.

"I have been charged with keeping an eye on you, son." No smile. "By someone I cannot fail."

He wiped his face dry with a paper napkin, settled back into the sofa, and returned to his meal.

End of discussion.

Dad steered us to a review of how the area around downtown Des Moines had changed over the years: bike and walking trails. Old warehouse and office buildings along the river now converted to lofts. New roads, new restaurants, great entertainment venues. I promised to take him to our massive Farmer's Market next spring.

As conversation wound down, I retrieved the oft-times elusive channel changer for the seldom-used fifty-inch big screen from under a sofa cushion. I'd talked myself into this media mammoth after spending too much time reading the Sunday sale ads in the newspaper on one of those lost weekends, shortly after the divorce.

Dad and I ate in comfortable silence, watching a rerun of "Frazier." Some of my colleagues are offended by the way in which therapists are portrayed on TV and in movies - warm and fuzzy idiots, or idiots with more issues than our clients. I figure if we're being made fun of, we've truly become a part of the culture. Anyway, Niles cracks me up.

And given recent events, the scriptwriters might have a point.

"It's good to hear you laugh, son. How's your head?"

"Humor hurts, but it's worth it."

I nudged him with my shoulder. "Thanks for staying."

"I'm under orders. Wild horses couldn't drag me away," he said, unaware he was quoting Jagger and Richards.

"Well," I said, looking at the remnants of the Chinese delights. "I imagine I've been awake now for at least two hours. I'm stuffed and pretty wiped out. It's bedtime."

"Good idea. You know how we country folk are, early to bed and early to rise..."

"Rests you up to cook burgers and fries." I finished his corny sentence, as I had for most of my speaking life.

After refrigerating tomorrow's leftovers, we headed for our rooms.

"Son. How's our security?"

"Damn!"

"What?" J.R. doesn't frighten easily, but it had been a rough couple of days.

"Sorry. It's just that I didn't update Belinda and Dennis on the latest Preacher sighting."

"It's not that late."

My face must have mirrored the time Dad made me go up the hill and admit I'd fed a laxative to Sir Bruce, my Chem teacher Mr. Whiteside's Corgi.

"No time like the present."

"Yeah." There was a decided lack of enthusiasm in my voice.

Of course, Belinda picked up on the first ring.

"What's wrong?"

After assuring her that everyone was safe, I gave Belinda the unedited version of the previous night, then held the phone at arm's length and waited to be chastised.

"Oh honey, I'm so sorry this damn fool keeps coming back. You worried about me?" Her pitch elevated to amusement.

"Hell, Haley, Gail and I are barricaded in a high-rise in West Des Moines. There's that very nice doorman who by the way, has a crush on me, and the security system in this building is state-of-the-art. Nobody gets in to see me without being announced unless they are known to the security person and aware of the code. You know that, you and Haley have been here a hundred times. You just watch out for you and that wonderful father of yours and I'll be fine. Now, go to bed and get some rest. Love you."

She hung up.

Best Belinda lecture ever.

On a roll, I dialed Dennis.

"Hello Hank." It was Jerry. "Dennis is in the shower. What's up?"

Deciding this was some twisted version of my lucky night, I gave Jerry the rundown.

"Oh, Hank. We are both so sorry that man came into your life. Are you worried about us?" All that was missing was, "you silly boy."

"You know that the lofts have a person at the door. The security system was developed by some kid genius. No worries. I'll tell Dennis everything and make sure he doesn't call and yell at you. You and J.R. stay safe and rest easy. We're fine."

He hung up.

Life was swinging in my direction.

I turned back to Dad.

"Done and done," I made a grand hand-wiping gesture.

"As far as security," I went on. "New door locks, front and patio. The windows and doors will be wired tomorrow. There will be camera involvement. James gave us an up-to-date garage opener system. The whole schmear will be connected to a company that can alert me, the police, and maybe the National Guard, if the alarm goes off and I don't call them within the allotted time. You and I will have the new codes. And Phil."

"That's reassuring, son. Would you be more comfortable sleeping down here tonight, on the first floor? I'll take the couch and you take the guest room. Most comfortable couch around."

His words said he was free from worry, but his offer smelled of watchdog.

"That sounds good, Dad. And will you tuck me in and read me some Dr. Seuss?"

"Only if you promise to read to me from my latest issue of 'Oysters and Other Culinary Aphrodisiacs' tomorrow night," he countered. The man looked old, but he was quick.

"Seriously," he said. "Maybe it'd be good to get a break from the second floor."

"Tell you what. I'll sleep on the sofa and you stay where you're at. That way I'll be within shouting distance if all hell breaks loose."

"It's a plan. And to be on the safe side, let's keep our phones real close tonight."

He got no argument from me.

TUESDAY AGAIN

I woke eight hours later to nothing but the crisp quiet of early light and the least physical pain I'd had in a while. No killers or narcs. No death dreams, at least that I could remember.

Dad was in the kitchen, brewing a fresh pot of the elixir of life. I grunted my good morning and ambled, rather than shuffled, into the shower, letting the hottest water I could tolerate beat against my lingering aches and stiff muscles. My ankle felt a mite more limber and the pounding in my head had subsided to a quiet, dull thud.

I secured the boot, hobbled up the stairs and dressed in blue jeans, a starched pale-blue chambray shirt, navy sweater vest, dark blue knit tie, and tan weaved loafers: the picture of counselor casual. At the bottom of the stairs, Dad greeted me with a travel mug of coffee, extra cream, and a tidy little breakfast burrito of egg, cheese, sausage, and green and red bell peppers.

"I may need you to move in and be my nanny."

"Be careful what you wish for. You ready to work?"

"I've got coffee, breakfast and a cane." I headed for the door. "What more could a fellow need?"

"A driver. I'll drop you off and then do a little grocery shopping," he said. "Your fridge looks like a barren wasteland."

"You keep talking like this and I'll report you to my Al-Anon sponsor for excessive oversight and caretaking. My hands are steady," I argued with Dad's frown. "I can get myself to work."

A stray thought arrived. I thumped the cane on the tile and stopped mid-stride.

"I totally forgot. Somebody needs to be here to let James from Day and Night in, to finish the security work. Can you do that?" I asked. "Then you can head for the Trader Joe's and go wild."

"A luxury we don't have in small-town Iowa." J.R. the cook's eyes danced. "You sure you're good to go?"

"I'm sure."

I headed toward the door before he could come up with any other ways to help me, promising to check in later in the day. Key fob and coffee in hand, I manage to crank up the Jeep, then navigate a quiet ride to the office, dropping in some early Pat Metheny Group to ease me through the traffic.

I arrived at the office unscathed and, in my limited capacity to suss out this stuff, unfollowed. I was still a bit nervous stepping to the pavement and into the view of the shiny, new security cameras on the parking lot. As I made my way slowly through the lobby and into the elevator, I noted the steely eye of security following my every move.

Belinda and Dennis were sitting across from each other at her desk as I moved through the open door.

"Good to see you, Marlowe," Dennis offered his best cheerful greeting.

"Morning, honey," Belinda said. "And thank you for calling last night. Everything was quiet at my place."

"Same here," Dennis echoed.

I turned to face them. "One favor, folks."

"Anything," Belinda and Dennis nodded in unison.

"Don't start acting too nice. I'm already traumatized by what's happened and it might push me over the edge."

Dennis smiled at Belinda. "I think he's getting better."

Belinda nodded. "Good, because I've got work to do. When are you going back to seeing clients, Hank?"

"Like you said on the phone, let's go back to regular scheduling tomorrow." I headed for my office.

Dennis trailed behind me and, uninvited, deposited himself on my new sofa, nearly matching the one that had been in my office before we were violated. The redecorating had returned the room to a place near its original physical form, but I wondered how the energy would be different as we all moved forward.

"OK. We did the pleasant hey-howdys," he said. "Phil also called me with the latest news on that thug. How are you, really?"

I felt the reassuring comfort of my undamaged leather chair. It was an anchor connecting me to a world before Kenny and Preacher and Jake.

"Really? Dreams, flashbacks, hypervigilance, fear, guilt. I kind of felt like a robot driving here today."

"Anger?" He was pushing a bit.

"Not much," I puzzled. "Right now, numb."

"When are you seeing Bob Rathburn?"

"For what?" I hedged.

"Like I said, no bull. You know the symptoms and you know the cure."

I conceded. "I'll call him today."

Dennis stood and moved toward the door. "As your old man would say, we need to practice what we teach."

Most of my phone messages were from clients concerned about what they'd heard or read in the news. Some were concerned about me. Most were concerned about how my situation might affect their therapy. Just as it should be.

Belinda had fielded each call with care and calm, then rescheduled.

I gave some thought to how I would respond to folks when they came back to sessions and asked about the drama. Whatever would refocus us on their therapy as quickly as possible. Piece of cake.

After Dennis went into session with his next client, I read a professional journal article about older therapists working with millennials. Although it was difficult to focus, the work gave me a sense of purpose. True to my word, I took a break to call Bob Rathburn late in the morning.

"This is Rathburn." After a hundred or so years of being the best therapist in town, Dennis notwithstanding, Bob still answered his own phone when not in session.

"Bob, Hank Anderson."

"Wondered if you'd call. Glad you did."

"Word travels fast."

"Especially if you read the paper."

"Oh. What's the headline?"

"Home Invasion Doesn't Pay," he quoted. "The spin is that a burglar was apprehended while attempting to rob your home."

"There's a bit more to it. I'd like to come in and talk."

"How about six this evening?"

"I didn't expect to get in so soon." I had called him and now I was resisting.

"It's meant to be. Think of it as a Higher Power moment. Come on in."

"I'll be there at six."

As I hung up, it hit me again that today was Tuesday, a week since this disaster had come into my life. A lot had changed; I just wasn't sure what that meant. As I sat back in my chair, however, I was certain of three things: seeing Bob would help, coming to work was a good thing, and I yearned for a cup of good coffee.

Like magic, Belinda walked into my office carrying a large biodegradable cup with the letters of my favorite gas-station beverage stop etched in bold colors. Brilliant.

"It's warmed in the microwave. I got it on the way in today. Not the best ever, but pretty good. Decided not to make my coffee. You've suffered enough."

"You're incredible."

"Oh, hush you," she said, depositing the reheated cup on my new desk. "I just want to say again that I'm sorry for what you've been through, and it's good to have you back. Now I'm going back to work and, dammit, don't bother me anymore." With moist eyes, she scurried from the room.

I spent as much time staring out my window, helplessly concerned for Kenny's wellbeing, as doing actual work. Dennis finished early and checked to make sure I had called Bob. Belinda closed shop and Dennis walked her to her car. She was heading home to my daughter and ex-wife. As promised, I also left before the advancing autumn evening, deciding to take a leisurely drive past the urban sprawl, toward Winterset. I had no specific route in mind. Just searching for two lane country roads and quiet.

Thankfully, Tuesday at six arrived without incident. I'd called Dad to let him know why I would be late. In turn, he let me know he had a new friend in James, who was explaining all the details of my new security rig as J.R. followed him around the house. He had even posed as an elderly bandit to test the system.

Don't tell him he's not supposed to be having fun with this.

Right on time, I found myself sitting outside Bob Rathburn's office, just off University Avenue, west of Drake University. Funky neighborhood. Old, but classy gray brick house, office to a venerable icon of the therapeutic community.

As I worked my way slowly up the dingy white ramp and stepped through the dark walnut front door, I reflected that this office was a perfect foil for Bob's therapeutic style. The waiting room was full of old, worn leather that had been expensive in its day. The plants were well cared for, the tapestry area rug both luxurious and ancient.

I recalled the first time I'd been invited into his therapy room. There probably was a desktop underneath all the papers and various implements of writing, but I was certain no one in the last twenty years had seen it. The office, likely a formal dining room in its first incarnation, was inhabited by weathered black-leather club chairs that would have been elegant in the days of Freud, Jung, and Frankl.

Bob himself blended well with the surroundings. A white, lightly starched oxford dress shirt with the first button undone. One hundred percent silk navy-and-pale-blue broad striped tie with the knot pulled down several inches from his collar. As always, he wore navy dress pants and spit-shined black wingtip shoes, the kind you probably had to procure from a wizened cobbler somewhere on the back streets of east Des Moines.

Bob had been somewhere beyond middle-aged when we first met. Now he was an elder statesman, with completely gray, bushy hair – some of it coming out of his ears – and lots of laugh lines on his heavily bearded face. He never seemed to gain a pound on his slender frame. I'd heard he still played a mean tennis game in the senior league.

Folks traveled from all over central Iowa to soak up Bob's legendary blend of empathy and irony. He was a transplant from Georgia, and I really didn't know how he'd found his way to the Midwest. But after several courses of therapy with him, I was grateful he had.

He met me in the waiting room and we walked the well-worn path to his office. He waved me to a client chair and assumed his position directly across.

"I'm glad you called." I knew he meant it; in Bob Therapy, economy of speech was essential. No fake compassion.

"This is physician heal thyself time. I'm not going to get through this one alone with a couple of Al-Anon meetings and a catchy list of affirmations."

"Have you told anyone the story?" Right to the point. I knew he meant the whole story, complete with feelings.

"I've piecemealed it. Gave Phil everything I could remember at the time. The best work I've done so far was with the ER nurse at Methodist."

"Juanita." He sounded sure.

"You know her."

"Best in town," he nodded. "She's like Belinda. Put us out of business if more people knew about her."

He had the floor and, as usual, continued.

"You know how this works," he encouraged, settling back in his chair. "You have as much time as you need."

Years ago, it would have taken me many weeks and many sessions to feel safe. In that place, with that man, I simply wept.

After a few minutes, or a long time, I looked up. "I'm not crying in sadness. It's the fear coming out." I felt comfort in my self-diagnosis, telling Bob something he already knew.

He smiled a Buddha's smile of acceptance and waited. Under Bob's scrutiny, I was clear.

Truth time.

"I'm glad he's gone. Not glad that I killed him, just that he's gone. In that moment, when I realized he had come to hurt Haley, I was all in."

In that moment, I realized I had not been crying for Jake. Perhaps he had earned his death many times over; I was not qualified to be the judge of that. I was crying for another man, the naïve man who was lost in a flash of terror and rage. The man who would never fully return.

Bob waited. Quiet. Tuned in.

I told my story in both technical and emotional detail, with the feelings I had as the disaster was unfolding blended into the emotions of this moment. Bob said little, only intervening to help me stay with the process, feelings intact, and to offer permission to go as slowly as I needed.

After an hour or so I'd had enough.

"You look tired," he said.

"It's always good to know I'm not the only therapist with a keen grasp of the obvious."

"Good, prickly Hank is still in there." He gave me a Cheshire Cat smile.

I sank a bit in the seat. "I'm beyond tired."

Therapy can be like running a marathon without ever leaving your chair.

"You know what may come next." Bob had learned a long time ago that he could get through to my personal side by appealing to my professional expertise. "You may begin to feel some relief, perhaps more sadness or other emotions. Perhaps more memory will surface."

He tapped the arm of his chair with his ever-present fountain pen to hold my attention.

"This is a very recent trauma. It takes time. You want to set another appointment?" He offered without taking a breath, Bob-talk for a strong recommendation.

"How about I call you when I feel a need to come in?"

"How about you call me later this week to let me know how you're doing?"

"Deal."

I left Bob's office carrying a bit less baggage than I'd walked in with. I even popped Curtis Mayfield, serious music for the sad, happy spirit, into the CD player and punched the advance button for "Move on Up." Bob Rathburn, the soothing fatigue of work well done, the rhythm section, and Curtis' driving falsetto were a potion for optimism through the pain.

As soon as the Jeep hit the street, the cell phone in my left coat pocket rang.

Two phones are at least one too many.

Distracted, without looking, I answered the phone.

"Doc?" A male voice.

With one hand on the wheel I slid into a parking lot on 42nd Street.

"It's Kenny again."

And the hits just keep on coming. I turned Curtis to silent.

"Kenny, how are you?"

"Better than Jake, from what I hear." He discharged a nervous laugh.

My tired feeling evaporated into the twilight.

"If you know about Jake, you know it's safe to come in, Kenny. Where are you?"

"No way I'm coming in, Hank." He gave the expected response, ignoring my question and jumping to his own. "Do you think Jake's the only guy they got out there? You didn't get his partner."

"The police know who he is," I countered, without offering any details. "They'll find him soon." Time to push just a bit harder. "Kenny, the police aren't just going to let this go."

"It's not my fault," he whined. "They said they'd turn me in to the company if I didn't carry packages for them. I didn't know what I was delivering. Honest."

That didn't match with what Kenny had told me several nights ago. I also knew it was not a good time to confront his lie.

"When I wanted to stop, they said they'd kill me, Doc! What am I going to do?" His whine buzzed like a maxed-out chainsaw.

"You're going to take a deep breath, let it out slow and tell yourself that you're alive and safe in this moment, Kenny."

A rush of air came through the phone, followed by nervous laughter. "OK, Doc, now what?"

"Now tell me. Who are 'they'?"

"The people that sent those creeps after me." I heard "what a stupid question" in the tone of his response.

"Kenny."

Use his name. Take things down a notch.

"It's time for you go to the police and tell them your story. You help them and then they help you."

"I told *you* my story!"

"Good start, Kenny. But you and I can't stop these people. The police can."

"They'll arrest me. They'll want to know where I went with the deliveries. Make me a snitch. I don't know why I bothered to call you!"

He was ready to bolt, again.

Time for the big truth. "And if you run, again, they'll eventually find you. Go in voluntarily. Tell them your life was threatened. I'll back you up. We'll work through it."

He paused, breathing hard. I could sense the wheels in his brain turning hot and fast.

"I'll only come in with you." His voice flipped to calm, radiating the pride of a boy who'd just deciphered a difficult math problem. "I don't want a bunch of cops shooting me down, like I see in the movies."

"That'll work. Just you and me, walking this through." I could hear the lecture that would come from Phil as my lips made the promise. "How about we meet in front of the police station?"

"No way. I know a place. I'll call and tell you when and where to meet me. Then we'll go to the cops."

He hung up before I could respond.

I checked my phone log. The ID: Private Caller. On the phone Jill told me to only answer for family and friends.

Turning the key to restart the Jeep, I thought back to a promise I'd recently been making good on.

Call Phil.

He'd help me develop some method to get Kenny to disclose his location and, hopefully, bring him in safely. Or, I could just let nature run its course. The police would eventually find him without my help. Unless Preacher – without anyone's help – found him first. In which case, Kenny might never make it into Phil's custody. Preacher would use Kenny in any way possible to serve his obsession of stopping more drugs from reaching the streets.

Plus, there were Jake and Preacher's employers. They were out there somewhere too. If they found him first, nobody would have to worry about catching up with Kenny – ever.

Consistent with my new policy, I grabbed the more secure phone and dialed Phil. Direct to voicemail. I gave him the scoop on my call from Kenny and let him know I was eager to hear back from him.

As luck would have it, I was minutes away from a late-night donut shop. It seemed logical to catch a snack while waiting for return calls. I could chew and think at the same time. I parked and in minutes, blueberry delight in hand, I was pondering the mishmash of available information.

It's all too tidy. I keep circling back. The story is just too perfect.

Maybe Kenny was smarter than I'd given him credit for; dropping the doorknob disclosure of "I've got a secret too big to share" by design. Showing me how scared he was at the end of the session to draw me in.

Why?

He knew he was in deep and wanted help.

But why hadn't he told Phil?

I played it out in my head. He was already in trouble with the court. He wouldn't take a chance on going directly to a police detective. He hoped my friendship with Phil would put him in the role of victim, not drug mule. Maybe this was his best, convoluted idea of a plan to escape his situation.

Good theory? The truth? Wild speculation? I could hear Dennis in my head, "Not enough clinical evidence yet, Marlowe."

I stared at the phone screen, willing Phil's number to appear as an incoming call.

Nothing.

Now what?

Saying goodnight to the solitary donut proprietor, I limped to the privacy of my Jeep, determined to reach Phil through the department phone line. Hell, I'd settle for Goodman, if necessary. Focused on my plan to reach the police, whether friend or foe, I opened the door.

No dome-light.

Reaching for the switch, I was frozen by Preacher's disembodied voice slithering from the back seat.

"Come on in, Doc."

It occurred to me later that I could have slammed the door. Hobbled back into the donut shop. Called 911. But, in that instant, anchored to the pavement, I knew he had a gun.

He just might shoot me.

I slid into the driver's seat, not bothering to ask him how he got into my vehicle. He seemed to have a knack for these things.

"How's our young man doing?

"What do you mean?"

"Where you headed?" He continued as if I hadn't spoken.

"Home."

"Maybe," he conjectured. "Seems odd you would leave an appointment, take a call, and then stop for a donut when your Dad's at home waiting for you."

He's been watching Dad.

"Just for chuckles, let's drive into the city. Keep that phone out. Maybe we'll get lucky."

He rapped my headrest with what was probably that same pistol he brought to our home.

I started the Jeep, pulled out of the parking lot, and turned south.

I concentrated on the cadence of my tires meeting the road, desperate to slow the lightening tempo of my heartbeat.

Don't get shot. Keep Kenny safe. Keep this maniac away from my family.

I wanted to scream, "HOW WILL YOU DO THAT, HANK?!"

My heart leaped to my throat when the phone buzzed again.

Please be Phil.

Private Caller lit up on the mini-screen. I wasn't sure I could speak. I allowed it go to voicemail.

"Let's return that call," Preacher said, as if we were cohorts in this travesty.

With mechanical precision, I forced myself to turn the wheel and pull into a deserted auto repair parking lot, unable to hit redial and drive at the same time.

"Why are you stopping?" Preacher's irritation echoed in the closed space.

"Would you like to drive while I dial?" My anger erupted before I could clench my teeth.
No response.

"No answer, genius." I was supercharged. "Then shut the fuck up."

The phone rang.

"Hi, Doc. You ready?"

Somehow, I'd hit the call button in the middle of my abbreviated meltdown. Kenny answered immediately.

"Ready, Kenny," I lied, fighting to refocus.

"I'm only going to give you part of the directions." I heard a change in his voice.

Relaxed?

"I don't want you to call the detective and next thing ya' know, I'm being read my rights." He chuckled.

"Dammit, Kenny." I spoke slowly to keep myself from hanging up on him and taking my chances with Preacher. "This is not pretend and it's sure as hell not funny. Keep it simple."

"Sorry, Doc. Long night. Drive to Walker-Johnston Park. Stop under a streetlight close to the main entrance. Get out of your Jeep and wait."

He hung up.

Yes. Relaxed.

I took a deep breath and exhaled loudly, uncertain whether Kenny's newfound composure was a good thing or a bad thing.

"Where we going?" Preacher impatience summoned me back to his presence.

"How about we call Phil Evans and ask for help with this?" It was worth a try.

"This is *my* deal. No locals to screw things up. Now, where we going?" He rapped his weapon on the headrest for emphasis.

I continued to prove that fear can make a person stupid.

"Listen, asshole. We're not going anywhere until I know you're not going to hurt Kenny."

"I always thought your kind of guy had more brains than guts. But with you, it seems like the other way around. Think about it. I need this kid. He's my ticket to the top. Not only will I not hurt him, if he cooperates, I can help him with the Feds."

I didn't believe him. History suggested Preacher would do whatever he thought necessary to get the information he wanted. It did make sense, however, that Kenny was relatively safe for as long as he held that information, and could testify at some future date.

Relatively.

I rubbed my eyes and rolled my shoulders to uncoil, buying a moment to think. There wasn't much more to do except hope. I'd made my stand. Preacher was unmoved. And, in control.

"Walker-Johnston Park."

"Perfect. Drive on."

I put the Jeep in drive, did a U-turn and headed for Urbandale. In another effort to recalibrate my hyper-charged body chemistry, I dropped Tangerine Dream into the CD player. Meditative electronica before it had a label.

"Good stuff," Preacher approved. "Let me know when we're a couple of blocks away."

Then he hunched down, out of view, and went back into ghost mode. I concentrated on getting us to Urbandale without pulling the steering wheel off the column. The Jeep made its way to the park and I crept toward the entrance, looking for signs of Kenny.

Nothing.

I parked as instructed, able to see only a few feet beyond the harsh burn of the streetlight. The largesse of the full moon had faded into the malaise of the past week and become no more than a sliver of hope. I checked my old school luminous watch, a 30th birthday gift from Dad. The dial said 9:57.

How has it gotten so late? J.R. is going to be beside himself. So sorry, Dad.

I slipped out of the Jeep, willing myself not to scan the area for company.

Plan's going well so far.

My phone vibrated and I almost power-hurled coffee and pastry onto the asphalt. I took a moment to steady my hands, then answered another call that was not from Phil.

"You're alone. Thanks." Kenny sounded relieved and a bit surprised.

"Where are you?"

"Turn around and look right across the street at the little house with the double porch light on."

I spotted a small, single-story house with an attached carport. It looked lonely and old-fashioned, tucked in amongst more upscale neighbors.

There was no vehicle in the drive.

The porch light was indeed emitting a soft LED glow. A good portion of the neighboring houses were dark, sleep coming early on a suburban school night. There was a narrow sidewalk leading up the slightly sloped lawn to a small porch covered with the green outdoor carpeting they use at miniature golf courses.

"The house with the porch light on," I repeated. "I see it."

Kenny wasn't in the park. He was watching me from the house.

What the hell? This is not his apartment in southeast Des Moines.

"What next?" I asked. Time for caution. No assumptions.

"Come on in." His tone was suddenly matter-of-fact.

I hung up, hesitated, saw no other choices, and crossed the empty street. My ankle boot and cane made for a slow climb up the sidewalk to the house. Someone had taken excellent care of this place. A nice little house trying to keep up in a nicer, redeveloped neighborhood. To the left of the door, a bay window offered no additional light from within.

Porch lights on and somebody's home.

Reluctantly, I leaned forward and touched the doorknob. It turned easily. I gave the door a gentle push, resisting any impulse to step inside. I shouldn't have bothered; the next push came from behind.

Preacher.

He must have made his way across the street, no doubt blending into the night. With his hand on my back, he was using me for a shield, pressing us both across the threshold and into a small living room.

"What the hell!"

With a bum ankle and my body propelled forward in high gear, I tripped over the cane and fell to my hands and knees. Momentum carried me forward and this time my head bounced on carpet, not much better than hitting wood. The flashes of light firing off in my skull immobilized me.

The all too recognizable and confusing sound of a handgun – somehow both loud and muted – echoed in the darkness, followed by the ominous thud of a person falling to the floor.

I flinched and flattened myself face down on the carpet.

Then I blacked out.

When I came back to consciousness, I was seated on the floor. Someone had pulled me forward, my back against sofa cushions. My head pounded, but that was nothing new. Directly in front of me, I saw a still form lying in the faint light of the entryway. Incredibly, that was nothing new either.

"Kenny? Preacher?" No reply from the inert body.

"Thanks, Hank." Kenny's voice came from the void on my left. "I owe you one," the voice continued. Deeper, smoother than I remembered.

I turned slowly to see Kenny's silhouette move quietly across the room. He was holding something in his hand. He kneeled and reached out to the immobile shape on the floor.

"A job well done," he chuckled. "Until tonight, I didn't know who the undercover guy was. Knew he was out there, just didn't know who. What luck, he found me. Say hey, Freddy."

As my eyes adjusted, I could see he was kneeling before the man I knew as Preacher. Kenny held a gun.

Preacher. Freddy. I doubted that was his real name. One thing was absolute – he wasn't moving.

The nagging awareness I had held from our first contact began to rise through the muck, unclogging my mental machinery.

"I could see from the start you were a bright guy, Hank." No longer "Doc." Now I was just Hank. "Something fishy from that first session, you're thinking, right? But you just can't quite get your head around it." He tapped his temple with the gun barrel.

"Well, curiosity got the best of you and here we are."

I tried to shrink into the sofa as he pointed the gun at me.

"You've arrived at the truth."

I could hear something in his voice. A smirk. Pride. I flashed back to our first session. Kenny the storyteller.

"But we're getting ahead of ourselves, Hank. First, we've got important work to do."

Kenny pointed a high-powered flashlight into Preacher's face. He was lying on his back. Blood on his chest. The dreary pallor of his skin was normal for the formerly very dangerous man, but the slouch of his shoulders and arms was not. His eyes were open. I wasn't sure if that meant he was alive or – like Jake – hadn't had time to shut them.

Kenny lifted Preacher's shirt and laughed.

"One to the chest. A little far to the right. But not bad with lousy backlight." Kenny complemented himself. "This guy is not a bright as he looks. He should have worn Kevlar."

Is?

"Just a little Glock does the job. Suppressor to mute the sound a bit," he explained, clearly full of himself. "Effective. Not too messy. We don't want to disturb the neighbors. They think I'm just a nice, quiet loner who works nights. Keeps his old-timey homestead up, and isn't around much."

Kenny picked up the handgun lying next to Preacher, the one that had surely been used to prod me in the door. Then he turned the beam directly into my eyes, blinding me.

"Stand up." My legs wouldn't move.

"Stand up!" he stepped close and punched my shoulder, gun in my face. "I doubt you're carrying, but I can't take any chances."

I flinched at the aggression, willed my body to move, and struggled up from the floor at the speed of a man twice my age.

"Turn toward my voice," he said, stepping back and keeping the light trained on my eyes.

"Now take off your coat and hand it to me."

On impulse, I tossed my light weight bomber jacket on the floor, hearing the muted thud of the phone I had stuffed into the pocket. An act of resistance amounting to nothing.

"Close enough. Now, do a nice little spin for me, so I can see you're not holding anything back."

I concentrated on keeping my balance, doing a sad little pirouette on my stronger ankle.

"Good. Now, take the phone out of your pocket, Hank."

I pulled a phone out of my pants pocket. I couldn't remember which phone it was.

"Throw it on the floor in front of me," he ordered.

I complied. The next sound I heard was Kenny grinding a heel into the phone screen.

"Leave the cane. You won't be needing it."

My spine felt like pudding.

He turned the flashlight off, leaving me night blind. "Now we're going for a short walk."

"What about Preacher?" I was surprised I could still speak.

"Preacher? Oh, Freddy. That's catchy, Hank." His voice was laced with sarcasm.

"Maybe he can still walk and talk. How about it, Preacher?"

"Help me up," Preacher eked out.

He's alive.

"Give him a hand, Hank. Two gimps in one."

It occurred to me that cooperating with the man I had known as Kenny was a bad idea, but I had no better plan. I willed my legs back to life and edged forward. It wasn't easy to stoop and wrap my left arm under Preacher. As best he could, he leaned in to me, sat up and groaned, then pushed his feet under himself and stood. We teetered but held our ground.

Kenny turned the flashlight to my face again, successfully alternating light and dark to disorient me. I could barely see the outline of the man at arm's length.

"Here's what we're gonna do, Hank. You're going take a hard right and walk ahead of me down the hall. I'll guide you." He aimed the beam toward our path. "And if you decide to work up some catchy scheme, keep Freddy in mind."

Preacher had just been added to the list of people I needed to protect.

Preacher and I slowly drifted in unison, limping ahead. Kenny stepped behind us and, with his free hand, steered me forward a few feet. As my eyes readjusted, I could see the silhouettes of a tiny kitchen to my left

Kenny gripped my shoulder to indicate, stop. The slight sound of a click came from his direction.

"There's a door directly ahead, Hank. Open it and down we go."

I turned the knob but it resisted.

"Pull harder, Hank. I unlocked it. It's a very special door."

Fighting to maintain my balance, Preacher's shallow breath in my ear, I pulled harder. The door emitted a sharp hissing noise and I startled, almost taking the two of us back to the floor. Kenny steadied me with a hand on my back.

"Easy. Just air. Sealed door. Special venting."

As the door eased open, I saw more LED emanating from a room below, just enough to guide me down the stairs.

"Like I said, down we go." I felt the steel barrel nudge me forward.

We shuffled down onto a landing. With both of my hands around Preacher's torso, we began a slow and painful descent down the rest of the stairs, one step at a time. As we all passed through the threshold, Kenny reached past me for a switch. The lights below flickered and the door closed with a whoosh that sounded final.

"Keep going, Hank," he insisted.

Each thump of our heels triggered a gasp from Preacher and a shooting pain on a direct path from my ankle to my head. I counted the steps, just to give my brain something else to focus on.

1, 2, 3, 4...13. Really. This had to be some deeply disturbed carpenter's idea of a joke.

At the bottom, the stairs opened to a large room that immediately erased the blue-collar aesthetic of the house's upper level. High tech was a fitting term.

I scanned the space.

Dialed down overhead lighting. Cool and dry. Whitewashed concrete walls with baffles for sound proofing. Two small, ground-level windows with blackout curtains. Thick, steel-blue carpeting and ceiling tile that was, without a doubt, also soundproof. The screen saver on a state-of-the-art laptop computer on a small worktable against the near wall blazed with fiery, burnt-orange explosions.

Tidy. No. Immaculate.

An old ceiling-high safe – black with gold scrolling – was edged into one corner. Flush against the side of the safe was a military style cot, bedding folded neatly. Stainless steel mini-fridge at the foot of the bed. Metal shelving against the far wall holding box after unlabeled box. On a large chrome table were enough handguns, rifles, and other weapons of urban warfare to make Ted Nugent drool.

A livable bunker.

The table also held several familiar items: our office computer. My lamp. Dennis' Serenity Prayer clock. And a hammer I recognized from camping, mallet head and multi-purpose claw ideal for destroying beautiful cherrywood desks.

Kenny was our B&E guy. One of those things that was obvious, once you knew.

Underneath the table were a hiker's backpack with various cords and pockets, tailor- made for hauling plenty of camping gear, and a compact dolly on wheels. Everything an enterprising thief would need for a short trip to the city.

The piece de resistance of this mini-fortress was hanging from brackets in an upper corner, answering the magic question of tonight's fiasco: how did Preacher and I get ambushed? TV monitors. Four of them, split screen, with views of the front door, the living room, the door from the carport to the kitchen, the hallway, and the rooms off the hallway. Plus, a full, frontal view of the park.

The security system I needed.

"The world's a dangerous place, Hank. Even one's home isn't sacred anymore. Just ask Jake. A little security is a good thing."

Kenny pointed to the screens, then punched a button on the laptop to duplicate the video. "First-rate warning system." More pride. "Installed in the quiet of night by yours truly."

The light in my fogged consciousness continued to sputter to life.

He extended his arm, gun in hand, and swept the room. "Hank. Freddy. This is Ken Central."

Not Kenny anymore. He sounded different. He looked different. Black leather jacket over a black T-shirt. Gold chain. Jeans over ebony, steel-toed cowboy boots. Now he was Ken.

We'd all been set up. The police. Preacher. Jake. Me.

Kenny was not Kenny, the delivery guy.

He wasn't Preacher's lead to the top of the food chain.

He *was* the top of the food chain.

Stunned didn't begin to capture my internal reaction. Staggered. I had both gotten close to the mark, and completely missed the target. I knew there was more to Kenny's story, but at my best, my intuition could not have carried me this far.

Breathe.

As I was finally awakened by the truth of this catastrophe, the answer to a question that had just arrived became obvious: Why had Preacher and I had not been pumped full of his leftover bullets; instead herded to this secret space?

He wants an audience.

I spoke for what seemed like the first time in hours. "A meth lab?" I croaked. Recent events had sucked all the liquid from my mouth.

"Been getting some details from the cops, huh? Good guess, but not quite, Hank." He lowered the pistol. "Do you smell the telltale smell of ammonia? No," he answered his own question. "If this was a meth lab, sealed in like this room, we'd be seriously brain screwed in no time. Or blown to bits."

I watched him survey the space.

"You see, Hank, I am not on the manufacturing level of the organizational chart. That's for the mind meltdowns. I'm upper management. Chief Operating Officer, you might say. I honestly confessed to you in the lobby of your offices – I'm into distribution."

He stepped to the shelf and patted one of the file boxes.

"As they say, that's where the real money is."

More money than he can fit in the safe?

"Your voice has changed," I said.

Keep him talking. Look for an opening. To do what?

I tried to telepath that question to Preacher as Kenny thundered on.

"Ah, yes, Kenny the loser. One of my many characters. Just a little charade to keep bums like your friends Jake and Freddy off-track. They had to believe there was somebody further up the line. They really thought they were recruiting me."

Doctor Watson would have called his laugh sinister.

"I hide in plain sight. Sometimes I show up in Podunk, Iowa, as Kip, the buyer. Or in Hooterville as K.D., the burnout. Different clothes. Different hair. Different voice. Different cars. I can be a lot of people, Hank. Keeps 'em guessin'."

"Must be hard to keep it all straight."

Play to his ego.

"I buy from rejects, nearly brain-dead from using their own product. There's nothing to keep straight," he explained, as if instructing a child. "By the time I arrive back in Des Moines, I'm Kenny the delivery grunt again. No one even notices an invisible wannabe coming through with his packages."

He smiled, then yelled "METH EPIDEMIC HITS OUR TOWN…FILM AT 10:00!"

The bile in his rant filled the room. Preacher leaned in to steady one, or both, of us.

"While our fine anti-drug force has been busy looking for the top dogs, I've been making drops for the small-time dealers. Most are so burned they wouldn't recognize me from one time to the next."

Time to feign interest.

"Seems like turnover and collections could be a challenge in this line of work."

His grin widened. He was loving the chance to finally show off his self-appointed genius.

"The applicants are numerous, and collections is what guys like Jake and Freddy are for." He flashed a false frown. "*Were* for. Anyway, word's out on the street that there's money to be made, if you're big and mean enough. There's a grapevine you're not exactly tapped into, Hank, even in a small burg like Des Moines. It's all done through the dark net. Encrypted email and prepaid cell phones. Social media for creeps. I'm the supplier and employer. And no one's the wiser."

The smile on his face didn't match the disdain in his tone.

"Money is delivered to P.O. boxes," he went on. "Payments made to the bad guys through other P.O. boxes. Simple. Efficient. Anonymous."

"These guys come with resumes and references?" The more we talked, the more I was able to think clearly and engage him.

"Very funny, Hank. Don't let anyone tell you that you're not hilarious. No, no resumes. But, as you are aware my friend, it's not that hard to tell the real goons from the fake tough guys."

He waved his gun hand at Preacher, whose eyes were riveted on Kenny. The lack of expression in his ashen face telegraphed hatred.

"So," I pushed forward, hoping for a better plan than talking him into submission. "Why the charade with me? Seems like a therapist's office is one of the last places you'd want to be, in this situation."

I made sure to say "situation," not ungodly horrifying calamity.

"Unexpected turn of events that was actually quite fortuitous, Hank. It wasn't in the original plan, but adaptability is key to all successful start-ups. The theft was just a little personal sideline. Everyone needs a hobby."

"You didn't plan to get caught," I pushed, guessing what his response would be.

"I didn't get caught." The threat in his words was absolute. "Kenny the Loser got caught."

This was more than simple role-playing – he was speaking of himself in the third person. Ken had spent years trying to split his sense of competence from the incompetent Kenny.

It hadn't completely worked.

"I knew there was heat coming my way, Freddy." He addressed my new ally. "Somebody on the streets was looking for the source. A cop maybe." His acknowledgement of Preacher held contempt.

"So," I continued for him, "you let yourself get caught, knowing you had contacts who would help with the court. You look hapless. Get sent for help. No time in jail."

"See, you are a bright guy," he said. "It could have gone the other way. But, first offense. A shirt-tail relative with pull who knows folks felt sorry about poor Kenny's childhood, and still doesn't know he did me a solid, far beyond his imagination, by asking the judge to cut me some slack. It was worth the risk."

"I still don't quite get where I fit in."

"I read about you, Hank," he said, confirming my guess. "In the paper. The article about you and our good buddy, Detective Phil. Some case with a bunch of religious fanatics. The bug was planted. I needed specialized help and you were the man. I was going to get therapy from a real celebrity and a friend of local law enforcement. That part of the plan also might have backfired, but every successful entrepreneur has to take a few chances."

"So, you knew I had contacts with the police. You pretended to be frightened, planted the idea that you were in danger and…"

His face almost burst with a self-satisfied grin as he gave me the punch line. "I became a snitch looking for myself."

Another bulb blinked on.

"Add in a little B&E..."

A bigger grin. "You're really getting it, Hank. A little something to increase the confusion. Bring more focus to Preacher, Jake, or alternative skells, as they say in the movies."

I felt disgust and wonder in equal measure.

"You painted those profanities..." I stamped down the words I wanted to pull off the office wall and use as my own. "It was all a ruse to find out who was looking for you."

"Almost. Originally, I was just looking to move the focus away from Ken by feeding them Kenny."

My questions leaped ahead.

"Why did you come back to the office Friday night?"

"Just building the narrative and having a good time, Hank. Tore my apartment up to make it look like I had a break-in. Drove by your office planning to handwrite a note and tape it on the outside door. Saw your light on. Every plan needs a little luck."

He feigned a frightened Kenny look.

"I figured, the more desperate I was, the more everybody would buy into the story. Then, that car showed up. I didn't expect that and I surely didn't want to bump into Jake and Freddy."

He nodded in Preacher's direction. "In all honesty, I did panic a bit. It was all added to the adventure."

He loves the risk.

"By the way," he asked. "Who was driving the car?"

I wasn't going to give him anything extra.

"So. The plan became: Kenny disappears into the night."

"Not exactly. Loose ends, Hank. I picked you to hear my story, and we were still a long way from discussing the most interesting stuff."

I shuddered. This was his stage. He had set up this meeting for a one-man audience. No exit sign in case of an emergency.

"Who knew," he went on, "that I'd get me my very own undercover cop as a bonus."

He assumed Preacher was a local cop. Kenny pointed to the screen that scanned the park, then to Preacher.

"Bad mistake not having the dome-light on, my man. When you got out in the dark, Hank, I knew something was fishy. Then the back door of your Jeep magically opened while you were crossing the street."

The devil's in the details.

"So, you concocted this story of Kenny and his childhood?" An old therapy technique. Even a wrong guess is likely to get a clarifying response.

"Wrong, Hank. Most of Kenny's sad story is true." He was referring to himself more and more in the third person.

"Divorce, alcoholic coked-up loser of a father, hostile bitch of a mother." He wasn't smiling any more. "I told myself every day that I'd get out of that hellhole. I wasn't going to end up like my old man."

Back to first person.

"I did one better. This, men, is the home of my youth. Mom conveniently changed back to her maiden name. No will when she died. I let it go to repo. Bought it with cash. No name association."

He stepped to the wall and slapped the sound baffling.

"Did the upgrades myself."

"Nobody remembers me," he went on. "A lot of new people. More money. And I forgot to tell you – I used to weigh 75 pounds more than I do now.

Nerd glasses. Hand-me-down clothes." The distain for his former self oozed from his voice.

Expanding his arms in another grand gesture, he took a bow and crowed, "Complete transformation."

My resolve was withering as Ken rattled on to his self-aggrandizing conclusion.

"I'm nothing like that pathetic kid," his tone held a touch of doubt. "I reinvented myself."

He was staring through me, his eyes fixed on a distant past when he had been forced to live the life he was so vividly describing. The result: rage without guilt. No compassion for the plight of addicts. In fact, he believed it was his right to contribute to their destruction.

The newspaper article about dead cookers.

"You killed them." I spoke with deliberation, the coldness of his act reheating the blood in my body.

He came back to the room and to eye contact, smiling his hate.

"Killed who, Hank," he pretended? "Well. Necessary complication. You read the paper. Once in a great while, people think they know me. Or ask too many questions."

He paused, gun at his side. "A little well-timed violence also reminds the help not to skim too much off their collections." He made eye contact with Preacher. "Anyway, it was time for those folks to move on down the road."

He called murdering desperate addicts moving down the road.

Preacher and I had clearly become the next folks he planned to move.

Belinda. Dad. Dennis. Gail. Phil. Jerry. Malcomb. Jill...HALEY!

People who the man I no longer saw as Kenny had decided I would never see again.

I shuddered, dropped my arm from Preacher's shoulders and launched my battered body forward with ill intent.

Momentum carried my shoulder into Ken's gut. He was a lot bigger but I was high on terror, and his hubris left him unprepared.

"What the...!"

Ken staggered back, dropping the gun to catch his balance against the steel table. Hitting the floor on all fours, my body screamed in protest, my vision foggy from the pain. Like some feral cat on his ninth life, I scrambled toward the pistol.

"STOP!"

Ken's boot came down hard, pinning the weapon to the floor. I froze as he wagged the second pistol, the one I had forgotten about, in front of my nose. Rolling onto my back in surrender, I saw that Preacher had collapsed to the floor and lay inert on his side. Ken retrieved pistol number one, took a step forward and placed it carefully on Preacher's temple.

"Now I have a story to tell you, Hank, and I intend to finish," he was breathing hard. "But I don't need Freddy to be with us when I do."

He looked over his shoulder at me.

"So, you decide. No more mischief, or I shoot him right now. I'm pretty sure one more bullet is his limit."

I sat up, leaned against the leg of the table, and raised both hands, palms out.

Ken waved me away from the table without eye contact, as he stepped back and ranted on. At that point, I realized the room could have been empty of real-life forms. We were just tools in the drama Ken was playing out. I groaned to my feet and went to kneel at Preacher's side. His breathe was coming in faint rasps.

"My father literally pissed his sorry life down the drain, just like these sorry sons-of-bitches that cook and use meth. You ever meet any of these people?"

Revulsion radiated from his question.

"The cockroaches are the cleanest things in the house. They don't bath. They don't eat. They don't feed their kids. Their yards look like something straight out of a demolition derby. Their houses smell like gas station bathrooms and cattle barns. Makes you sick."

Not me. It had made Kenny sick. And robbed him of his heart.

"As for me. Clean and sober."

It got quiet. Ken came back to the present. Eye contact with me, as if Preacher was invisible.

"I can't tell you how refreshing it's been to finally tell somebody the real history of my life, Hank. I've had to keep this all a secret for so long. You're the first person I've told the truth and, thanks to you, I truly feel better. Sorry you won't be fully reimbursed."

His vicious attempt at humor painted a clear picture of the future.

"Unfortunately," he said, morphing into an officious tone. "Our time together must come to an end. Though the relationship has been brief; you've been helpful beyond my wildest dreams." He mocked me with a standing ovation.

The surge of terror ran from my toes to the top of my head. I closed my eyes and pushed the anger coursing in my belly through the fear.

My turn.

I stood, opened my eyes, and stared into his.

"This isn't just going to go away, Kenny. People have been murdered."

"As it goes in the free-market economy, Hank. Every day there are winners and there are losers. I win. You and Freddy lose."

"It's a bit more complicated than that, Kenny." I made it a point to use the name he had rejected.

Was it my stubborn hope, or did I see a flash of that chastised boy from our first session?

"Oh, good," he clapped his hands again and the image was gone. "The great psychotherapist, Hank Anderson, intervenes. You hatching a plan to confront Kenny about his errant ways? Maybe bring him to a spiritual awakening, as you 12-Step hacks put it?"

"Not quite, Kenny. There are a couple of details you missed."

A depth of undeniable concern crossed Ken's face for the first time since his diatribe began.

"Bullshit. What details?" His bravado faded into a frown.

I pointed to Preacher, who lay still in noiseless rage.

"Two in particular. First, you keep calling Freddy an undercover cop. Here's another truth. He's a DEA undercover informant. You have hit the big time, Kenny."

My turn to applaud.

"Federal law enforcement is interested in you, and they don't just get frustrated and go away. By the way, they work in all fifty states, and across borders. Now, I don't have a whole lot of experience with this sort of thing, but I'm guessing if you kill Freddy, it will really upset them."

Ken was thrown. I knew something he did not and he was finally at a loss for words. I pushed on.

"Second, I'm not a lost soul cooking drugs twelve miles from the nearest incorporated town. People will miss me immediately, and some of them are tenacious police types. When you fail to resurface, my favorite cop, Detective Phil, and his DEA pals will know just who to come looking for. They'll find this house. They'll find us. And, then, they'll find you."

I paused for effect. Genuine fear flashed across Ken's face. He got quiet as the wheels turned inside his head, retreating into a downcast look that I'd seen in clients who spoke of pervasive loss.

Some of the first session was not an act.

Ken worked to gather himself. He looked up, attempting to restore his body to an imposing six feet.

"Well. All good things must come to an end. Opioids are the hot thing anyway," trying to sound as if he was discussing a new brand of toothpaste. "I proved my point, Hank."

He stepped to the shelf, his effort to insert the energy back into his tirade fading to wooden.

"I've put more than a little back." He patted one of the boxes. "And so, it's time for me to close up shop and relocate. But, where?" He murmured, yoyo-ing back to his own thoughts.

He hadn't planned for the next stage of his delusional saga to be life on the run.

Ken's eyes drifted with his confusion, scanning his make-believe castle. I followed his motion, watching for one more opening, a last chance for Preacher and myself to live.

Instead, Ken froze, drawing both of us back to the surveillance screen from whence we came.

Like some horrific sitcom, we were met with the live action picture of three inexplicable figures, softly illuminated as they edged through the front door and into the upstairs living room.

Dennis. Jerry. Dad!

My vision went fuzzy and I lost the feeling in my legs. From some otherworldly place, I heard Preacher find the strength to whisper from the floor, "Steady."

I turned to him. Blood trickled from the side of his mouth; a feverish light burned in his eyes.

"What the hell!" Ken reawakened.

I watched, unable to move, as he launched himself up the stairs, taking two at a time. He punched the door opener with his left fist – gun in his right – as he pushed into the hallway. The "whoosh" of the door opening and automatically closing, again, jolted me. I looked at the screen as the rear view of Kenny entered the picture, pistol pointed at our makeshift posse.

No one reacted as I screamed, "STOP!" My shriek was locked in the insulated basement along with the rest of me. I wanted to look away from what would happen next, but instead stood transfixed, like a race day spectator drawn to a fiery, multi-car crash.

The crash didn't come. Instead, the movie went into slow motion.

Dennis, Jerry, and Dad froze, then began the measured dance I had completed a short time ago. As one, they raised their hands, tossed off their jackets, and began to rotate. I couldn't see Ken's face, but I knew he was the director, his voice emitting ominous threats as he dictated the action.

"This show is already on re-runs," I said to no one, an even deeper dread creeping to the surface.

How the hell did they find us?

Via live video feed, I watched Ken give the upstairs trio what I assumed were the same instructions that had landed Preacher and myself in the basement. Not a place I wanted the rest of the gang to be. Nevertheless, in single file, my fearsome threesome began moving toward the door, Dennis in the lead, followed by Jerry, then Dad.

I couldn't immediately comprehend why Ken hadn't just shot the whole crowd. His story was told. He certainly had no reluctance to kill anyone who interfered with his grand plan. And he now knew he would have to run, so a few more bodies didn't seem an insurmountable problem for his madness.

One more last chance.

I surveyed the room. Guns. Lots of guns. Even Ken was capable of real panic and, in his rush to deal with my crew he had locked us in with a room full of deadly weapons.

Simple plans are best in crisis. Grab the biggest, ugliest gun. Run up the stairs, burst into the hallway, shoot this monster before he could kill my loved ones. I had an instant before they arrived at the door, but no cogent thoughts regarding the complication that my loved ones had just become human shields.

One more problem: Iowa is a state full of properly licensed hunters. My family fished. The last gun I'd shot was a BB gun, and that was decades ago. With bargain-bin Abba and Bread albums for targets. Not people. Still, Dennis would be the first to say I have never been bound by the restriction of having to know what I'm doing.

While these thoughts flashed in rapid succession, Preacher seized the moment. He rolled to his belly and drug himself from the ground to his knees. Silent agony was etched on his face, blood oozing from his chest and mouth, iridescent, wet streams migrating down his black shirt.

Without regard for any of this, he urgently clawed his way under the stairs. With a deep gasp and a massive effort, he pushed himself upright, resting his back against the inner wall. He smiled something close to genuine and gave me a thumbs-up.

What the hell does that mean?

Deciding that encouragement was the right move, I gave him a thumbs-up right back. Energized by his determination, I squared my shoulders, turned as quickly as my ankle would carry me and hobbled to the table for the nastiest weapon in sight.

Two plans. Maybe the odds were better than desperate.

I cradled the heaviest, deadliest, long semi-automatic whatever that I could lift. It was the type of assault weapon I'd seen in action films, identified by letters and numbers I couldn't remember. I found a trigger and then wondered how it worked. Limping back toward the steps, I heard the sickening sound of the vacuum-sealed door opening.

"Hank, you guys still there?" Ken called out, his unhinged humor and sense of power over us restored. "I've got some old friends come a callin'. Just thinking you all should have a few moments together before I have to leave our fair city."

The dull thump of Ken's boots hit the landing.

"Oh, by the way. If you made it to the gun table, they're not loaded. First rule of gun safety, gentlemen – always store your ammo away from your firearms."

I looked at the underbelly of the gun, guessing that's where the ammo clip would go if I happened to have one.

"OK, men, move on down."

I turned to the video screen to see Ken's back as he prepared to follow the troops. Chances were better than excellent that he wouldn't be in the mood for a retelling of his story when they got past step thirteen. Arriving at yet one more useless awareness, I realized he was simply enjoying the mental torture of drawing this nightmare out, making us face one another with the reality of our helplessness.

The muted shuffle of men moving cautiously down the carpeted stairs refocused my attention. Standing there with the leaden weight of the impotent gun in my now shaking hands, I frantically searched for another idea.

Dad had slowed down over the years and he was going to take some time getting to the bottom. Imitating Preacher's resolve, I ignored the pain of my recent injuries, twisting the gun and grabbing the barrel like a broadsword, with both hands. Maybe I could catch Ken as he moved around the corner, hit him with the butt of the gun, and disarm him.

It was a lousy strategy, but surviving Jake had taught me the value of tilting at windmills.

As I braced myself, Preacher snapped his fingers to catch my attention. He smiled again, laboriously turning to point at the underside of the steps. It took a moment to track on his pantomime. Then I noticed the glare that appeared between the boards. Each step was a wooden plank, separately carpeted, open in the back.

Yeah. Bad carpentry.

I shrugged my shoulders. He pointed at the rifle and beckoned me to hand it over. The tumblers in my head connected.

Why not?

I moved close and laid the rifle in his lap. In a feat of superhuman strength, he grimaced, lifted, and rested the butt end on the back of the stair plank level with his eyes. He gripped the barrel end with both hands. Then he motioned me closer. One more whisper and a riveting look was all he could manage.

"My wife. Meth. She died. I'm Victor. I'm sorry, Hank." He called me by name, the tears on his face revealing the pain he felt, and perhaps, the pain he had caused.

Then, he melted into the wall, retreating to hold vigil over those slivers of possibility.

The cliché is that time slows in the milliseconds that proceed disaster. It's more than a cliché. Muffled shuffle of feet. Muffled shuffle of feet. Muffled shuffle of feet and the sound of my labored breathing. As I saw the shoes of my friends and family finally begin to show between the steps, I poised to rush Ken, fists clenched.

First came Dennis, followed by Jerry, trailed by Dad. As Ken's boots reached my new partner's eye level, Preacher—Victor-- leaned in, rammed the gun through the opening, and hammered the heel of our captor's left boot just as he lifted his right foot.

Ken stumbled, missed the next step, and pitched forward into his line of captives. An uncountable series of suppressor pops echoed in the closed space of the basement.

The gun!

In a mass of arms and legs and torsos, the group amoebaed down the last three stairs. With a series of thuds and outcries of pain, the whole crew – including Ken – ended their ride in a jumbled pile at the bottom.

I had to make myself look at the tangled heap in front of me.

Ken was on top, face down. His ever-twitchy body was completely still. The remainder of the pile groaned en masse, and a "damn" that sounded a lot like Jerry leaked from a low point in the stack. The mound gradually started to shift from an amorphous mass to definable heads and appendages.

Stumbling forward, I tentatively poked Ken in the side. He was, at the very least, unconscious. His grossly bent form resisted as I tried to push him off the top of the mass of bodies. Finally, he rolled to the right, crumbling onto his back into the concrete corner. The handgun was locked in his grip, held against his chest. His left arm was twisted, clearly broken in several places. There was blood patterned all over the front of his shirt, like crimson tie-die.

Whose blood!?

"Dad? Dad!"

"Son."

Bodies began to slowly sort themselves, rolling into the crevices of the cramped space, and, once again, becoming my dad, Dennis, and Jerry. J.R. gingerly reached out for my hand. I carefully took his elbow and helped him up. Then I gathered him around the chest as we struggle to stand.

"Are you OK?"

"I'm breathing, son."

Jerry moaned, rolled further to the left, and pushed himself up, which sent Dennis, face first, onto the carpeted floor.

"Dennis! Hank!" Jerry was kneeling next to Dennis, who was silent. "He isn't moving!"

"Don't try to turn him," Dad said, grabbing the side banister for support.

In that moment, the upstairs erupted with the deadened sound of a legion of footsteps, loud enough to barely leak through the soundproofing. Almost immediately, the door exploded and two men in blue helmets, visors and guns drawn, crashed through the shards and came bursting down the narrow stairwell.

Right behind them came Phil, gun in hand, with the closest I'd ever seen to terror on his face.

Goodman was huffing and puffing right behind, like he'd run all the way from the police station to save us.

"Step back!" The lead cop gave the orders.

As we gave way, Dad and I leaned on one another for balance. The SWAT commander moved to Ken and put his fingers to the carotid artery, as the second man squeezed through and went directly to Dennis.

"No pulse," the commander announced.

"Pulse," the second officer yelled. Dennis exhaled. "And sound."

The first officer was already speaking into the mic attached to the upper left side of his vest.

"Ambulance needed at site. Two men down. One has no pulse. Three more with injuries."

"Wait!" I yelled, pointing under the stairs.

The second officer moved quickly to check Preacher, who was slumped against the wall. I could see that his eyes were closed. The officer punched his mic again.

"Update. Three men down. Two with no pulse."

My legs started to wobble. I let go of Dad, aimed for the carpet, and lowered myself carefully to the floor. As I closed my eyes, I wondered whether the cops would have to update again.

"Damn, he fainted." I heard the grating sound of Goodman's voice calling me back.

"Nope," I said, blinking my eyes open. "Just resting from a busy night."

"Shit."
Dad, Phil, and Goodman stood over me. My old EMT friend Jeff knelt at my side.

"We've got to quit meeting like this, Mr. Anderson," he quipped. He raised his eyes to the gang. "Butt bruise perhaps. We'll need to make sure he didn't reinjure his head."

"Might be an improvement." At that Goodman was warned off by Jeff's eyes. Compassionate but stern.

I tried to sit up. "Dennis?"

"Easy, stay down. He's on the way to the hospital, probably has a broken arm and a concussion to match yours. No gunshot wounds. He'll be checked out top to bottom. He was conscious and cussing like a sailor when they left, telling his partner not to fuss so much."

Dennis was being Dennis, a good sign.

"Jerry went with him in the ambulance," Phil reassured. "He'll have plenty of bruises too, but he's going to be fine."

"Dad?" I was working my way through the list.

"Just a little tumble, son. Your friends made for a nice soft-landing pad. I'll be a bit stiff in the morning, but you can't keep an old man down." Oddly enough, he sounded pleased with himself.

Jeff added, "We'll need to check you out, sir. I'm thinking you may have at least bruised some ribs." He turned to me. "He refused to leave until he knew you were OK. We'll transport both of you to the hospital and get him his own personal x-rays."

"That seems a bit extreme, young man," J.R. countered.

"Just a precaution, sir. How about it."

"Dad."

"If it'll make you feel better, son," J.R. acquiesced.

I became aware that both Ken and Preacher had been removed from the basement.

I'd heard the cop, but still needed to ask.

"Victor?" I owed him his real name.

Phil just shook his head.

"He saved our lives. Mashed the rifle into Ken's heel and sent him tumbling down the stairs."

My wife. She died. Meth.

"Ken?" I had to make sure.

"He's dead, too. Most of the blood was his, Hank."

I later learned that Ken had reflexively pulled the trigger during the fall. With his gun hand turning inward as his other hand reached out to catch his descent, he shot a bunch of small holes into his own body. Ken had mocked Preacher for not wearing Kevlar. Certain of his superiority, he had no protection from his own bullets.

Intense sadness passed over me like a harsh rainstorm.

"Give you a set of stairs and a bad guy, you people are hell on the wheels, Anderson." Goodman was having a good time in a very sick way.

"Dale, do me a favor and go upstairs to wait for the forensic crew." Phil didn't sound like he was asking for a favor.

Goodman stalked upward, yammering about "lame-ass touchy-feely types."

I stretched out my hand for Phil. Jeff, ever the professional, gently laid his hand on my chest.

"Let us carry you and your father up the stairs, Hank. Just to be on the safe side."

That worked for me. As I lay on the carpet, quietly waiting for the gurney, my thoughts returned to Ken.

"We've got a lot to talk about." Phil intruded on my thoughts. "Like, why did Belinda call me, then load these yahoos up in her car and drive them to this house after I told them to stay home and let us handle this?"

His bulk expanded to fill the stairwell as he frowned at Dad. Then he seemed to will himself to shrink back to regular human size.

"But it can wait until you're all checked out," he sighed, giving way to Jeff and his team. "I'm just glad you're all alive. Let's get out of here."

The EMTs took Dad first. As they were loading him up on the gurney, he turned to me.

"By the way son, the rest of the security system is in. And the refrigerator is full."

I looked at Dad.

Phil looked at me. "You are a truly unique family."

Then, for the second time in a week I was gently loaded onto a rolling bed. After the crew had Dad safely inside one of the fleet of ambulances that was currently serving our needs, I was carefully moved up the narrow staircase.

This being a blue-collar neighborhood, the before-dawn working folks were already up and about, shivering in their robes, making for a fair amount of front yard gawking at the sea of law enforcement vehicles and personnel surrounding us. The SWAT team got special attention. A part of me wanted to say, "Go back to your homes, people, there's nothing to see here." I knew that wasn't true, and it was clearly inappropriate for me to speak like a TV cop, so I let it go.

Just as I was being loaded into my personal transport vehicle, I spotted the aura of a special face penetrating the crowd. She was standing across the street, next to a gleaming Lexus. Her hands were pressed together as if she had been praying ferociously. I waved and gave my guardian angel a Victor-style thumbs up. Belinda wiped something from her eyes and waved back.

How did she get here so fast?

Overwhelmed by the muddle of a complete adrenaline dump, I was enveloped by the careful glow and comforting warmth of the ambulance. Lights, no sirens. Jeff maintained his calm presence throughout the ride as the events of the interminable evening tumbled through my exhaustion.

In short order, the whole Anderson Never Deputized Anti-Drug Unit had arrived back at the hospital. Sadly, Juanita wasn't working that morning, but young Dr. Randisi was. We shared a cordial moment as he checked me out. I thanked him. He told me he was very pleased I was alive, and that all my friends and family were safe. He told me he hoped my life would slow down. I wished him the same. We traded tired smiles and shook hands.

WEDNESDAY AGAIN

I woke up in my own bed to the sound of the doorbell and a subdued greeting to the ringer of said bell, after what seemed like very little sleep.

I replayed the previous evening's closing festivities. In turn, Dennis, Jerry, Dad, and I had all been checked out by the doctor. Dennis was put in a temporary arm cast and given a follow-up appointment; no surgery necessary. No concussion. Jerry, the local tough guy, had barely a scratch. Dad had bruised, not broken, several ribs and received a long list of cautions and instructions for a safe recovery. Issues with breathing and pneumonia were genuine risks for my senior citizen bodyguard.

My head barely believed the report that I had not suffered another concussion, but avoiding all contact sports for an extended period was recommended as a good thing for both my brain and ankle.

My jacket was returned to me and I found the extra cell phone in a pocket. A lot of good that did us.

We were then collectively pronounced beat to hell and upright, and sent home. There was very little conversation, but Phil assured us all that we would be discussing the error of our most recent ways in the very near future.

Doorbell again. Might be Phil dropping by to check on me. Probably should get up and see what's going on.

I fell back to sleep. I was awakened shortly by more ringing, went back to sleep, was awakened, and so on and so forth. After the fifth or sixth arrival, I decided I might as well get up, or they would just keep coming. I dressed in a well-worn Morningside College sweatshirt and sweatpants, a gift from Phil's Sioux City alma mater. Then I trudged downstairs, sans cane, giving only brief thought to Ken, Victor, Jake, and the events that, in this moment, seemed far away.

The house was buzzing with activity. Gail and Jerry were scurrying hither and yon, bringing mugs of hot coffee into the living room, where Dad, Dennis, Phil, and Jill all sat in quiet conversation.

"Did we wake you son?"

"No, the broken doorbell that kept going off woke me."

Jerry scurried my way. "Here's your coffee. Sit down. Phil called us all together to get the whole story straight. Dennis has a headache and his body aches all over. I'm fine, due, of course, to my athleticism and excellent conditioning. Your dad is tough as nails. How are you?"

"Where are Haley and Belinda?" I figured this peculiar family reunion might include everyone.

"Belinda took Haley shopping for new earrings," Gail answered tersely. "Plus, she had to cancel another day of your clients, based on your latest bonehead move."

It appeared that Gail had to force the next sentence from her lips.

"Then, she actually told me that she's proud of you," she fumbled. "And that she hopes she did the right thing."

Damn straight, Belinda.

"I told her in no uncertain terms that she had taken a ridiculous chance," Gail said. Her glare dared me to disagree.

My shrug was non-committal.

As we all settled into various pieces of furniture, Phil shifted gears.

"So," he began. "I…"

"What were you thinking," Jill interrupted, giving me the full force of her recrimination. "I just got your butt out of one jam and…"

"What *were* you thinking," Gail interrupted Jill's interruption. "You're a father, a therapist, not some SWAT commando."

"It all turned out for the best, honey," Dad offered.

Bad move.

"And you three!" Gail turned on J.R., Dennis and Jerry in unison.

"Go ahead," Jill deferred to Gail.

"I expected better than this from you, J.R., the grandfather of my daughter, for God's sake. You're a sensible man. Usually."

I hadn't seen Dad blush in a long time.

"And Dennis," Gail railed on. "You go on and on like you're Mr. Voice of Reason to Hank's Mr. Loose Cannon. Then you decide to play Marlowe, too. What the hell!"

"Now dears," Jerry started. I gently shook my head and he got quiet.

Before Dennis could open his mouth in defense, Jill turned to Phil.

"And where were you while all this was happening, Detective?" Phil's early truce with Jill was ancient history.

It went like this for the better part of several minutes, with Gail and Jill playing tag-team. They didn't sound like a psychologist and a lawyer. They sounded like my mom reproaching me for the time I secretly drove my ancient Impala ninety miles to Omaha with Mark and Lou, in a blinding southwest Iowa blizzard, to see R.E.M. in concert.

Great show.

Bottom line from our panel of judges: we had messed up, taken absurd risks, and were far more than lucky to be alive.

Mom had been right. Gail and Jill were right, every word propelled by the fear that was grounded in love and concern for a member of the foolish five.

In turn, we each issued an inadequate apology; even Dennis, who rarely regrets anything he does or says and Phil, whose only crime was trying to keep us from doing the very things we were in trouble for. No matter, guilt by association.

Jerry and Dad went to the kitchen and refilled coffee mugs, just to do something productive and break the tension.

Then we got down to the rest of the story.

"So, the magic question is…" I directed this at my fellow fools. "How did you find me?"

Dad took a risk and opened his mouth.

"Turns out that new phone of yours has a tracking system. While I was sitting around waiting for James to finish all the new security, I got to reading your instruction manual."

He looked around to test the lay of the land.

"So..." J.R. was going for broke. "When you didn't come home for dinner and I didn't hear from you, I called Dennis. He hadn't heard from you either. I called Belinda. Not a word from you. We all got worried."

He rocked gently on the sofa as he revisited that moment, looking everywhere except in Gail's direction.

"Gail and Haley were out having mother-daughter time. Belinda left a message for Gail that she was going for a visit with Dennis and Jerry. They came here."

I noticed that Dad winced as he took a breath in to continue the story. Bruised ribs are no joke.

"We figured out how to lock into the phone's general whereabouts. I guess it was the new one that was in your jacket."

"Belinda called Phil. He didn't answer." No recrimination in Dad's voice. "Then she called Detective Goodman, who told her Phil was at a church function with his family. She gave him the information about your phone."

A weak but valiant attempt to imply they had done the right thing.

"And he told you to hold tight, that he would let me know there was an emergency, and that we'd respond immediately," said Phil. Plenty of recrimination.

"You surely did, Phillip. But this is Hank we're talking about."

No further apologies.

"I decided to look for my son." He scanned the room, as if daring anyone to challenge his decision.

And then, J.R., man of grace and civility was back.

"Dennis and Jerry were resolved to keep an eye on me." He nodded his gratitude.

"Belinda deemed it necessary to provide safe transport," he smiled. "And we all know Belinda does as Belinda choses."

"We didn't know exactly where you were, but the tracking got us to the neighborhood. Jerry spotted your Jeep. We wandered around and saw that the door to a house across the street was open. Figured you might have gone there. Something had to be wrong. None of us could think of any good reason for you to be near that park at night. We went to the door. Spotted your cane and coat lying on the carpet. We didn't see any people."

Dad gave Phil a respectful, palms up acknowledgement.

"In that very moment, Dennis' phone rang and it was the detective."

Phil chimed back in, his patience meter hitting the red zone. "And, what did I tell you?"

He answered his own question.

"I told you we were on the way with all hands-on deck. Go back to the car. We would take care of things."

"I got more nervous," J.R. ignored the reminder of the original order he had ignored, continuing to take the heat for the whole crew. "I was determined to go in and poke around."

"Belinda waited on the street to tell the police what was going on. Dennis and Jerry just followed me. They were looking out for a father who needed to find his son. Then that unfortunate man with the gun showed up."

J.R. sat back, relinquishing the floor to whatever came next.

Instead of more anger, I saw the tears of what Gail's imagination told her might have happened to her family rush to her eyes. Dad reached to his left and covered her hand with his own.

It's difficult for this crowd to be at a loss for words, but it happened. Given my recent behavior, I was in no position to defend my rescuers. My choices had set this whole living nightmare in motion. The sensible people in the room were still in shock. The rest of my crew had nothing to add to Dad's compelling synopsis.

We were alive. It was a miracle.

After a few seconds of interminable silence proved that time is, in fact, relative, Phil re-broke the ice. Being the only person in the room who was qualified to participate in a police raid, and the only one of our team who had not acted recklessly, he began to fill in the blanks.

"Fortunately, we were only moments behind these characters. I was on the line with Belinda as we approached and she got us to the right house immediately. We, the police," he riveted each of us, in turn, to our seats with his cop glare, "took a few minutes to deploy and secure the area before storming the house."

"It turns out," Phil continued, "that Ken's story had a lot of truth to it. He was driving for IP both as a cover and to deliver shipments of meth to street dealers. He was living in his apartment as the IP delivery guy and in the house as the non-descript neighbor who wasn't around much. Guessing that Jake and Victor had ransacked his apartment, he was hiding in plain sight in his old neighborhood."

He gave us context, bringing a kernel of sense to this insanity.

"These meth labs are all over the rural areas. Addicts who cook and sell mostly to support their own habits. Word goes out among these people that there's a buyer. It was easy to stay ahead of being identified. He randomly bought from lots of people, using different personas. Those folks don't ask for ID."

Dennis turned to me. "When Victor came to Hank's house that night, he was looking for some organizing force tapping into a network of labs and dealers," Dennis said. "And there was none."

"Exactly," Phil said. "What looked like anonymous string pullers was basically a one-man operation: buy from addicts who wouldn't recognize him if they saw him in the local grocery store, deliver packages as the invisible IP man, and use out-of-town bad guys to collect on the streets and pay off via P.O. boxes."

"Creative," Dennis said. "But, how did he keep from getting ripped off by street dealers, most of whom are also addicts, or a low-life like Jake?"

"Best guess, he knew he would be. As Ken, he never dealt with anyone face-to-face. He paid top dollar for collections and lived with the fact that most of the people would skim some drugs, money, or both, off the top. The cost of doing business."

"And," Phil added. "He recently sent a message for effect."

"What message," Jill asked?

"Ken admitted he killed those three sad people out in the country," I finally spoke. "He told me conflicting stories – that he wasn't afraid of being recognized and that he'd killed them because he might be."

"An object lesson for people who would rip him off," Phil surmised.

"Yeah, he mentioned that, too."

Phil went on. "He really did have some shoestring relative who remembered his rough childhood as Kenny and called in a favor with the court. Ken remembered reading about Hank in the *Register* and passed this on to the court, who passed it on to the Captain, who passed it on to me. Ken got himself referred for counseling with someone who might have an inside track with the police. He told himself it would help protect his operation."

"So, he sees Hank for a while, does his probation, keeps the separation between Kenny, delivery guy, and Ken, drug dealer," Dennis said. "How the hell did it get so crazy?"

Phil looked to me to explain.

"Enter Victor," I said. "Victor had gotten himself on the inside, with Jake as part of his cover. Hired to do collections. They were duped into believing that Kenny was just a vulnerable kid being used by a higher source. When Victor came to my room the night after Jake died, he said he believed Kenny would be his link to the power behind the meth distribution. He didn't know he was already following the man in charge."

"This is not meant to be crass," said Jerry. "But, why didn't they just beat the information out of the young fellow. They would have known right away that he was the linchpin."

I felt my amateur detective skills resurfacing. "It's complicated. Victor couldn't afford to have the delivery guy running back to the people he believed were pulling the strings. He was juggling a lot of balls. Keep his contact alive and scared into silence. Make sure Jake didn't figure out Freddy was his cover and he was a DEA informant. Keep the lid on the plan he was orchestrating to tap into the drug distribution network that, it turns out, didn't even exist."

Victor's image passed through my thoughts.

"So, Victor wanted to get me out of the way. Afraid I'd stick my nose into the wrong place."

"Imagine that," Jill said, getting a nod from Gail.

Gaining courage, I continued. "Then, when Ken disappeared and I didn't go away, Victor hoped I might know something more."

"What about this Jake coming to the house," Dad asked?

Phil answered. "Maybe Jake's plan for getting Hank out of the picture was more direct. He didn't seem like a deep thinker. But more likely, what Victor told Hank was the truth; they were increasing the fear factor to see what Hank knew. Letting you know they could come into your house and threaten your whole family."

"We're just speculating here," Phil added. "But Victor probably went along to keep from blowing his cover."

I shivered again, put my face in my hands, and flashed on that night.

I felt the comfort of soft hands on my shoulders. Gail and Jill had both stood up to console me. Something passed quickly and silently between the women. Shock, embarrassment, jealousy? They both stepped back.

Fortunately, the doorbell rang.

Phil stepped up and opened the door to a whirlwind on legs.

"Uncle Phil!" Haley smashed herself into a hug from the big man, leaped over the steps, careened into the living room, and came to a sliding stop.

"Mom told me Belinda wanted to spend more time with me. Belinda told me Dad and Grandpa were kind of busy today. Belinda told me Mom needed to drop something off at Dad's house." She panned the crowd. "Hi, Dad. Hi, Mom. I knew something was going on."

She blew Dad a kiss.

"Grandpa J.R., why are all these people here? And who is that pretty lady with the red hair?"

Once again, Jerry saved the day. "Sweetie. Let's go into the kitchen and find you a juice box and a snack. Your Mom and Dad are having a family meeting and then they're going to explain everything." His look could only be described as hopeful. "And this is our new friend, Jill."

Haley, ever interested in new friends, approached Jill, said, "Nice to meet you, Jill," and reached out her upward palm.

"Same to you." Jill seemed a bit mystified, as she high-fived my daughter.

"OK, Jerry. Let's hit the fridge." She held up her teacup pinkie and put on a Queen of England voice. "I am feeling a bit peckish."

Off they went.

The crowd smiled as one.

Jill made eye contact with me.

"She's even funnier than you."

"Oh my!" Belinda directed her sympathy toward Dad, but she was looking at me. "Is that what it was like to raise that man? She's unstoppable. So, what did I miss?"

Jill stepped in, suddenly the voice of peace and serenity.

"No more, for now. My little gang of miscreants are exhausted from their ordeal. Time to wrap up; let them rest and heal."

She was speaking to the group but looking at Gail.

"Yes," Gail echoed. "Let's all clear out. Belinda, I'll catch you up on the whole ridiculous story when we get back to my place." Her hands went to her hips. "Including your part in this deception."

"Dear." There was no repentance in Belinda's tone. "I saved these men, one and all. You'll have to take any other concerns up with Mr.'s Anderson and Greenberg. Now, let's collect that baby of yours and give folks a chance to recuperate."

She made it sound as if leaving had been her idea.

Gail took her marching orders in the spirit of love. She leaned in again and squeezed my shoulder.

"We'll talk more later. I'll handle Haley's questions and we can decide how much more she needs to know when you've had time to mend."

She'd gone from anger to fear to empathy in the blink of an eye. I tried not to think too hard about what that meant.

"One more minute," Belinda directed.

She walked to the sofa, sat next to me, and leaned into my arms. She rested her head on my shoulder and I felt the slight quake of her sobs. I held her tight.

"You wonderful, crazy-assed man," she cried softly.

"Thank you for coming to find me," I whispered.

It was the safest I had felt in more than a week.

As Haley's curiosity drew her back into the room, Belinda released me and looked at the pattern in the rug as she lightly backhanded her tears away.

Dennis took charge of diverting Haley's attention, delicately getting to his feet with an oversized groan. "Holy shit, I'm getting old."

"Uncle Dennis!" Haley admonished.

The whole troop laughed.

"Time to get the Tough Guy home," he added.

Jerry beamed at his new nickname.

Jill collected Jerry and Dennis. Arm in good arm, they all walked out after Jill shook Phil's hand, having reinstalled some type of uneasy armistice.

Gail and Belinda gathered Haley, who garnered careful hugs from her Grandpa, feigning bruise-free ribs, and from me, then leaped back up the stairs and out the door.

Phil stood, promising to run interference with the DEA for a couple of days. He also relayed that they would eventually insist on getting the full accounting of events, straight from the team. They'd lost a man.

I wanted to know a few things, too, like the rest of Victor's story. Phil suggested I would probably have to learn to live with my questions unanswered. The Feds were unlikely to be in the mood for filling in the blanks.

I stood and walked him to door. In the most un-cop-ly thing I had experienced in my years of knowing the closest thing I had to a big brother, he leaned down and buried me in a hug of mammoth proportions, then stepped me back with his hands on my shoulders.

"No one could have put the pieces of this tragic puzzle together any faster than you did, Hank." He held me at arms-length. "I've been doing this for a long time."

True.

"I'm good at my job."

No false humility. True again.

"You got close, but we could only know the whole truth when Ken faltered."

"Faltered?"

"Like a lot of misdirected people, he overestimated himself. Complex plan with no exit strategy," he explained. "You couldn't have prepared yourself for him."

"That's true."

"And, my friend," he stepped back and popped his fedora on for effect. "He was most definitely not prepared for you."

Without another word, he thumped me just a little too hard in the chest and stepped through the threshold.

The return to quiet was sudden. Settling back into the sofa, I felt nothing except the weight of a numbness that seemed roughly equal to the planet's entire gravitational pull.

Dad stood slowly and began picking up the remnants of our brief caffeine high.

"That can wait Dad."

"I need to move a bit, or the kinks in these sore muscles will settle right into this old body."

He stopped, cups in hand, and looked at me.

"What?"

"Well, my AA sponsor says everything happens for a reason."

"I'm still struggling to find one in this, Dad."

"For a while, at least, there are some horrible drugs that won't make it to the streets," he said hopefully.

"Yeah. Lost lives to save lives is a big stretch for me."

"Me, too," he admitted.

He went another direction. "When was the last time you had two beautiful women competing for you?"

"You noticed."

"Everybody noticed. Especially the two of them."

"So, the lesson to be learned from the week is that women dig an idiot who accidently busts up a drug ring?"

He shrugged.

"We'll grieve, son. This poor soul Ken chose his path a long time ago. Just like that man Jake. They wanted to take you, and the people you love, down with them. We got in the way of that. It surely could have turned out a whole lot different."

"What about Victor?"

"He was a haunted man. He also was somebody's husband and son, maybe a father. It's very, very sad. He saved our lives. We owe him a gratitude that is beyond any words, and the hope that he is restful."

I clasped my hands, as only the uncertain and prayerful do.

"There may always be a reason," he went on. "Sometimes I don't understand what that reason means. I know that I'll pray for another sober day. I'll reach out to help another alcoholic. I'll miss your mom. I'll be proud of a son who seeks to help others heal the destruction that addiction brings into this world."

He looked into the bottom of an empty coffee cup as if to see the universal truths, then looked me in the eyes.

"And I'll consider it a miracle that I was able to keep the promise to my grand-daughter to watch out for her dad."

Now I knew why he had come for me.

"And, what about the women?" My confusion was genuine and thinking about it distracted me from the whole family and friend's near-death thing. "I don't know whether to feel guilty about how long I've held on to the fantasy that Gail will take me back, or thrilled that Jill might be interested in me."

"A therapist I admire tells me to allow all of my feelings to pass through me," he nodded my way. "They all matter. And, they're all temporary."

"Anyway," he finished. "The women are just an unexpected bonus. And complication."

The Sage had spoken.

EPILOGUE

There was a mild winter bite in the air. Mild for Iowa anyway. A light snow fell in slow motion, flakes like God's diamonds dusting the grass and immediately disappearing as they touched the yet unfrozen concrete. Inside the local Court Avenue tap, a decent crowd of hardy Midwesterners, undaunted by weather, was jumping to the sounds of Slippery When Wet.

James looked very much the rock star in his Buddy Holly glasses, a red satin sport coat, skin-tight black chinos, and what men older than me once called Beatle boots. He power-strummed a vintage fire-engine-red Fender Telecaster as the band blasted through their super-charged version of the Traffic classic, "Freedom Rider," complete with bass, keyboards, drums, sax, and trumpet. They followed with the Avett Brothers, minus the cello, then a nitro-powered tune that sounded like The Who meets Bob Marley, which had to be an original.

James and I had struck up a bit of musical friendship and he dedicated the next song to our group. The band segued into a striking, understated version of The Impression's immortal "People Get Ready." The drummer sang lead while the spaces between the notes of James' crisp, clean lead guitar work filled the room. I had a slightly silly vision of

Curtis Mayfield, sitting on a cloud in heaven, smiling and swaying with immense pleasure as he looked down on this young diverse band keeping the faith. Between songs, James waved at us.

On the table sat a combination of ice waters and sodas. Phil and his wife Catherine were teetotalers by religious choice. Dennis and Jill were cohorts in sobriety. Jerry and I drank soda out of deference to Dennis' recovery. This annoyed him to no end. A bonus.

We were having a belated everybody-in-the-family-is-alive-and-well gathering.

Dad was here in spirit, recuperating nicely back in southwest Iowa, where he was flipping burgers and letting the customers know he had been significantly involved in assisting in a police matter in the capitol city, but was unable to offer the specifics of his role. I checked in with him weekly and still drove down at least once a month, weather permitting, for the Al-Anon meeting. Recent events suggested I still had work to do on the 12-Step slogan, Keep It Simple.

Belinda had declined our invitation, citing a disinterest in spending the evening listening to, "that damn loud music," but I knew the real reason. She disapproved of my invitation to Jill. Still holding out for a sea change with Gail.

I had chosen not to invite Gail. Court Avenue had several familiar haunts from our past and, except for co-parenting Haley, we had been keeping a greater distance since the events now called "that mess in the fall." There was no penultimate communication. I accepted, with time and Dennis' help, that the knee-jerk, possessive response I had seen in her was, as I'd guessed, brought to the surface by our family crisis. It had just as rapidly disappeared into a faraway place in the past. Exactly where it belonged.

Haley had been open with me about her feelings – frustration, fear, and love – around the events she was aware of, having been given an edited account of the situation. As always, she deciphered enough detail to require a level of honesty that reminded me I was still a dad-in-training. She had been ushered, without any choice, into a world of uncertainty and danger far beyond her years. It would take time, more conversation, and a whole lot of good decision-making on my part, to heal the pain of this invasion. As a start, we were keeping extra close track of one another's whereabouts these days. I had also retired the now weaponized CD player and switched to an up-to-date online streaming music service, which indicated I was still willing to learn.

Haley also sensed a change in the weather between her mother and myself, enough to slip the name of "Walt, the new friend who went with mom to a movie," into our conversation. It was a good sign for all involved that I didn't cringe, ask additional questions, or lose any sleep over this information.

Then there was Jill.

I tell clients that one of the great myths of romance is this: the best way to get over a relationship that has ended is to find someone new. More likely, unrequited love that lingers will infiltrate the next relationship. Not in a good way.

As I moved further into resolving my past with Gail, I was making room for a future. I was very attracted to Jill. She appeared to think that I was an interesting challenge. We'd been speaking regularly since Ken's case had been closed. For a while, she ran interference for me with law enforcement and the press. I once again became semi-famous for all the wrong reasons. At the conclusion of her work as my advocate, she sent me a bill of $1 for services rendered, refusing to take more, refusing to take less.

I'd sent her an invitation to join me tonight. She accepted.

Jake. Victor. Ken.

Bob Rathburn continued to help me retrieve some sense of groundedness, as I struggled to find meaning in the madness that had changed me for all time. I had witnessed the violent deaths of three men. I learned that a young man I hoped to help was, in fact, a drug dealer and a killer. My sorrow for Ken, Victor and even Jake, clashed mightily with the havoc they had visited on our lives. They were men whose attempt to gain mastery over their own demons had brought them to rain suffering on others, over and over.

In our considerable joint experience as therapists, neither Bob nor I had any framework for the impenetrable nature of their grossly misdirected paths. We were crafting my path forward as best we could.

Bob had also helped me revisit a flawed childhood dream. Detective Anderson. Skilled though I was in assisting those who come to me with a sincere desire for health, or at least a willingness to struggle in the direction of honesty and healing; I was not in possession of a special ability to uncover truth in a life dedicated to deception and destruction.

Another lesson in humility.

The DEA had their time with us. We told them everything that had been reported to Phil. They didn't much like it, although they also seemed more than willing to help me keep a lower profile in return for the DEA taskforce taking complete credit for breaking through Ken's elaborate scheme. Even in this time of phone video and social media, most of the story did not reach the outside world. In return, they extracted my pledge to keep Victor and Jake's covertly sanctioned damage a secret. There were no explanations, no apologies, and no thank-yous. I was curious about the amount of cash Ken had accumulated in that basement and what would become of it. I was told in no uncertain terms that I could keep all my questions to myself.

This included the fact that I would never know if anyone came forth to claim the remains of Victor, Jake, or Ken. All the sadder.

Both Phil and Jill assured me that the best we could hope for was that all those government types would go away and leave us alone.

I didn't tell anyone about my final, brief connection with Victor. No one got to know that I had learned how the match of his fanaticism had been lit – by the death of his wife to drugs. I had decided to invoke the sanctity of the moment we faced together when he lost his life and saved four others.

That worked for me.

We got a nice check from the insurance company for the B&E damage, along with a super nifty discount on rates for all the high-tech security we had James install. That discount offset the increase in rates that came shortly after the nice check, due to filing a claim for the B&E damage.

Dennis, Belinda, and I decided to donate the insurance check to a nearby addiction treatment center specializing in services to economically strapped rural folks. It was an anonymous donation in honor of Victor and wife. No last names, just Victor and wife.

I like to think that would have worked for him.

The sanitized DEA version of Ken's story hit the Internet, papers, and television. I'd changed my cell phone number again, and Belinda was carefully screening calls at the office, ruling out people who were just curious onlookers.

Sadly, it was our good fortune when a local high-profile businessman quickly captured the headlines by leaving town with his administrative assistant and several million in assets from his supposedly bankrupt company. Folks moved on to the next neo-reality show.

Our house had been restored and rejuvenated. The bullet in Haley's ceiling was removed and the hole patched, all without her knowledge. For now, I had decided to keep us in our home. More time would tell. I kept the squeaky boards in the entryway. They were an additional, homespun safety alarm, one I hoped we'd never need again.

I was working some. Several new clients reminded me that good people have difficult challenges and, with rare exception, folks work toward healing with honest intent. As J.R. says, "Most of the time, getting help helps."

One concession to family and friends was that I now carried my cell phone everywhere, fully charged and locked into the "you can find me, anywhere, anytime" position. This seemed little enough, given the realities that a phone with tracking had saved my life and those of my team. Those in the know believed immediate phone access would assist them in the future, as I would most definitely find some form of unusual trouble to immerse myself in somewhere down the road. Progress, not perfection.

And so, I was feeling somewhat better.

I was feeling a nudge of something else, too.

This was the first time I had seen Jill in casual clothes. Form fitting blue jeans, black cashmere turtle neck sweater, simple onyx earrings set against her pale skin and red hair.

I hadn't thought much about any woman's body, other than Gail's, for what seemed like a very long time. From hair to heeled black leather boots, Jill was, consciously or not, issuing a serious challenge.

I thought I matched up well, in a My Morning Jacket inscribed Henley, black jeans, and brand-new black Chuck Taylors.

"You look good," Jill interrupted my musings. "Well rested."

"I certainly aim for the well-rested look, whenever I can," I said, smiling my way back into the room.

She playfully punched my arm as she turned from the music. "You know what I mean."

"Yeah. I do."

Maybe she'll want to ride on the Register's Great Bike Ride Across Iowa next year. Traveling town of bicyclists, more riders than people in most of the towns we pass through. Cheap pancakes, excellent watermelon, all the free water you can drink.

"Maybe back to tent camping. Two sleeping bags, of course," I mumbled.

"What?" Jill furrowed her gorgeous, unique strawberry brow, unable to read my lips through the pulse of the bass player's riff.

"Just thinking out loud about RAGRAI."

"Sure. Thinking about bike riding. You are a unique character, Hank." Her smile warmed another room. "I like tents," as if she'd read my mind.

She likes tents.

I didn't know much of Jill's story, yet. It was clear we were both working from a tentative place, romantically speaking. Tents was a place to start.

The band took a break between songs.

"I've biked all my life," I told her, as the room quieted to conversational buzz. A careful disclosure.

"I ran track to stay out of the house, away from my dad's drinking."

A fellow escapee from family troubles. With her own vulnerability, she was telling me she had divined the meaning of my love for the outdoors.

I leaned close to her ear.

"I'd like to hear more of your story."

She elbowed me in the ribs, like pals do.

"More will be revealed in time, super sleuth." She turned, as if to engage Catherine in conversation.

It's a start.

Given the circumstances of the past several months, one might think I had become risk averse.

I edged my chair closer and interrupted.

"By the way, you look rested, too. Perhaps too well-rested."

I waited.

She smiled another devastating smile at the very moment James and his gang recaptured the stage and launched into some early Big Head Todd and the Monsters.

"Stick around. Maybe we can tire each other out sometime."

She took my hand in hers and turned back to Catherine.

Everything happens for a reason.

ACKNOWLEDGEMENTS

Much love and appreciation to my early readers: Aimee, for helping me clear up my overuse of jargon; Nathan, for helping me clear out the repetitious language; and DiAnne, for always being the first person I trust to read everything I write.

More love to Aimee for becoming my Social Media Coordinator. Hank's mild aversion to technology may have some parallel to my own, especially in the social media world.

A boatload of gratitude to my friend, Mary, who edited this book into something far better than my almost final manuscript. Your clarity of language and sentence structure, combined with maximum skill in deepening the emotional force of the book has been nothing short of amazing. The value of your ideas for strengthening the female characters in Hank's story was immeasurable.

Thanks to Tony, who reminded me that my introduction into reading mysteries was The Hardy Boys. Old school.

Thanks to Ralph, who did me a solid with a final read through.

Thanks to the family and friends who remind me of the beauty and underappreciated cool factor of Des Moines.

To the degree that my depictions of other professions have had authenticity, I am indebted to the wide range of callings and occupations that friends, family and clients have brought to my life over the years: farmers, EMTs, firefighters, musicians, nurses, police officers, baristas, custodians, fellow therapists, delivery persons, cooks, doctors, lawyers, teachers, and so many more.

Thanks to the editor of my first non-fiction book, published more than 30 years ago. The message you gave me, "You're a pretty good writer for a social worker," was all the encouragement I needed to continue to write.

Raymond Parish is a pen name. Parish is a psychotherapist, and the author of four non-fiction books and multiple non-fiction articles. *Overnight Delivery* is Parish's first work of fiction.

HOLD ON FOR THE NEXT HANK ANDERSON THRILLER!

HIGHER EDUCATION

A prequel to
Overnight Delivery

The origins of a friendship forged in spiritual mayhem.

Made in the USA
Coppell, TX
22 November 2020